The Bone Thief

Claire Buss

Other works by Claire Buss:

The Roshaven Books
The Rose Thief
The Silk Thief
The Bone Thief

The Interspecies Poker Tournament – The Roshaven Case Files No. 27
Ye Olde Magick Shoppe

The Gaia Collection
The Gaia Effect
The Gaia Project
The Gaia Solution
The Gaia Collection (Books 1-3)

Poetry
Little Book of Verse, Book 1 in the Little Book Series
Little Book of Spring, Book 2 in the Little Book Series
Little Book of Summer, Book 3 in the Little Book Series
Spooky Little Book, Book 4 in the Little Book Series
Little Book of Love, Book 5 in the Little Book Series
Little Book of Autumn, Book 6 in the Little Book Series
Little Book of Winter, Book 7 in the Little Book Series
Little Book of Christmas, Book 8 in the Little Book Series

Short Story Collections
Tales from Suburbia
Tales from the Seaside
The Blue Serpent & other tales
Flashing Here & There

Anthologies
Underground Scratchings, Tales from the Underground anthology
Patient Data, The Quantum Soul anthology
A Badger Christmas Carol, The Sparkly Badgers' Christmas Anthology
Haunted, The Sparkly Badgers' Halloween Anthology
The Last Pirate, Tales from the Pirate's Cove anthology

Sea Witch Shanty

There once was an evil witch o' sea
Who would gladly try to capture thee
When the winds whipped up and the boat sank low
She'll stretch her hand and strike her blow

Chorus:
Beware when you sail on the seas so brave
Or you'll end up in her evil cave
Pay your tribute and pay it quick
Or you'll be drowning in the drink

This witch o' the sea she speaks to the dead
Never satisfied she wants your head
Collecting souls, she's black to the core
A necromancer always after more

Chorus

The sea witch she did lose her lover
Never will she ever find another
She'll whip up a storm in the blink of an eye
And we'll never hear your dying cry

Chorus

With blackened eyes and scales of green
It's a sight you'll wish you'd never seen
Her smile is lined with razor like teeth
She'll dig in her claws and sink you deep

Chorus

This witch rules the sea with an iron fist
And always demands sacrifice as gift
It cannot be paid with jewels or gold
Give her souls before their body grows cold

Chorus

Chapter 1

Ned Spinks, Chief Thief-Catcher, slumped his shoulders in dismay at the pile of reports spilling over his desk. Things were not well in the city of Roshaven.

'And these are all from this week?' Ned asked as he gestured at the pile.

'Yes, Boss.' Willow, a tree nymph and one of Ned's catchers, nodded her head so vigorously, her leaves rustled. 'There's been multiple instances of people claiming their magic has been stolen and a report from the Sailors' Guild that unexpected sea-related deaths have risen sharply.'

'Have you spoken with them?' asked Ned.

'The Guild? No. We thought it was just their standard report. Was we supposed to?' Willow bloomed uncertainly.

'No, not the Guild – the people who think their magic was stolen.'

'Not yet, but we've set up interviews with some of them this afternoon. But Boss... how can we prove if someone's had their magic stolen or not?' she asked.

'The best thing you can do is find out why they think it's happened in the first place. If we can discover a common element between each experience, then we might be able to pinpoint why it's happening,' replied Ned.

He was mildly concerned. In all likelihood, the people who thought they'd lost some magic had inadvertently used more than they expected or had some other ailment that was preventing their ability to cast.

But magic skimming, taking small amounts of power from others, was illegal, so if these were legitimate claims, then the catchers would need to find and arrest the culprit before they caused someone permanent damage. Skimming was dangerous for both parties.

'Let's hope it's kids messing about so we can nip it in the bud or, better yet, maybe they all have a nasty cold affecting their casting. See what you can find out.' He shuffled through the paperwork. 'Is that everything?'

'There's the paper,' said Joe helpfully. He was Ned's only fully human catcher, besides himself.

Ned waited for the lad to expand but nothing else was forthcoming so he examined his paperwork pile more closely and sure enough, a copy of *The Daily Blag* lay between reports. He eased it out of the stack and read out the headline.

'Death at the Beach.' He glanced at Joe.

'There's a bit more, Boss.'

'Yes. Thank you, Joe.' Ned stiffened the paper with a flick of his wrists and read on. 'Towns and villages up and down the coast of Efrana are reporting an increase in mysterious deaths linked to the ocean. Officials are baffled why it is suddenly not safe in the water and are urging locals and visitors to stay away from the beach.' Ned read on in silence, but the article lacked any further facts.

'What do we think – mermaids?' asked Ned. 'They're not exactly the friendliest creature in the ocean.'

Both Willow and Joe shook their heads.

'True, but they are territorial, and this is happening all over.'

'Plus we spoke to Pearl,' said Joe. 'She said it wasn't them.'

Ned nodded. The mermaid Pearl was an honorary thief-catcher and helped out from time to time with sea-related cases. If she said it wasn't the mermaids, then it wasn't.

'Sparks thinks it's *her*, Boss,' said Willow, her leaves fluttering.

Sparks was another of Ned's thief-catchers and a firefly with many contacts in and around Roshaven because of his huge bug network of friends and relations.

'Her?'

'You know, from the song,' supplied Joe. '*There once was an evil witch o' sea...*'

'Yes, thank you, Joe.' Ned cut in. Now he would have that song stuck in his head for the rest of the day. Everyone was singing or humming it these days.

'Anything else I should know about?' he asked. He was due at the Palace for the weekly meeting between imperial officials.

'Just the dragon,' replied Joe with a smirk.

Ned groaned. The dragon. Jenni, his second-in-command and usually the most down-to-earth, pragmatic person you've ever met, was convinced that she kept seeing a small golden dragon on the streets of Roshaven.

'Whatever it is Jenni is seeing, I am very sure there is no baby dragon roaming around town.' Ned stood and gathered in the reports. 'Tell Jenni I've gone to the palace if she gets back before me.' He left Willow and Joe getting ready for the interviews and walked downstairs into The Noose, semi-reputable inn and location of Thief-Catcher HQ.

With a nod to Reg, the barkeep and owner of The Noose, Ned headed over to the Imperial Palace and his second progress meeting of the day. This one should have cake which usually made up for how long it could drag on for.

Upon entering the second-best meeting room, he was impressed to see Ma Bowl's excellent ginger cake together with a pile of what looked to be meltingly good honey cakes on the table waiting, and then he paused. Two types of cake meant they did not expect this meeting to go well.

Ned sat himself at the table and nodded greetings to the others. On his left was Jimmy Fingers, the Lower Circle, responsible for imports, exports and maintaining relations with Roshaven's trade partners. On Ned's right sat Madame Silk, the Stalls, who looked after the varying aspects of Roshaven's nightlife and next to her was Griff, Ned's recently revealed father and loyal subject of the empire. As far as Ned was aware, Griff hadn't been given an official title yet, but he was in talks with imperial advisors the High Right and High Left, both of whom were in attendance and were sitting either side of Rose, Ned's wife and Empress of Roshaven.

'Things are not well in the city of Roshaven,' intoned the High Right. 'The Sailors' Guild have reported an increase in suspicious deaths and reports from our neighbouring towns suggest that mysterious sea-related deaths are on the rise. You all saw today's paper, I assume?'

There were mumbled agreements from around the table. Ned added his own, mentally adding a note to thank Joe for his diligence, although he and the other thief-catchers knew Joe only got the paper for the crossword.

'It looks like the Sea Witch is collecting,' remarked Griff before humming a few bars of the sea witch shanty tune that had seeped into everyday life.

'There's no doubt it's a popular song, but do we

really think it's based in fact?' asked Rose.

Griff shrugged.

'These things often have a kernel of truth within them and you and Ned both know the Sea Witch exists, eh?'

Ned could feel the back of his ears heating as all eyes swivelled to him.

'It's true we gave the Sea Witch a tribute when we crossed the bay in Fidelia, but… that's what you do, isn't it?' He looked to Fingers for support.

'Yeah, I mean, usually if you want a sea voyage to go well, you'll offer a tribute to the Sea Witch for fair winds and no funny business, but that's what condemned criminals are for, right?' Fingers gestured back at Griff, who confirmed with a nod.

'So why do we have an increase in suspicious deaths if the Sea Witch is getting her usual payment?' Rose looked around the table at her advisors, but the only person who had any response was Griff, who replied in a sing-song voice.

'This witch o' the sea she speaks to the dead
Never satisfied she wants your head
Collecting souls, she's black to the core
A necromancer always after more.'

'Really? We think the Sea Witch is hell bent on collecting more souls? For what, exactly?' Ned couldn't help but be a little scathing. The shanty had been getting on his nerves for days now.

'Her necromancer magic demands souls. Perhaps she's planning something that requires more power. I confess, I don't know what that could be, but I do think we should be worried,' replied Griff.

'For now, let's look at practicalities. Fingers – can you increase the number of patrols on the docks at night?' Rose asked. 'You can borrow from the Palace Guard ranks if you need to. That should deter any further night-time accidents and then we'll warn everyone to be extra vigilant and avoid the sea unless absolutely necessary.'

'Yes, I can do that. The Sailors' Guild are advising their members to stay in groups and double check safety measures.' Fingers bobbed his head. 'We can pass the advice onto our trading partners as well. The last thing we want is for shipments to be delayed, or worse, cancelled.'

Rose nodded her thanks and turned her attention to Griff.

'Can you contact the Sea Witch? See if we can find out what she's up to?'

'As I said, I don't know what she's up to, but I think I know what's she after.' Griff flashed a glance at Ned. 'She wants the bones.'

'Bones?' asked Ned.

'The ones Jenni stole from the Spice Ghosts,' replied Griff.

'Allegedly stole.' Ned could feel his ears burning again. 'You know as well as I do Jenni didn't steal those bones.'

Everyone at the table avoided Ned's gaze except for Rose, who was looking at him sadly.

'I'm telling you, she didn't steal those bones,' he repeated. 'I asked her, and she denied it. Emphatically.'

'No disrespect to you, but the sprite will be here soon to answer to the Imperial Council,' said the High Right.

Ned's heart sank. That explained the extra cake. He couldn't help feeling a little stung at not being told the council was calling Jenni in for questioning, but his rational mind pointed out that they had to ask her about it directly. But he still felt his wife could have given him a heads up.

'We may have another land-based problem,' said Ned. 'There have been reports of magic stealing. My catchers are interviewing those affected today to see if there are any similarities in the how and the when. We could be looking at a case of skimming.'

That got everyone's undivided attention. Skimming was dangerous. It was possible to take power from other practitioners without their permission by skimming a little off the top. It usually went unnoticed, but the problem with skimming was that it was highly addictive.

'If someone is skimming, then they are going to take more and more power in order to get the same rush as the first time they skimmed.' Ned looked at the grim faces in the room. 'But we all know that can never be recreated. And the people they keep skimming from run the risk of being sucked dry, having their magic stolen for good.'

'Let's wait for the statements to come in before we do anything. We don't want to cause a panic, but if it is a skimmer, then we need to quash them.' Rose waited for Ned to agree before asking if there was anything else.

'Erm...' Ned really didn't want to mention this but knew if he didn't, it would come back to bite him. 'Apparently there have been sightings of a small golden dragon running around the streets of Roshaven.'

'A dragon!' gasped Rose as the rest of the council looked suitably aghast.

'Alleged dragon. It's only been reported by one person, so I don't think we need to be too concerned,' replied Ned.

'And who has reported these sightings?' asked the

High Left.

'Er… Jenni.' As soon as Ned said her name, he realised what he had done. He had cast her as an unreliable witness, the very thing the council had been accusing her of.

The members of the council broke for a comfort break before Jenni was due to arrive and Rose headed straight for Ned.

'I'm so sorry, my love. The Highs, and Griff, felt it prudent to call Jenni in for questioning after the rise in suspicious deaths. They asked me not to tell you because of your personal connection. You understand, don't you?' Anxiety creased her lovely face, and Ned knew he couldn't stay mad at her for long. It wasn't entirely her fault that she just happened to be his wife and the Empress.

'I'm telling you, Jenni didn't steal those bones,' he said.

'What about the dragon?' asked Rose.

It was Ned's turn to frown with worry.

Chapter 2

'It weren't me.'

Jenni the sprite shifted slightly in her chair. Her new blue coat was still taking a bit of getting used to. The tail hole didn't feel the same as her beloved old red coat.

'Look, Jenni. You're among friends here. If you did something on the side you're not particularly proud of, it's okay to tell us.' Fingers smiled encouragingly at her.

Jenni glared at him.

'If she says she didn't do it, then she didn't.' Ned made his point again firmly. It was the third time he'd vouched for his second-in-command and Jenni could see he was feeling annoyed that his role as Chief Thief-Catcher wasn't carrying any weight here. He kept cracking his knuckles.

'Can you tell us the message again please, Griff?' Rose asked the seasoned smuggler. Jenni watched the two of them interacting. She knew Rose was still coming to terms with the fact that this long-time friend of her empire was also Ned's father - a fact that even Jenni hadn't known.

'You have to understand that they communed with me while I was in my magical suspension, half-way between life and death, so nuance may have been lost,' Griff replied to Rose's request. 'But the general gist was that the Babet sprite has stolen our magic bones, and there'll be hell to pay if they're not returned. More or less.'

'Let 'em come. I ain't got nuffink to 'ide. I didn't steal no bones. When they get 'ere, they can look in me coat pockets.'

'I wish it were that simple, Jenni. I really do. But the Spice Ghosts are likely to raze Roshaven to the ground if they don't get what they want.' For once, Griff had a sombre look on his face.

'Why are we so scared about the Spice Ghosts? Aren't they just a bedtime story told to frighten children?' Ned sounded dubious, as if he couldn't understand why Griff was taking the Spice Ghosts so seriously.

'The Spice Ghosts look after the realms, making sure the dead remain dead and their spirits stay in the spirit realm. Neither dead nor alive, they travel across the seas from country to country, maintaining the balance,' replied Griff.

'Why have we never seen them?' demanded Ned.

'You may not have, but I've seen them. And I think young Fingers has had dealing with the Spice Ghosts in the past, eh?'

Fingers swallowed and nodded, his face pale.

'We don't see them because they don't linger much in the real world,' said Fingers. 'They're sort of half in and half out. Plus, water is a conduit between realms if you have the power to make the connection. It makes sense that they stay on their ship most of the time.'

'I didn't know that about water, but even so, why should we be so worried? We don't have the bones,' reiterated Ned.

'They don't know that. All they know is that a sprite from Roshaven stole them...'

'Allegedly,' interrupted Ned.

'... allegedly stole them, so they're coming here to retrieve their bones. We'd be wise not to stand in their way. They have destroyed towns in the past.'

'Momma K'd never let that 'appen.' Jenni looked directly at Rose. 'I swears it.'

'I've seen them in action. Sailed in their wake for a time. I would never cross them,' said Griff. 'And if I'm right about all these suspicious deaths, then the Sea Witch has her claws on the bones or one of her minions is delivering them to her. All that extra soul-power together with the Spice Ghosts' bones will give her enough power to do, well, pretty much anything.' Griff leaned towards Jenni across the table. 'Are you sure you don't know where they are?'

'I ain't got no bones. I ain't never 'ad no bones. I don't need bones to do magic.' Here Jenni faltered slightly. 'Leastways I never did afore. And now I know my limits, I'd never use a living fing without permission. Never.'

The room went quiet. They had circled the problem several times and each time it came back to the fact that Jenni did not know why the Spice Ghosts thought she had stolen their bones.

'Maybe we're looking at this from the wrong angle,' said Rose.

'Ow do you mean?' asked Jenni, eager to explore every other plausible idea.

'Well, according to the message Griff received, the Spice Ghosts are looking for a sprite with the surname Babet. Do you have any siblings, Jenni?'

All eyes swivelled to her.

'Nah. Just me. But…' Jenni started tapping a finger to her lip as she thought. 'I got the same name as me Dad, so it could be 'im they're looking for?'

There were smiles of relief all round.

'Great.' Jimmy rubbed his hands together gleefully. 'Tell him to go see the Spice Ghosts and clear up this mess. Job jobbed.'

'I would only I ain't never met 'im. I don't even know wot 'e looks like.'

The momentarily high spirits in the room sank back down. Ned tried to rally them.

'But at least now we have a lead. He must be the sprite the ghosts are talking about. I'm sure Momma K will know where he is.'

Jenni snorted and cast a doubtful look in Ned's direction. But she was grateful for his positive attitude.

'Awright, I'll go talk to me mum. See wot she's got to say about 'im. I'll let you know if I 'ear anyfing.' Jenni stood and gave a little wriggle. The new blue coat really wasn't that comfortable.

'Shall I come with you? Strength in numbers and all that,' offered Ned.

Jenni thought about it for a moment.

'Nah. Probably best if you don't. She gets ever so cagey about 'im and if we wants answers, we want 'er to talk. Catch up with you at HQ laters.'

Knowing that the people she left behind were probably talking about her, Jenni tried not to mind. She'd been as helpful as she could. There was absolutely no way she'd ever stolen bones before. Furs, jewels, wine, and some jellied eels, yes, but never bones. Bone magic was on a different path than the one the fae in Roshaven followed. They could use it, at a pinch, but why try to bend a circle into a square when you yourself are round?

Jenni knew Ned was trying to help, but she needed a bit of space herself to figure out exactly what she was going to ask her mum. Father questions had always been met with indifference and in the end, Jenni had stopped caring who her dad was. He wasn't here, and that was that. But now, with this apparent enormous threat hanging over the city she called home, she would have to find a way to get Momma K talking before it was too late.

With that in mind, she made a small stop at the confectioners. Ned's previous gift of sugared snails had gone down so well, they were now Momma K's favourite crunchy snack. Jenni bought two bags. It never hurt to be doubly armed with candy, especially on sensitive subjects. She added in some caramelised grasshoppers, just in case.

The fae realm was quiet when Jenni arrived. Usually there would be fae flitting around, music tinkling through the air and the smell of exotic things tantalising the taste buds. Today there was nothing. Jenni knew this was a terrible sign. Momma K was in a bad mood.

Spying an unfortunate brownie, Jenni darted over and pinned him against a toadstool.

'Wot gives?' she asked.

'Momma K is, er, busy?' You had to give the brownie props for trying to sound casually nonchalant. Unfortunately for him, the shaky hands and quaky voice gave him away that Momma K was much more than busy.

'Wot's got into 'er bonnet this time?' Jenni wondered if it was an actual bee. She'd never really understood the phrase, but she supposed a bee in your hat would be annoying.

'Someone came to visit.' The brownie clasped both hands together in prayer and sank to his knees. 'Please, Miss Jenni, he travelled through the portal. He knew the way, he brought cake. We didn't think there was anything wrong. Just a visitor, that's all.'

Jenni snorted at the mention of cake. It was a

brownie weakness, and the reason so many of them made their homes beneath large kitchens and bakeries. There was always a constant food supply, and, in return, the brownies did small favours for the humans. Clearing out spiders, keeping the milk fresher for longer and removing any and all crumbs.

'This bloke, you seen 'im before?'

The brownie shook his head firmly and Jenni stepped back a few paces. Leaping to its feet, the brownie tugged its forelock in Jenni's direction and made a dash for freedom.

Now Jenni had a tough decision to make: interrupt her mum in what was apparently a very unwanted visitation or leave it until everything had calmed down here in the fae realm, putting Roshaven at genuine risk.

'Snails!'

Stuffing her hands into the pockets of her coat, Jenni stomped towards Momma K's inner sanctum, hoping that her sugary gifts would at least offer her a modicum of protection from whatever was going on.

It was icy cold in the arbour. Infused with Momma K's magic, the foliage and flowers, colours and smells usually reflected the season and Momma K's mood. Right now, there were beautiful frozen fractals all over the trees and their leaves. All the flowers had shut their pretty blooms, and the grass stood to stiff attention. The whole place was hushed, as if waiting to exhale and move. There were no insects or birds or other animals. Just Momma K and her visitor.

The man had his back to Jenni, but she could see the haughty fury on Momma K's face. Despite being seated, the queen of the fae was rigidly still, her wings folded, hands clasped on her lap in front of her, and not a muscle moved in her face.

Jenni saw Momma K's eyes flicker to her presence and widen slightly before returning to stare at the visitor. It looked like a sprite to Jenni. Dirty blonde hair on his head and the same pointy, hairy ears that she had. He wore a tatty brown jacket that was patched, and his tail stuck out a convenient hole – just like Jenni's did. She frowned. She knew all the sprites in Momma K's kingdom, but she didn't know this one.

Jenni took a risk and spoke.

'I bought you summink.'

'Chil' now be not de time for bringin' tings,' snapped Momma K, her eyes remaining on her visitor.

'Yeah, I fawt you might say that, but we got a problem in the big city. A proper one. So I need to speaks to yer an'all. Alone.'

Momma K flicked her gaze between the two people in her arbour.

'Ya bring dis wid ya?' she asked the man.

He shrugged his shoulders and said nothing. Jenni risked walking a few steps closer to the others, bringing out the bags of sugared snails and caramelised grasshoppers as she did so. Momma K's head snapped up at the distinctive rustling paper bag sound and there was a glint of pleasure in her eyes as Jenni placed the bags of sweets gently on a nearby tree stump.

'Got yor favourites,' she said by way of explaining.

'Wat ting is so important ya disturb me, den?'

'The Spice Ghosts are coming. They reckon I stole a bone, and they wants it back. Threatening to burn Roshaven to the ground if I don't.'

Momma K's attention was firmly back on the man.

'Ya stole bone?' Her wings fluttered, the only sign of her agitation. 'Ya lost wat mind ya had?' Momma K glared daggers at the man but he said nothing in return.

She turned her focus to her daughter.
'Ya in dis too? Ya steal da bone?'
'I ain't stole no bones. Why would I?'
Momma K sucked her teeth.
'Jenni, meet ya fadder.'

Chapter 3

Jenni stood gaping in astonishment.

The dishevelled sprite had turned and gave her a nervous wave. Jenni looked at him more closely. On his head he had tufts of the same dirty blonde hair Jenni did, just not as much. And his tail was thicker. He wore a brown suit that had seen better days and nestled in his jacket's breast pocket was a grubby orange handkerchief. The same tufty hair sprouted from the backs of his hands and feet. He was larger than Jenni in both height and girth. He flashed his daughter a smile and a wink and it was there that Jenni caught a hint of the cheeky rogue her mother must have fallen for.

'Wha…?' began Jenni, but her brain hadn't caught up with events yet and she didn't know what to ask.

'It's good to finally meet you, kid. Call me Norm and getting whatever you need's the game.' He glanced sideways at Momma K. 'Leastwise that's what I do, normally.'

'You don't sound like me,' observed Jenni. 'Wossat about?'

Norm bounced a little on his heels in excitement.

'You're descended from a proud lineage, my dear. I hear you're powerful.' He darted another side glance at Momma K. 'You must have inherited the accent and the magics from Nan June, gods rest her soul. She would have loved to have met you, kid.'

Momma K didn't agree with that at all.

'Her magic come from me and mine. Ya jus' da lucky relative.' She sniffed and fluttered her wings at him.

Jenni decided that there must have been a great deal of revelry the night they conceived her. A very, very great deal.

'So wot's going on then? Where's this bone fing wot you stole? And why'd you steal from the Spice Ghosts?' Jenni peered at her father. 'You gone in the 'ead or summink?'

His eyes filled with tears and his smile got wider.

'Ah, the old tongue. It's like being in the same room as Nan June.'

Twin glares from Momma K and Jenni soon wiped the reminiscence off Norm's face.

'I'll admit there might have been a slight disagreement with me and the Ghosts.' He puffed his chest out a little. 'I was part of their crew for a while, you know. Was even thinking of joining when they did their last lot of recruiting. They had a Spice opening, you see. Would have been perfect for me.'

'So why didn't you?' Despite herself, Jenni was a little intrigued. She hadn't known you could apply to become a Spice Ghost.

'I, er... borrowed their bones for a small game of chance. Purely for show you understand. I wasn't planning to use them as collateral...' Norm trailed off under the disbelief emanating from both women.

'Lemme get this straight. You lost the Spice Ghosts' magic bones in a game of poker and instead of sortin' it out, you ran?' asked Jenni.

Norm nodded miserably and looked down at his feet, mumbling something.

'Wot?'

'I thought I was going to win,' he replied in a small voice.

'Yeah well, you didn't, and now the bloomin' Spice Ghosts wanna destroy my home. Wot you bring all this on me for? They ain't looking for you – they're looking for me. What's that about?'

'I might have erm disguised myself when I was playing.' Norm beamed at Jenni with pride. 'I heard about your win in the Interspecies Poker Tournament, by the way, very impressive. Quite a big prize, I hear?' He gave his daughter another wink.

'That weren't me, it were me boss. I was just the muscle.' Jennie eyed her dad up and down. 'They really fawt you was me?'

'Obviously they've never met you, my blossom. Three times the sprite I am, I'm sure.'

'Try ten,' remarked Momma K. 'Ya bring all dis to me door. Why ya not stand up and speak de truth? Tell em youse de one, no Jenni. Do de right ting for once in ya life.'

Norm's ears quailed in response to Momma K's wrath.

'You're right, absolutely right. But I panicked. And before I knew it, I was hundreds of miles away from the poker game and the Spice Ghosts. I thought I'd get away with it.'

'Well, you didn't, so now you gotta sort it out. Fast!' said Jenni. 'Just tell 'em it were you and get 'em off me trail. Send the ghosts to whoever won the bones at the game. Simple.'

'I can't.' Norm's ears were pressed flat against his skull, and his face was deathly pale. 'I'm on the lam as it is. I can't go to the Spice Ghosts. They'll kill me on sight and I can't risk going to find the person I lost to. I am wanted everywhere along the Efrana coastline.'

'You ain't wanted 'ere,' commented Jenni,

unimpressed.

'Give it time, chil', give it time.' Momma K was even less impressed than Jenni. 'Ya can't stay here. Me kingdom is a place of freedom for fae not wanted for crimes. Me no harbour criminals.'

Norm looked like all his hopes had been utterly destroyed. Jenni felt a reluctant pang of filial responsibility.

'Come with me. If you do wot I say and straighten out who is wanted, the Thief Catchers can 'elp you sort out this mess.' Jenni could feel her mother's eyes burning into her, but she refused to acknowledge that.

'Oh, would you? Oh, Jenni, love, that would be fantastic. I couldn't ask for more. Except for somewhere to stay, of course. And maybe a hot meal? I haven't eaten in days.' Norm's tufty ears were pricked up in hope.

'Yeah, sure. Ned'll 'ave summink at 'is place. We'll go there first. Come on.' She gestured for Norm to go in front and leave the fae glade. As he stomped past, he winked at Momma K and sketched a bow.

Momma K grabbed Jenni's arm before she left.

'No trust him. No one inch. No one second. No believe. Look afta ya heart.'

And then she gave Jenni a little push as if to say, hurry – get this over with. Whilst she was grateful for her mother's warning, Jenni had no intention of trusting her father. She just wanted to straighten things out and get the Spice Ghosts off her tail.

Chapter 4

Jenni glanced sideways at her dad as they came out of the fae realm. He caught her looking and gave her a nervous smile.

'Is Gariboldi's still the best pizza place in town? They used to do a mean fungal surprise.'

'Yeah and yeah.' Jenni scratched her nose. 'We can order one if you like? Catchers got a tab, s'not a problem.'

'Oh, that would be grand.' Norm changed the subject. 'Is it far to your man's house?'

Jenni frowned at Ned being called her man.

'E's not my man, 'e's my boss and nah, not far. 'E might not be 'ome yet but I got a key, so it's awright.' She shoved her hands into her pockets and hunched her shoulders. Thankfully, Norm took the hint and said nothing until they got to Ned's place.

He wasn't at home. Jenni yelled for Sparks before she went inside. It didn't matter that the firefly was nowhere nearby. One of the other bugs in the city would pass the message on that Jenni was looking for him. Bugging was an excellent way to find out where people were, but you had to have a man on the inside.

If Norm thought it was odd that Jenni shouted 'Sparks', he didn't mention it. Instead, he looked around the place with hungry eyes.

'Don't even fink about it,' warned Jenni.

'About what?' Norm had plastered an innocent look on his face, but Jenni didn't buy it. She'd seen that face too many times in the mirror.

'Everyfink. Everyfink yor finking – don't. I brung you 'ere as a curtsey an I'm trusted that yor not a fool all the time. Stealing from Ned is stealing from me. Got it?'

Norm nodded quickly but didn't stop eyeing the place up.

Jenni began biting her nails, wishing Sparks would just get here. Finally, the firefly whizzed in a nearby window and flashed hello.

'Awright, Sparks. Look – can you take an order to Gariboldi's for a fungal surprise and put it on the Catcher's tab. I'll square it wiv Ned.'

Sparks responded with a complex light show and then added some extra flashes and flickers. He was telling Jenni that Ned was waiting for her at the office and that he felt sure Ned would definitely want to know about Norm.

'Wait a minute. 'Ow do you know 'is name?' asked Jenni. She watched for the answer, then turned to her dad in surprise. 'You knew Spark's great-great-great firebug?' she asked.

Norm puffed out his chest with pride.

'I used to know a lot of people in my line of work,' he said with a wistful look in his eye and giving Sparks a nod as the firefly flew out the window.

Jenni didn't want to get into that right now. She needed to let Ned know who it was that had stolen the bones and what had happened to them, so they could send word to the Spice Ghosts. Hopefully, that would prevent the destruction of Roshaven. They might be half human, half not, but surely they had some kind of code.

'Right, Sparks is gonna whizz off to Gariboldi's and put the order in for you to eat summink. Then 'e's gonna come back 'ere and keep you company. I'm gonna go get Ned, but we'll be back.' She paused for a moment. 'I can trust you, right? You ain't gonna do anyfink?'

'Leave me with something to drink, my dear, and I'll be right here when you return.' Norm waggled his fingers at the fireplace, and it burned merrily.

'Right. There's a bottle of scumble in the wood basket.' Jenni nodded towards the hearth. 'That yor power – fire?'

Norm puffed his chest out again.

'I can work a little elemental magic here and there, nothing too powerful of course.' He leaned conspiratorially towards her. 'I skim, a little here, a little there.'

'That ain't legal. I could 'ave you for that.' Despite herself, Jenni was intrigued. The Fae Council had curtailed her own powers, and she was still figuring out what she could and couldn't do without drawing on the life force of things around her – whether by accident or on purpose. Skimming could be the answer to her problems. Yes, skimming was outlawed, but when it was magic people weren't using anyway, was it really all that bad? Trouble with skimming was, you needed someone to show you the ropes and Jenni hadn't had the gumption to walk down that alleyway yet. Now there was someone in Ned's front room who knew what to do.

'Go on, then. Show us 'ow you do it,' she asked after checking that Sparks was definitely out of earshot.

Norm walked to the window and peered out into the street. There were a few people around.

'What you're looking for is a quiver, a slight resonance in magic. Do you know what I mean?' he asked.

'Yeah, yor talking about when people's have magic – how it sorta rings out. I knows what you mean.'

'That, my dear, is the first step. That shows you who

has magic. Next, you have to sort of peel the lid off, so to speak. It's easier if I show you.'

Jenni watched in fascination as Norm focused on a man stood on the other side of the road. He was waiting outside the dressmaker's shop and looked fed up. She reached out magically herself, looking for the ring or resonance and felt it hum back at her. The man on the street felt nothing. Now that she was hyperaware of the surrounding magic, Jenni watched as Norm sent a magical swipe in the man's direction that came away with a faint burst of colour.

'Is that it?' she asked, feeling slightly disappointed, although she didn't know what she had been expecting.

'You try. Stretch out your magical awareness, think of wiping over the top of something and go for it. It's a swiping motion, not a dip. You must never dip.'

Jenni took a breath to focus herself and reached out towards the man, imagining that she had a cloth in hand and was just going to wipe over the magical top of him.

As her power connected with his, there was a tremendous rush of adrenalin. Jenni felt like she was buzzing with energy. Everything was clearer and sharper. She felt more alive, more real and full of life. Her heart was thudding in her chest and her skin was tingling all over, but in that good way, not the bad way. Jenni didn't know how long it was going to last, but it felt amazing. She glanced over at the man to make sure he had noticed nothing and he was still stood outside the shop in moody impatience, waiting for whoever was inside.

'That were amazing,' she breathed.

Norm smiled indulgently at her.

'The first one is always fun. You wait until you try a multiple sweep. The energy boost is just intoxicating. It will last a few hours, that first time.'

At those words, Jenni came back down to earth. She was a thief-catcher, not a magic skimmer. She upheld the law, not broke it.

Filled with sudden guilt and remorse, Jenni figured it was crucial she spoke to Ned as soon as possible so they could sort everything out, which was why she was going to go get him rather than sending Sparks. She didn't want to talk about Norm in front of Norm.

Her father was humming happily as he helped himself to a measure of scumble. He eased himself back into the chair closest to the fireplace and propped his feet up on a stool.

'Did you want any food saving?'

'Wot?' Jenni frowned, then remembered the pizza order. 'Yeah, I'll 'ave a slice. See you in a bit.'

On the way to Thief-Catcher Headquarters, Jenni couldn't quite shake the feeling that she'd done the wrong thing, but she put it down to having finally met her father and not really knowing what to do with that feeling. He was sort of what she expected but also, not really. She thought it was comforting to know she was like one parent at least as she clattered up the stairs to Catcher HQ.

Ned looked up as she entered the office.

'Alright, Jenni? What did Momma K have to say?'

'It's me Dad. 'E's the one wot stole the bones and brung the ghosts on us. 'E's at yors now, 'aving a pizza. But the problem is, 'e lost the bones so we gotta figure out 'ow to get 'em back and sort it all out. Quick like, afore the ghosts get 'ere.'

Before Ned had a chance to respond, there was a familiar clatter on the rickety stairwell up to the catchers office. Some heavy breathing outside the door could be heard before the entrance of Fred, the Palace Guard.

'What's up, Fred?' Ned shot a warning look at Jenni, which she noted for once.

'Mr Spinks, Sir. I got here as quickly as I could, but I had to avoid Second Street because of the orange festival. There are spherical obstacles up and down that street. It's not the best place to traverse when you carry a ceremonial spear. I found that out yesterday. Did you know if you don't clean pith off straight away it sets like concrete?' Fred cocked his head, clearly expecting an answer.

'You got a message by any chance?' Jenni asked, keen to move Fred along.

'A ship has been spotted on the horizon. It's flying the Star Anise. Fingers says they'll be docked in a couple of hours. The Empress, Long May She Rule, wants you both for an emergency meeting.'

Ned had leapt up and was throwing his long coat on.

'Fred, son, that's the sort of thing you should lead with. Not oranges on Second Street.'

Jenni led the way as they all left the office.

'You say that, Mr Spinks, but how do I know you're not planning to get to the palace going that way. You'd take two steps in that citrusy malark and anything could happen. There's peel, pith, juice and seeds just waiting to do a man injury. Just waiting.'

'You forgot the smell,' sniggered Jenni. Despite the tense scenario they were about to get involved in, she couldn't resist.

Fred took it seriously.

'Absolutely right, Miss Jenni. Orange allergy can be terribly powerful. Mam's Uncle Trevor gets laid up every festival with such swellings. It's a wonder he survives it at all.'

Fred continued in this vein for the duration of the walk to the palace. Jenni wished she could talk to Ned more about her dad, but she didn't want Fred earwigging everything she said, so she grumpily held her tongue and pointedly ignored every opportunity for a good orange gag.

Ned sent Fred briskly on his way once they got to the Palace grounds and beckoned Jenni closer.

'Let me get this clear, your dad stole the bones, then lost the bones and now we've got to go find the bones.'

'Summink like that, yeah.'

They were walking through the inner atrium now, hoping to be scooped up by one High or the other as they weren't exactly sure where to go. As they loitered near the largest potted plant, Jenni tried to fill Ned in on everything.

'I left Sparks wiv 'im, so that should be fine. Afta 'e comes back wiv the pizza. But I fink 'e's gonna drink all yor scumble. Sorry, Boss.'

'Sparks doesn't even like scumble.'

Jenni huffed.

'Not Sparks, me dad. E's at yors ain't 'e, 'aving pizza and that. Promised me e'd stay put while I came and filled you in.'

Ned rubbed his chin, which Jenni knew meant he was thinking of the right way to say something.

'Jenni, do you, ah, think we can trust your dad? I mean, what does your gut tell you?' He looked at her with a slight squint, as if expecting a big reaction.

'Onestly? I ain't got a clue. I fink I shoulda brung 'im wiv me now that the Spice Ghosts are 'ere. Or nearly 'ere. I 'spect 'e ain't gonna be too keen on chatting wiv 'em.' She didn't dare mention the skimming.

Ned mused on this for a moment as a High appeared

on the other side of the atrium and beckoned them sharply to follow.

'At least Sparks is there, Jenni. He won't let him out of his sight for a second.'

They couldn't talk any further as the High was accelerating down the hallway at top self-important advisor speed and they both had to hurry to keep up. He ushered them into the third best meeting room where Rose, Jimmy Fingers and Griff were waiting for them.

Chapter 5

Rose took a half step towards them when they entered the meeting room.

'What did Momma K say? Does she know anything?'

Jenn shuffled her feet, waiting for Ned to speak, but he was silent. At least he hadn't left her standing on her own.

'It's me Dad.'

'What! Norm?' asked Griff in surprise. 'Last I heard, he'd fallen off the edge of the world. Literally.'

'Yeah, well, 'e says 'e was working wiv the Ghosts and was meant to be joining them or summink, becoming a new spice but then he took their bones to a poker game for collateral and ended up losing 'em. So 'e ran.' She left out the bit about potentially going to get them back. Ned hadn't exactly agreed that they should, but she felt mostly confident that he would.

Everyone digested her explanation for a moment. Ned had the first question, as he'd been cogitating on things for longer.

'Why are the ghosts after you if Norm stole the bones?'

'I can answer that one, son.' Griff gave Jenni a friendly wink. 'When they realised their bones were missing, the Spice Ghosts would've cast a magical resonance spell based on the thief's essence left behind. For some reason that attached to Jenni and not her father.'

'Rubbish spell then, innit?' Jenni decided she

wanted to sit down for the next bit and took a chair at the meeting table. The others followed suit.

'Fred said the Spice Ghosts have been spotted?' Ned asked.

'We've had reports in from the eagle-eyed scouts that confirm a sighting,' replied Fingers.

'We got eagle scouts?' Jenni shook her head. 'Wot's next? Mermaid messenger fish?'

'It's funny you should say that actually,' began Fingers but he caught the look on Rose's face and cleared his throat before changing subject. 'We could try to get a message out to their ship before they land, but Griff says a welcome party at the harbour will pull more weight. Show respect and that.'

Ned nodded in agreement.

'Who's going to be there?' he asked.

'Me, my Highs, Fingers, you and Jenni. Oh, and Griff, of course,' replied Rose.

One of the Highs coughed.

'And some guards,' added Rose.

'Why are you coming, Griff?' Ned's ears flushed a little as he asked the question.

Jenni knew he hadn't really got used to calling Griff Dad and felt that Father was too stiff and formal. The two of them had been friends for years before Griff finally revealed the truth after his fake death. Jenni wished she'd had years to come to terms with the fact that her dad was called Norm.

'I'm Roshaven's new Warmonger.'

Jenni noticed that both Rose and Fingers looked a little uncomfortable at that statement. The Highs were staying well out of the conversation. They'd retreated to the furthest corner of the meeting room so they couldn't accidentally be called upon to take part. They were still listening, though.

'Does Roshaven need a Warmonger?' Ned was focused entirely on Griff now.

'That depends. Do you want neighbouring countries to carve up your little kingdom piece by piece without so much as a by your leave? Are you going to protect your Empress from every military incursion whilst walking the city beat? Know much about training people to kill, do you?'

'Well, I…'

'Enough!' Rose slapped her hand on the table. 'Ned, you are my Chief Thief-Catcher and I rely on you to keep the peace within my city. But Griff is right, we are a tiny empire. Easy pickings for anyone with half a mind to have a go. I don't have a war council or an army or even a general. So I appointed Griff as Warmonger. He will advise me.' She glanced around the room. 'As will you all. I trust I can rely on you to speak for the fae, Jenni?'

'Yeah. I'm sure Momma K will tell you if she don't like summink.'

'Will she not want to be here to greet the Spice Ghosts?' Fingers sounded nervous. 'I sent a messenger to tell her they were on their way.'

'If she does, she'll be there, but she didn't say nuffink spific.' Jenni felt like squirming in her chair. She didn't like it when people questioned her about Momma K. Just because she was Jenni's mum didn't mean Jenni knew better than anyone else what she would or wouldn't do. Yes, they were both fae, but Jenni was a sprite and Momma K was a full-blown faery. There was a difference not only in size but also temperament, magical leaning and affinity for things. You wouldn't catch Momma K dipping fries in milkshake, chasing gnomes or working as a thief-catcher.

'Well, we'd better go, if we want to be there before the ship arrives,' Fingers stood. But of course, it is never that simple to move an Empress from one place to another.

'We ain't gonna 'ave no city left to save at this rate,' Jenni muttered to Ned, who was drumming his fingers on the table while they waited for the Empress and the two Highs.

Finally, Rose appeared wearing the exact right headdress and associated finery. She proceeded with the others out to the courtyard, where at least someone had had the presence of mind to tell the stable boys to get the carriage ready.

'We ain't going in that, are we? It's practikally round the corner.'

'No Jenni, we're not. But the Empress has to make an impression,' said Ned as he watched Griff climb into the carriage as well. 'And apparently, so does my father. Come on, we don't want to get left behind.'

Ned, Jenni and Fingers fell in with the Highs who were solemnly trailing the slowly moving carriage as it came out the palace courtyard. The Palace Guards marched in a mildly co-ordinated fashion behind Ned. Jenni could see a small smile playing on Ned's lips, so she did her best not to catch his eye. Otherwise, they'd both start giggling. As it was, smiles grew on all three of them as the carriage went down Imperial Row towards the docks.

The procession had brought out the crowds; well-wishers, nosy neighbours and opportunistic pickpockets who at least had the decency to look semi-bashful as they caught Ned and Jenni watching them. Some even returned their picks.

The excitement of the expectant crowd rubbed shoulders with the uncertainty that hung over the imperial delegation, neither one knowing what to expect.

33

Chapter 6

A crimson mist rolled into the harbour, bringing with it ever-changing scents. There was ginger, cinnamon, nutmeg and cloves, - among others all aromatically combining, weaving in and out until the smell of mixed spice lay heavy in the air.

A vessel loomed in the mist. Shouts from crewmen could be heard as sails were furled, the anchor lowered, and lines thrown to moor the ship along the Dead Pier.

On the pier, skulls hung at jaunty angles along railings made of femurs and tibias. Some skulls were painted blood red, others black, but most had been bleached white and were highly polished. They all had deep, dark, empty eye sockets and grinning teeth.

Hastily Rose stepped down from the imperial coach onto the decking and beckoned Ned, Jenni, Griff and Fingers to stand with her, the Highs half-a-step behind them with the Palace Guards suitably arrayed. She squared her shoulders, ready to defend her city and empire, not really sure what she was about to face.

Boots thumped down the pier, echoing louder and louder until four shadowy figures materialised into physical people. The tallest among them had warm brown skin and a kind face. He wore trousers and a shirt in muted tones with a worn, weathered trench coat. Flanking him were two women. One had fiery red hair and a face full of freckles. She wore tight black leather trousers and a crisp white shirt with ruffles. A sabre was buckled to her waist. The other woman was ebony black with large, almond-shaped eyes. Her tightly curled hair

lay close to her skull, and she wore tiny dagger earrings
that dangled in her earlobes. Dressed in a red dress, she
stood out from the others who were more piratical.
Behind them all, the last figure was short and squat. He
had nut brown skin from sun exposure and was dressed
in a yellow silk shirt and brown trousers. As they came
closer, the three taller Spice Ghosts parted, letting the
shorter man stand before them. They all stood at
readiness, eyes alert and hands close to weapons.

Rose inwardly thanked the Highs for urging her to
change to ceremonial garb as she glided towards the
visitors, her imperial blue gown making her at least look
the part, even if she didn't quite feel it there and then.

'Welcome to Roshaven. I am Empress Rose. Whom
do I have the pleasure of addressing?'

The squat man spoke.

'We are the Spice Ghosts. Represented by Nutmeg,'
he pointed to himself. 'Clove.' The ebony woman.
'Ginger.' The redhead. 'And Cinnamon.' He jerked his
head back towards the tall man before focusing on Rose
again. 'We've come for our bones.'

Rose inclined her head at the introductions and
introduced her own retinue.

'We are pleased to meet you. May I introduce my
Warmonger Griffin Finglas, my Lower Circle Jimmy
Fingers, my Chief Thief-Catcher, Ned Spinks and Fae
representative Jenni.'

Nutmeg's eyes narrowed as he looked at Jenni. Rose
continued.

'I'm afraid we do not have your bones, but we
believe we may be able to discover who does have
them.'

Nutmeg raised one finger, causing Rose to stop
speaking in surprise. He extended the finger towards

Jenni and inhaled deeply.

'You took our bones. We've smelt you before.' His voice descended into a menacing hiss. 'Thief!'

Hurriedly Rose took a step to the side, throwing her arm out to stop Jenni from retaliating. She saw out of the corner of her eye that Ned too had put a restraining hand on Jenni's shoulder.

'I can assure you, Mr Nutmeg, Jenni does not have your bones. We believe it was her father who mistakenly took the bones and has since lost them. If you would accompany me to my palace, we will bring him in for questioning and together we can discover the exact location of your bones.'

Ginger, Cinnamon and Clove conferred too quietly for Rose to hear what they said, but as one they nodded at Nutmeg, who had half-turned towards them. Spinning back to face Rose, the short Spice Ghost pursed his lips, staring up at her intently for a moment.

'Very well. We accept your proposal. But be warned, you do not have long.'

Together the Spice Ghosts moved forwards, showing they would come to the palace and causing Rose to rapidly backpedal herself into her coach and the others to scramble after it as they travelled around the corner back to the imperial palace. She frantically beckoned Ned over.

'Can you get Sparks to bring Jenni's father to the palace? As soon as possible?'

Ned gave her a curt nod and sent Jenni running. With a bit of luck, she'd return quickly, and the Spice Ghosts wouldn't be kept waiting.

Rose's carriage and her guests arrived at the palace together and there was a period of intense diplomacy as the Spice Ghosts were shown to the second-best meeting room and refreshments called for. The diplomacy was mostly on the side of Rose, Ned and Jimmy. Griff eyeballed the Spice Ghosts while they themselves clumped together and regarded the others in silence.

Polite conversation had already mentioned the weather four times when Rose finally heard running footsteps in the corridor. She smiled at her guests and glided to the doorway. One of the Highs poked his head around the door.

'Your Eminence!' he puffed, out of breath at having had to run for the first time in a long time. 'Urgent message from the sprite. Her father has gone missing. She's trying to track him and will report back soon.'

'Snails,' snarled Rose under her breath, pinching one of Jenni's favourite expletives. She acknowledged the High with a nod and glided back to where Ned stood close to a plate of chocolate biscuits. He'd just taken a bourbon.

'He's done a runner, hasn't he?' Ned asked as he stopped levering the top of the biscuit off.

'How did you know?' whispered Rose.

'Because nothing is ever that simple.' He put his half-deconstructed biscuit down on his saucer. 'What's the plan?'

'Apparently Jenni is out looking for him, but who knows how long that will take.' She peeked over at the Spice Ghosts. There were signs of restlessness; a tapping foot, drumming fingers, and increasingly sour faces. 'What am I going to tell them?'

'I'd go with the truth.' Ned picked the biscuit back up. He hadn't had a decent bourbon in ages. There was a slim chance he might get to eat this one. 'People respect the truth.'

'For goodness' sake, finish eating that biscuit and

come with me. Who knows how they're going to react.'
It was Rose's turn to wait impatiently as Ned crunched
the final bourbon layer and brushed his hands clean of
crumbs.

At Rose and Ned's approach, the Spice Ghosts
turned their attention as one towards them and four sets
of eyes fixed on Rose. Trying to ignore the ball of slimy
dread in her stomach, Rose held her palms out
placatingly.

'It seems that the man we want to question has…
gone for a walk. He obviously did not know you would
arrive today. As soon as he returns, we will bring him to
the palace. You have my word.' She waited to see how
the Spice Ghosts would respond.

'Didn't see that one coming, did we?' snapped
Ginger, her sarcasm biting.

Cinnamon held up one finger and Ginger retreated,
still seething.

'In deference to your hospitality, we will give you a
second chance, but we cannot stay here any longer. You
will bring the thief to our ship within one hour,
otherwise we will take the daughter hostage or else you
can forfeit something equally valuable. Your
warehouses, perhaps?'

He spoke with such quiet authority that everyone in
the room, save the Spice Ghosts themselves, had leaned
in closer in order to hear every word, and it was in deep,
respectful silence that they watched the Spice Ghosts
leave.

'Ned?' Rose didn't have to say anything else.

'On it. Fingers, send out runners to your network.
I'll speak to Queen Anne. Jenni will have covered the
fae and will probably be running a tracking spell. I'll
send Joe over to the Runners Office and the coaches and

get Willow to put eyes and ears on the gates.' There were two sets of gates in and out of Roshaven, both more decorative than anything else and both equally covered in greenery. 'Willow will know the instant someone tries to leave the city, thanks to her plant vine.'

Rose smiled inwardly. Ned was so dashing when he took charge like this.

'Why do you think they can't stay here any longer? Did you hear them when they left the Dead Pier? They said we didn't have long.' Ned looked pensive. 'Do you think they can't stay on land for too long or something? Explains why they can't go looking for Norm themselves, I suppose.'

'I don't know, but maybe. It's said that they exist half in, half out of the mortal realm. Perhaps that's what it means,' replied Rose as she gave Ned a quick kiss before he hurried off.

A touch on her elbow brought her attention to Griff, who was standing just behind her.

'Do you think they really will destroy our warehouses?' she asked.

'I think they are desperate to get their bones back and we need to prepare for the worst, my liege. Get extra sandbags and buckets ready, just in case.' His face was sombre.

'I trust you to see to it,' Rose said, grateful for the advice and support. Fingers and Ned had already left. Now that Griff was hastening away, it left Rose in an empty meeting room. She spied a lone bourbon biscuit left on the plate and, taking it, headed slowly for her own office where she could think in peace about what to do next if Jenni's father couldn't be found.

Chapter 7

'I can't believe 'e's not 'ere,' said Jenni as Sparks buzzed behind her while she double checked every room in Ned's house. 'E's gotta be 'ere.' Jenni's heart sank. Of course he ran. Now she thought about it, it was obvious he was going to. She should've sent Sparks to get Ned or put a stay-put spell on Norm. But it had discombobulated her meeting her father for the first time. And then he'd shown her how to skim, which was illegal, but she'd done it anyway. She'd been having conniptions about Norm meeting Ned and how that was going to go down, but now there was no father. Norm had vanished.

Remembering that Ned had a power well in his bedroom, Jenni decided to use it to fuel a locator spell. What would have been an easy click of her fingers prior to her coming-of-age ceremony now demanded a stable source of energy for her magic and she'd already killed all the plants in Ned's house, much to Willow's disgust. Her new magical limitations were taking some getting use to. But when Jenni reached into the well, she discovered it was empty.

'Snails!'

A shout outside caught Jenni's attention. There was a group of lads kicking a ball around on the street. I could just do a quick skim, she thought. No one would notice. Taking a deep breath, Jenni reached out like Norm had taught her and felt the energies of the lads. It was crackling with enjoyment, but only two of the five actually had any magic to skim. Jenni swiped across and gasped as the stolen magic from two people swept into her. This was more like it. A quick glance out the window showed no ill effects on the lads. Or at least nothing she could tell. Now she could cast her spell.

A green arrow blinked in front of Jenni as she trotted down the stairs. With Sparks buzzing along in her wake, Jenni took the arrow's directions, turning right out of Ned's front door and then left at the top of the street.

Ned met them there.

'Locator spell?' he asked.

'Yep.' Guilt snaked in her stomach as she hoped Ned wouldn't ask where she got the juice for the spell from.

'I'm going to get Joe to check the Runners Office and coach yard while Willow activates her plant vine on the city gates. Then I'll ask Queen Ann to keep an eye out. We'll find him.' Ned paused and asked the obvious question. 'Er... what does he look like?'

Jenni's arrow spun to point in the opposite direction to Thief-Catcher HQ.

'He's got 'air like me, same ears and tails. Bit bigger and wearing a brown suit. I'll send Sparks back to you if I find 'im first.'

'Okay. Um, Jenni? The Spice Ghosts weren't too happy. They've given us an hour to hand him over otherwise...' Ned scratched his head.

'Overwise wot?'

'They want you as hostage or they'll destroy the harbour warehouses.'

Jenni bit her lip and nodded.

'Better get on wiv it then.' And she peeled off, following her arrow with Sparks glinting along beside her.

*****

41

Ned regarded them for a moment, wishing he'd been able to say something more comforting. Deep in thought, he hurried over to The Noose. The sooner he got the other catchers on the case, the sooner they'd apprehend Norm and sort out this mess.

Nodding a greeting over at Reg, proprietor of The Noose, Ned ignored the daytime patrons and scrambled up the back stairs to the Thief-Catcher HQ office. Willow and Joe were doing the paperwork that had accumulated after their interviews and looked up hopefully as Ned came in. No-one enjoyed doing paperwork.

'Alright, Boss?' asked Joe.

'No. Jenni's father has done a runner, and the Spice Ghosts want him for the theft of their bones. We've got to use every tool at our disposal to find him in the next fifty minutes, otherwise the Spice Ghosts will retaliate. Willow, I need you to activate your plant vine at the city gates. I want to know if anyone fae leaves the city. Joe, I need you to run down to the Runners Office and put a stop to any coaches due to leave. I want manifests for those already gone. Use all the authority of the Empress if they give you any trouble. Got it?'

Joe's mouth had opened at the mention of Jenni's father, and Willow's tendrils were all a quiver, but they were well trained enough to know that wasting time now by asking questions about what Ned had just told them would have a negative effect.

'What does he look like, Boss?' asked Willow.

'Sprite with dirty blonde hair, wearing a brown suit. Bit bigger than Jenni.'

Ned rummaged in his desk drawer for the imperial seal to give to Joe, while Willow went to the window and reached out to the lichen carpet she'd been cultivating. Ned watched, fascinated at the way she worked. Willow pushed her hands deep into the filaments as she began releasing a communications chemical. If any fae left the city, the plant vine would report back. Pulling her hands out, she entwined some tendrils for permanent contact. Allowing them to grow out meant she could return to the office but still be in touch with her network.

'Here you go, lad.' Ned gave the seal to Joe. 'Don't hang about, get going!'

As Joe dashed out, Ned took a silver bit out of the kitty and pocketed it.

'Willow, stay here and if by some miracle, Jenni's dad comes here, escort him to the docks.'

'Yes, Boss. Um… Boss? Something came up in the interviews, with the people claiming they'd had their magic stolen.' Willow fluttered her leaves. 'Only everyone said they remembered seeing an older sprite in a brown suit.'

Ned paused at the door. That was unlikely to be a coincidence.

'Don't worry about that at the moment. Let's focus on catching him. Once we've got him in custody, we'll question him about the bones and the magic thefts. Send word if you hear anything.' Then he hurried out and down the stairs. He was going to go straight to Queen Ann's court on the far East side of Roshaven. She was queen of the beggars, the best information network around and her subjects probably already knew what he wanted to know. All he could hope for was the Norm didn't have any previous agreements with the beggar queen. She was loyal to a fault.

As always, there was little movement to suggest Ned

had arrived at court, nor much indication that anyone was in residence, but Queen Ann famously never left. Not bothering to even announce himself, Ned headed straight for the semi-concealed doorway and knocked twice. It opened immediately, and he stepped through.

Queen Ann had changed since he last visited. This woman was younger than the last and, unlike the queen before her, was not wearing her beggar disguise in her inner court.

'You do not have an appointment.'

'It's a matter of some urgency, Ma'am. I'm looking for a man, he mustn't be allowed to leave the city.'

'And what is this man wanted for?' The young queen's voice was tightly controlled, but she couldn't hide the flash of anger Ned saw in her eyes.

'He has stolen the Spice Ghosts' bones and if he doesn't return them, they will retaliate.'

The queen's shoulders relaxed, and Ned realised she had been holding on to a great deal of tension.

'I brought a silver bit for the information, as is customary.'

The queen regarded the coin and allowed Ned to put it inside the worn wooden collection bowl on a nearby table.

'Customs change. The network is under new management, and you have not paid fealty.'

Ned tried to suppress his irritation. He didn't have the time nor inclination to jump through hoops to satisfy a new beggar queen. He'd had a good relationship with the last one.

'If I may ask, what happened to your predecessor?'

The queen turned away, hiding her face from Ned's question.

'She has been replaced,' came the eventual reply.

'My condolences. The agreement with the catchers stands, if the terms are acceptable.'

It was an ancient pact between law enforcement and the beggar network that had been in place ever since Roshaven had been a truly great empire.

The queen inclined her head in agreement.

'I will happily return with a new agreement for us to sign, if that's what you require. But I really need the network now.'

'Leave your description. It will be done.'

As Ned scribbled down what few facts he knew, his hope lay in the network's immediacy. The beggars found things out well before others, and a new arrival in the city should have been already noted. He hoped.

Fae, sprite, goes by the name of Norm, recently arrived. Dirty blonde hair, tufty ears and wearing a brown suit. Visited the Fae Grove and Ned Spink's house. Seen in the company of Jenni. Wanted for theft. Maximum bounty.

The queen had moved closer to Ned and he saw her eyes widen as she read his note.

'I'm sorry I don't have more information.'

'This is fine. Those who don't want to be found often shed their appearance several times. But maximum bounty, are you sure you can pay the fee?'

Ned felt a slight tickle of apprehension at the question but hoped that the coffers of the Empress would back him up as he nodded.

'We'll let you know once we've found him.' The queen waited for him to leave, her face impassive, having dismissed Ned from her court.

'The new fealty?' he asked.

'We'll let you know.'

Ned didn't want to outstay his welcome any longer,

so he supposed that would have to do and left the inner court. He wasn't sure how the beggar network passed information so quickly, but he wouldn't be surprised if, by the time he returned to the palace, the entire city would be humming and looking for Jenni's dad.

Chapter 8

Jenni's locator spell was having difficulties. First it spun left, then right. It travelled up, then down, and finally settled on a repeated wonky loop.

Sparks buzzed tentatively.

'No, my magic ain't on the fritz again. E's gone is all.'

Jenni checked the ley lines and saw that the locator spell was stuck on a convergence of power. With her coming-of-age power restrictions in place, Jenni had been learning more and more about how to harness what was available naturally. Something her father clearly had experience with.

There was another buzz.

'I don't know, mate. I can't track 'im from 'ere. I guess we heads back to HQ, see if the ovvers got any leads.' Jenni thought it unlikely. Surely Norm wouldn't be stupid enough to pop to somewhere else in Roshaven. He must have known the entire city would be looking for him by now.

She had just finished telling Willow what had happened when Joe came gasping in.

'No sign of anything down at the Runners Office,' he puffed.

Jenni chewed on a fingernail. Nothing much she could do until Ned came back.

'It's silent on the plant vine. Minimal fae presence across the entire city,' commented Willow.

Jenni knew that was Momma K's doing. She would have told all fae to stay within the realm, keeping out of the way so as not to be implicated in Norm's actions.

She was just wondering if she had time to nip to Aggie's for a cinnamon twist when Ned came through the door holding a bag of the very same baked goods.

'Great minds!' exclaimed Jenni as she took one eagerly, the others not far behind her. 'What did the Queen say?'

'It's a new queen, and she wasn't thrilled about us expecting previous agreements to stand,' said Ned.

'But it's always been that way. It's fing, innit. Can't change fing. Bred in the bones of the city.'

Ned was nodding in agreement as he ate.

'She agreed in the end. If the network sees your father, they'll let us know. I'm guessing you didn't get on too well?'

Jenni scowled.

'I lost 'im on Bucket Street. 'E just vanished, so popped, I reckon. If he can do that. I dunno. If 'e don't surface again then that's it, I can't find 'im.' But as she said it, Jenni realised there was one other thing she could try. She kept it to herself for now. Blood magic was nothing to trifle with and in order to power a spell of that magnitude, she'd need to do a lot of skimming. Hopefully, someone else would get lucky.

'We haven't got long left before we're meant to deliver Norm to the Spice Ghosts. We'd better get over to the Dead Pier. The Empress can meet us there.' Ned screwed the cinnamon twist bag up and threw it in the bin next to this desk.

'Wish it were that easy,' Jenni nodded towards the rubbish and shared a small smile with her boss. The real Cinnamon and cohorts wouldn't be so easy to get rid of.

It was a sombre walk to the harbour. No one felt like talking, Jenni, least of all. She was mad at herself for leaving Norm at Ned's and for not being able to find him. Being able to find wanted criminals was kind of her wheelhouse. That it was her own father made her feel worse. That and the guilt swirling round in her stomach for skimming magic, not telling Ned and wanting to do it some more. She actually thought she might be sick.

Rose, Fingers and Griff were waiting for them in a small pavilion that had been erected on the Dead Pier to add some imperialness to the proceedings. The Highs were tucked in towards the rear.

'Anything?' asked Griff.

Jenni shook her head for all the catchers. Their despondency was plain enough that she spoke for all of them.

Rose squared her shoulders, readying herself for what would come next.

'Jenni, I have no intention of allowing the Spice Ghosts to take you hostage in lieu of your father. We will find an alternative solution.'

Jenni nodded her thanks, not trusting herself to answer. She was touched.

Like before, the red mist rolled in from the docked vessel and four figures strode towards them with confidence echoing from each bootfall. Again, Nutmeg spoke for them all.

'Do you have him?'

''E escaped.' Jenni stepped forward, causing the Highs to tut at her baldness. 'I lost 'im. The 'ole city's been looking for 'im but 'e's done a runner.' She saw no reason to sugar coat the truth.

'We will not stop searching for him. You have my word,' said Rose, who had stepped forward to stand with Jenni.

'Then we shall take his whelp as hostage until he

returns the bones to us,' declared Nutmeg.

'I wouldn't advise that.' Ned had moved to stand on the other side of Jenni. He put a hand on her shoulder. 'She's the only one who will be able to find him.'

'But we have no assurances. We warned you what we would do if you did not bring us the thief.' Cloves sneered down at them.

'My word is the only assurance you need,' Rose said calmly.

'That is unfortunate,' spoke Cinnamon. 'You leave us in an untenable position.'

Ginger was rubbing her hands in glee and her hair had taken on a life of its own, growing redder and dancing about her shoulders. There was a crackle of energy and an intense gingery smell filled the air as the woman began levitating, her eyes gleaming. She raised her arms to point towards the group of warehouses on the left bank of the shore and fired. Two enormous fireballs shot out of her hands and rushed towards the buildings.

There was nothing anyone could do but watch as the fireballs hit their target and the buildings went up in flames.

'We shall return in four days' time. You will meet us here, at the Dead Pier, at first light. If the bones are not returned to us by then, we will raze this city to the ground,' said Nutmeg. 'A warning to others for allowing thieves to roam their streets and a deterrent to anyone who thinks of stealing from the Spice Ghosts in the future.'

The Spice Ghosts turned as one and returned the way they had come, their red mist retreating with them. Shouts could be heard from their crew as they made their vessel ready to leave.

'Why ain't we fighting back?' asked Jenni, her hands balled into fists.

'We don't have the firepower to take on the might of the Spice Ghosts. They are the defenders of the realms, not just sailors on the sea. And we must heed their warning. Remember the Port of Arnlisle?' asked Griff.

'No,' replied Rose.

'Exactly.'

Ned span round to Fingers.

'How can we help put the fires out?' he asked.

'Teams are already in place.' Fingers half bowed to Rose. 'I'd better see how they're getting on.'

As he hurried away, Ned looked at Rose for an explanation, but it was Griff who spoke.

'Whilst you were busying running around the city looking for a vanishing needle in a haystack, I took the liberty of emptying the warehouses of goods, people and livestock whilst stockpiling sandbags and water buckets for the inevitable.'

'But 'ow did you know wot the ghosts were gonna do?' asked Jenni.

'I am the Empress's Warmonger. It's my job to anticipate the enemy, prepare our defences and organise a counterattack.'

'And the Spice Ghosts did threaten to blow up warehouses,' added Rose.

'Fair play.' Jenni decided not to ask any more questions in case Griff decided she was the enemy. 'Wot are we gonna do now?'

'Find your father,' replied Rose firmly.

Chapter 9

Ned was knackered. Despite Griff's forward thinking at the dock warehouses, it had taken hours to completely put out the fire. Some stock had been lost. It was inevitable given the short time the Spice Ghosts had given for their deadline, but Rose had made sure Fingers worked out compensation packages for all those concerned. She couldn't give coin to everyone - her coffers weren't bottomless - but she had authorised Fingers to replace merchandise where possible and find other ways traders could profit in the long run.

Ned had also spoken to Fingers and offered some of his own recently acquired wealth. The huge payment Griff had bequeathed him in his fake will had still been transferred, despite the fact that Griff hadn't died, which made Ned one of the wealthiest people in Roshaven. Except for Griff, of course.

The other members of the thief-catcher team had called it a night an hour ago, Ned was just doing a last sweep of the area. It was all quiet. And damp. His boots squelched as he walked away from the docks towards home. Hopefully Jenni would have the fire built up and there would be something to eat.

A warm glow met him when he opened his front door.

'Well done, Jenni. I can't wait to sit in front of that fire. What a day.'

But when he looked over at the sofa, it wasn't Jenni sitting there. It was an older male sprite.

'Norm, I presume?' asked Ned, not sure whether to

raise an alarm or try to capture him. He decided he would find out why the sprite was here and then formally arrest him.

There was a clatter from the kitchen and a surly looking Jenni stomped through with two cups of tea.

'Kettle's boiled,' she snapped as she saw Ned. 'Don't worry, 'e ain't going nowhere. Apparently 'e wants our 'elp.' The tone of her voice suggested she didn't think he deserved it.

Ned decided against taking his boots off and instead made himself a brew with an extra spoonful of sugar. Then, perching on the arm of his easy chair, which he wished he could sink into, he regarded the two sprites. One radiated hostility, the other sipped his tea as if nothing in the world was amiss.

'What is it we can help you with?' Ned thought he'd better do the questioning, as Jenni looked like she was ready to murder. She was even drinking her tea aggressively, despite how hot it was.

'As you know, the Spice Ghosts think I stole their bones when, in actual fact it is a huge misunderstanding. I merely borrowed the bones.'

'Why ain't you given them back then?' asked Jenni.

'Someone else has them. Temporarily. I just need your help to retrieve them.' Norm moved his focus onto just Ned. 'I hear you won the Interspecies Poker Tournament. You know, a talent like that could win you big money in the games up in Braso Amia.'

'I'm not interested in playing any more poker,' said Ned. He had broken out in a cold sweat at the reminder of that game. It had been intense playing against the shapeshifting fae serial killer. But worth it. Ned always got his man.

'Shame. Well, that's where we need to go. To get

the bones back. I er… lost them, temporarily, and the person who is um… holding on to them for me, needs a bit of persuading to return them. Once we've managed that, you can take them back to the Spice Ghosts for me.' Norm slurped his tea and looked expectantly at Ned over the rim of his cup.

'You keep saying temporarily, but how do we know the person who has them will actually give them back?'

Norm squirmed on the sofa before replying.

'He's a gambler. He'll play for the right stakes.'

'And what about the skimming? Is that all a big misunderstanding as well?' asked Ned, figuring he might as well put the sprite on the spot. He watched as Norm flashed Jenni a look.

'Entirely my fault. I forget it's illegal here. I've been travelling for so long.'

Ned snorted.

'It's illegal everywhere, Norm. Consider yourself officially warned. Should any further skimming occur, you will be charged accordingly.' Ned wanted to arrest him. Skimming was dangerous, but all he had was hearsay at the moment, no proof, so hopefully the warning would be deterrent enough. He needed Norm focused on the Spice Ghost's bones. Ned stood.

'Jenni, a word in the kitchen, please?' And he walked through without waiting for her.

Putting the cup on the drainer, Ned began searching the cupboards for the half bottle of scumble he kept for emergencies. He had several emergency stashes dotted around the house for stressful times and this certainly felt like one of those.

'Way I sees it, Boss, is that we go in and out. Get the bones back, job jobbed and then the ghosts and 'im can bugger off.'

'We'll have to get imperial approval to take Norm to Braso Amia and negotiate getting the bones back.' Ned had found the scumble and was exchanging the tea in his mug for it. 'Do you think he's telling the truth? That this person who has the bones currently will want to give them up.'

'Yeah, I reckon that's where the bones are, but there's probably more to it.' She leaned closer to Ned. 'I don't fink we can trust 'im an 'alf inch, let alone a whole one.'

'I agree. The man is skimming, Jenni. Skimming!'

Jenni blanched with what Ned hoped was disgust at her father's magical choices. He didn't have to worry about Jenni doing anything like that. Ned's throat burned from the last of the scumble he tossed back and together they headed back into the front room. An empty sofa greeted them.

'What…?' Ned looked around in case Norm had changed chairs, but he definitely wasn't in the room. 'Has he gone again?' He asked Jenni.

'Yeah.'

Ned could tell she was fuming as actual smoke was coming out of her nostrils. He'd only ever seen Jenni this angry once before, and they had never spoken of the fishing trip again.

'Jenni… maybe you could calm down a little, eh?' He suggested cautiously.

''E left a note.' Jenni held it out to him, stiff-armed and tried taking deep breaths. It just made the smoke look even more impressive.

Keeping one eye on his enraged sprite, Ned cast a quick look over the note.

Meet me at the high tables in Braso Amia tomorrow evening. I'll get us a spot in the game. N.

'I guess we're headed for Braso Amia,' said Ned. 'Pack light.'

Chapter 10

It was half a day's travel to Braso Amia. Ned and Jenni had booked the first carriage headed that way from Roshaven, which did not leave until late morning, giving them plenty of time to be scolded by Rose in front of both Highs and Griff.

'Why couldn't you raise the alarm? You knew we were looking for him and that our city's very safety depends on handing him over to the Spice Ghosts.' Rose breathed heavily through her nose.

Ned decided it would be better to answer in empress-subject role, rather than take the romantic partner role.

'I'm very sorry, my liege, but Norm said he wanted our help to get the bones back, and we thought that would be the best course of action: return the bones and lift the threat.'

'Oh, don't you 'my liege' me,' huffed Rose, which was when Ned realised she was mad at him on every level.

'If I may, I think they did the right thing.' Griff ventured his opinion, which earned him a sharp look from Rose. 'Allowing Norm to lead us to the person he lost the bones to makes sense. To get them back, we can make them an offer they can't refuse. Certainly the most expedient course of action given Norm's reluctance to be captured and handed over.'

'I'm sorry, you said we?' asked Ned with a sinking feeling.

'Griff will go with you, to represent the empire and

keep you two out of any more trouble,' snapped Rose.

Ned finally understood where her aggression was coming from. She wanted to be part of the team. After the excitement of going on a quest to catch the rose thief, Rose had confessed to him a taste for adventure, but as Empress, she couldn't just disappear for a few days. He flashed her a small smile in sympathy and whilst she said nothing, her frown lines relaxed a little.

'Right, well, the carriage leaves in two hours so we'll just meet you there, yeah?' Ned said to Griff. It was the best he could do in the circumstances. Ned wasn't too impressed with having to take Griff with them. Ever since he'd come back from the dead and revealed himself to be Ned's father, Ned had found it difficult to rekindle their former friendship. He still felt like that part of their history was dead and buried. He would much rather be travelling with his love than his father. Ned caught the hurt look that flashed across Griff's face before he covered it with bravado.

'Wonderful! It'll be a grand adventure, eh lad?' Griff clapped Ned on the back and smiled widely. 'I've got some business to conclude in Braso Amia. Happy accident, no? Winning all round.' His forced jocularity was grating on Ned's nerves. Rose saved him.

'I just want a word with my thief-catcher before you all leave. Don't let Roshaven down. We're counting on all of you.' Rose dismissed the room except for Ned.

He wondered if he was going to be shouted at again. As the door closed behind the last person, Rose closed the gap between them. Instinctively Ned drew her into a hug, and they stood like that for a few moments, each savouring the close warmth of the other. Ned dropped a kiss on the top of Rose's head. She looked up at him.

'You will be careful, won't you? I can't lose you

after everything we've been through.'

Ned smiled.

'Don't worry. We'll all be back in one piece, with the bones, before you know it.'

'Good, because we have our future to plan.'

Ned's stomach flipped again, so he said nothing, just held on to Rose for a little while longer.

They were both a little misty-eyed when Ned finally left the palace, but his cheeks were warm and his heart felt light. There was a lot to be said for goodbyes with loved ones. He couldn't wait for the home coming reunion.

The lengthy goodbye to Rose and then waiting for Jenni to meet him at the Palace gates meant they ended up running late. As it was, they barely made the coach, and it had only been down to some fast talking from Griff that it had waited for Ned and Jenni at all. In all fairness, they were haring around the corner towards the coach courtyard at the exact moment it was due to go and the driver could see that they were running towards him. Plus, they had shouted, yelled and hollered. But coach drivers were strict with their timetables. Their rules and regulations made them a success, and even though today's driver had only had to leave forty-five seconds later than he was meant to, it meant he grumbled about making up the time for the entire journey.

When they pulled into Braso Amina exactly on time, Ned couldn't help but feel a little smug. He pushed down the urge to say told you so. Jenni, however, had no compunction. She offered a handsome bribe to the driver if he deliberately waited a minute and a half before leaving to return to Roshaven. He declined.

'Save your money, young Jenni. You'll need it once

we get into Mannon's Lair.' Griff was rubbing his hands in glee.

'Mannon's Lair? Sounds like the one place we want to avoid,' replied Ned doubtfully. He didn't know if he could trust Griff to have Roshaven's best interests at heart in a place like this.

'Trust me, lad. It's where the high-stakes games will be played. And where we'll be able to find Norm, I have no doubt. Come, let's go find us a place to stay. And then, we play.'

Griff was enjoying himself far too much for Ned's liking, but he let him lead them to a suitable hostelry. Despite himself, Ned couldn't help but be impressed at the number of people Griff knew and greeted like long-lost friends. They all responded warmly. He was clearly a well-known, well-liked person.

The hostelry Griff chose was called The Maiden's Blush, which made Ned frown as they entered. It seemed respectable enough; clean, brightly lit, with the smell of freshly baked bread wafting from somewhere. It reminded Ned's stomach that he hadn't eaten since breakfast.

'Ah, Meester Griff! So good to see you again. You staying longtime? I have your usual ready for you?'

A very tall, thin tree nymph beamed at the group from behind his welcoming desk. If Ned had to put money on it, he'd say the nymph was some kind of reed. But really plants weren't his thing.

Looking over at the other guests, the reed seemed to dismiss Jenni and Ned at first, but then, upon seeing a human and fae together, and clocking their Thief-Catcher badges, he came swaying from behind the desk.

'You are Spinks, are you not? And Miss Jenni? From Roshaven? My cousin has told me much about you.' The reed leaned in a little closer. 'We are proud, so proud to have Willow working in law enforcement.' He spread his arms expansively. 'Delighted to have you staying at the Blush. Anything you need, you just ask Remmy. I at your service.' He bent low, forehead nearly touching the floor.

'Thank you, Remmy. That's very kind. We will need three rooms for the night, please.' Ned hoped the reed stopped bowing soon, as they were drawing attention.

Remmy sashayed back to his desk, and with delicate fingers, began flicking through his book.

'Ah! I have a suite for you. Four bedrooms and rumpus room in the middle. Perfect for chatting.' He leaned a little closer to them. 'I send welcome basket.' He passed the keys over to Ned.

'Thanks, Remmy. Appreciate it.' Ned nodded, uneasy about exactly what a rumpus room was, and glanced at Griff, who quickly hid a grin. Wondering what that was for, Ned followed him to the stairwell.

'Top floor is only two flights. Still the largest place in town. It's wide, see.' Griff pointed at the room numbers painted on the door they passed. It read 21-40. 'The top floor has several suites. We're lucky they've got one to spare.'

'How's that?' Ned wondered if Griff always stayed in a suite.

'There's a big game tonight. Here.' Griff handed Ned a flyer he'd picked up from somewhere. It read:

Tonight in Mannon's Lair
TRY YOUR LUCK
Your chance to test the cards against the best
It's Open Season!
Will there be a new champion or will Landis 'The Blade' Kane reign supreme?

'Did you know about this?' asked Ned.

'Ned, my lad. Of course I knew about it. We'll have some fun, eh?' Griff double checked the number on the door and rapped his knuckle on it. 'This is us.'

Scowling, Ned opened the suite and let out a low whistle. It was huge. The Thief-Catcher's office would fit three times over in this space. The rumpus room, it turned out, comprised half a dozen comfortable chairs, a bookcase, a chess set, an open fireplace and a drinks cabinet. Two doors lay either side of the room. Jenni headed for the nearest one on the left and revealed a huge four-poster bed which she proceeded to go jump on.

'Uh, which room do you want?' Ned asked Griff.

In answer, Griff took the nearest one to the right. Deciding that keeping Jenni nearby wasn't such a bad idea, Ned walked towards the far-left door. He too, had a four-poster bed. And a desk, two chairs and another door, which revealed a bathtub. Idly, Ned wondered whether Rose would like to stay in a place like this, then shook his head. She was probably used to rooms much more extravagant than this. He'd barely had any time to explore the imperial palace since moving in and had kept his old house, so he had somewhere to decompress. Plus, it was handy for working late.

Dropping his bag on the floor, Ned went back to the sitting room. He felt more comfortable calling it that.

'What shall we do until the poker game starts?' he asked.

'I'm starving, Boss,'

'Yes, let's eat and decide on a plan for this evening.

We need to co-ordinate our efforts. While we are here, there is something I need to procure.' Griff rubbed his hands together. 'Ready? I know a great place.'

I bet you do, thought Ned as he followed Griff and Jenni out of their rooms, careful to lock it securely behind them.

Chapter 11

Griff took them to a food court. When he'd told them that was where they were going, Ned had been a little apprehensive. He wasn't sure what a food court was. However, on arrival he decided it was just like market day, only instead of vendors shouting out lots of different wares, they were shouting out different food. The thing he liked the most about the food court was that they didn't all have to eat from the same place. The thing he liked least about the food court was having to endure other people's weird food choices. And the smell. There was a powerful mixture of aromas going on.

Jenni had opted for her all-time favourite dish, beetle cheesecake, and Ned wasn't about to question whether she should be eating just dessert. Griff had chosen a seafood medley that looked a little too lively for Ned's liking. He was sure he'd seen the tentacles move. He'd played it safe and gone for a pizza, figuring you can't do much wrong with a pizza and, to be fair, it wasn't bad. Just the wrong shape. Everything in the food court was connected to Mannon's Lair and gambling. Like his pizza, for example. In the shape of a playing card. Quite what was wrong with a circle was beyond Ned.

'Coins are circular,' he muttered, pulling another slice apart to eat.

'Wossat, Boss?' Jenni's cheesecake was decorated with hearts, diamonds, clubs and spades.

'Fun place to eat, eh?' Griff spoke but wasn't really paying any attention to Ned or Jenni. He was too busy scanning the crowds.

'What are you looking for?' Ned asked.

'Opportunities are only missed if you don't look for them and I'm always on the lookout.' Griff shot a grin at Ned and took a large scoop of his medley.

Ned grimaced. That tentacle had definitely moved. He pushed his pizza away, appetite lost.

'You done, Boss?'

Ned nodded and Jenni helped herself to a slice.

'S'not bad this, 'cept for the funny shape.'

Ned was feeling antsy. He told the others he was going to get some air and left them to their dinner. Walking out of the cacophony of sounds and smells, he at once felt more settled, as if he could now finally hear his own thoughts again. Outside it was getting dark, and there was a faint nip in the air. Ned felt in his pockets until he found his tobacco and pipe and lit up, leaning one-legged against a wall, watching with interest the different people streaming in and out of the food court.

There was a generous mix of fae amongst the humans. Ned saw a couple of pixies and a dryad, a gnome, a pack of goblins and - if he wasn't mistaken - an imp. The humans were just as interesting. They'd obviously travelled from all over as he saw thick winter coats and fine thin silks. There were high hems and trailing cloaks, masks and veils, gloved hands, bare hands, even blue hands. Mannon's Lair attracted people from everywhere.

No wonder Griff seems right at home here, thought Ned. Braso Amia seemed to be the perfect place to conduct a little smuggling.

Ned was coming to the end of his smoke and was knocking the wattle from his pipe as Griff and Jenni emerged from the food hall.

'You ready for this, eh? Just follow my lead,' said

Griff with a wink.

'What exactly are you leading us into? Are you planning to go straight in and ask for the bones back? Or is this recon?' Ned wasn't happy with the notion of not having a proper plan. Granted, his plans were often made up of let's go see what happens, but at least he admitted it.

'Let's get the lay of the land, eh? See what's what. We've got to meet your man, Norm. Did he say where?'

'No. He's going to find us.'

'Well, all the more reason to go blend in, eh?' Griff chuckled and led the way.

'Don't worry, Boss. We can always pretend we don't know Griff if fings go south.'

Ned had to smile. Whilst he would never actually leave Griff behind, it was an amusing thought.

Mannon's Lair was set back from the other establishments in Braso Amia. An avenue of streetlamps burnt merrily, lining the path to the entrance. It was a large dome-like cave, and despite his best peering as they walked up the avenue, Ned couldn't make out what was inside. As they drew closer, he could see dark red curtains hanging back from the open archway. People a few feet in front of them walked calmly through the curtains and Ned heard laughter and tinkly music.

'Relax, lad. We'll find your man.' Griff strode confidently through the curtain, Jenni scampering happily behind him.

Ned was more cautious. He looked left and right, noting the discreet guard huts on either side of the entrance. They were half in, half out of the curtains, obviously there to watch for trouble within and without. The guards were run-of-the-mill brutes who clearly knew their job; they didn't react to Ned's scrutiny outwardly, but they put pen to paper. Ned walked in with a touch of pride. He'd made it to the lookout list.

Inside, multicoloured smoke hung in the air, low lighting added to the cave-like atmosphere, and the walls sparkled. He'd already lost Griff and Jenni. They were nowhere to be found. Happy screaming to his left grabbed Ned's attention. A woman with purple skin and black hair had just won something. She seemed very pleased.

Ned put his hands in his pockets and hunched his shoulders. He tried to ignore the operating pickpockets, the bartender watering down the whiskey, the floating ladies of the night and the sleight-of-hand dice swapping. This wasn't his city, and it wasn't his job. He disarmed three people of their shoddily concealed weaponry and accidentally knocked into a seedy-looking man, about to add some white powder to his companions' drink on the sly. Some things couldn't be ignored.

After two turns around the main room, Ned found Jenni near the bar, atop a stool, drinking a beer.

'S'awright 'ere ain't it, Boss? Got a real flavour to it,' she said.

If Ned didn't know better, he'd say she was drunk. But Jenni never got drunk. He squinted at her. She looked different. More… sparkly. Ned shook his head. Jenni had probably walked through a glitter fountain or something.

'Yeah, this place is delightful.' Ned deposited the confiscated weaponry on the bar and signalled for a drink. 'Any sign of your dad yet?'

'Nope. Not a sausage.'

'What's Griff up to?'

'Dunno. I lost 'im in the crowd. But I'm sure e'll

come find us if 'e needs us.'

Ned thought it was very convenient that Griff had lost them. A short man jostled him, making him spill his drink.

'Hey, watch it, mate!' Ned clocked who it was. 'Thanks for that, Norm.'

'Mr Spinks, Jenni, dear. I see you both made it. Wonderful, wonderful. And with the full consent of the Empress, I hope? Ready to right wrongs and stick up for the little guy.'

'More or less,' replied Ned. 'Let's get on with this. Who did you lose the bones to?'

Norm's gaze darted around the room.

'He's not here yet. Erick the Diamond is a big player. He'll want to make an entrance. The big money games don't start until Erick gets here.'

'You seem very nervous, Norm,' remarked Ned, wondering what other trouble Jenni's father had brewing.

'Let's just say, having the Spice Ghosts on my tail isn't the only problem I'm dealing with.' He regarded Jenni, head tipped to one side. 'You look positively glowing, are you... safe?'

Ned watched the interaction curiously. Why would Norm be asking if Jenni was being safe? There was something going on here.

Norm finally looked Ned straight in the eye. 'You haven't got any string, have you?'

Ned, being an upstanding citizen of Roshaven whose boots lasted longer than his laces, reached wordlessly into one of his coat pockets and passed a ball of string to Norm, whose face lit up.

'Capital. This will do nicely.'

Ned watched with interest as Norm performed an

intricate version of cat's cradle with the string, securing different bits of junk from his own pocket in various places and muttering all the while under his breath.

'Jenni?' whispered Ned. 'What's he doing?'

She peered over Ned's arm to take a better look.

'E's making a tangle. Hedgewitch magic for taking a peek into the future. Never got on wiv it meself but I 'eard it can work well.'

'Why was he asking if you're being safe? Is something going on?'

'Nah, Boss. It's all good. Don't worry about it,' replied Jenni, looking a little glass-eyed. She was definitely drunk on something.

Norm muttered under his breath and adjusted a few bits of rubbish before letting the entire thing unravel. He scooped all the composite parts back into his pocket, taking Ned's string with him.

Ned waited, but Norm was not forthcoming.

'Well?' he prompted.

'What? Oh, too many variables to tell for sure. Could go either way.' Norm looked Ned square in the eye. 'Do you have a lucky talisman?'

'What? No.'

'Pity. We could have sacrificed it to the gods of fate.' Norm licked a finger and held it up. He sniffed. 'Not that it would've done much good. The energies are all off.' He muttered under his breath some more.

'Jenni? What's your take on the energies?' Ned wasn't sure if this was all an act on Norm's part. He looked around, taking in the excited chatter of the patrons, the buzzing of the card tables, stressed out waitresses trying to serve drinks and snacks, beady-eyed security guards sizing everyone up, winners and losers rubbing shoulders together, all of them trying to get ahead of the house.

'There's desperation and 'ope, Boss, in buckets. 'Ard to tell if there's ought else,' she replied. 'Lots of opportunity though…' Jenni trailed off and earned a sharp glance from Ned.

Opportunity for what exactly? he thought. Two no-neck security guards were making a beeline for where Ned stood. He cast a glance sideways at the rapidly disappearing throng of people.

'You two, with us,' grunted the larger of the two behemoths.

'Two of us?' queried Ned before realising that Norm had made his escape with the thinning crowd. 'Where are you taking us?'

'The boss wants to see you.' And with that one heavy grabbed Ned, the other Jenni, in a vice-like grip and began steering them towards a pair of double doors.

Ned braced himself for what might be behind the doors and hoped fervently that it wasn't a beating. The doors swung open to a small chamber where a single poker table was set up, six occupied chairs around it.

'Mr Spinks, I've been expecting you.'

'You have?' Ned was trying to see if Griff sat in one of the chairs, but it was hard to tell. The room was shadowy, spotlights picking out just the players' hands, the cards played and a pile of gold bits. 'And who are you?'

'I'm Erick, proprietor of Mannon's Lair. And you, you have come to play me for a pile of old bones. Come, join in. We have an opening.'

At that point, a body toppled sideways from one of the chairs. One of the brute squad hauled it away and Ned saw a jewelled dagger sticking out of the deceased player's eye.

'I'm not here to play. But I'll happily negotiate the release of the artefacts. For a fair price.' Ned had stepped closer to the table and could see Griff sat with a modest pile of coin in front of him.

'Come now,' coaxed Erick. 'Not even a simple coin toss? Fifty-fifty chance.'

Ned glanced at Jenni, but she was walking around the table, sizing everyone up. The other players weren't sure who to keep an eye on. The roving sprite or the man who refused to play.

'Maybe I'll come back tomorrow. When you've finished your little game.' Ned glared at Griff as he spoke. 'Jenni.'

The sprite capered back to Ned's side.

'We'll see ourselves out.'

Ned stalked out of the private room, ignoring the brute squad escorting him across the gaming area and out the entrance. He wasn't sure if he was madder at Erick, Griff, or Norm.

A simple coin toss would have been rigged. He didn't need to be a thief-catcher to know that. And there was no way he was sitting down to play cards at that table. His poker experience was minimal at best and Ned was certain he had used all his luck last time he played. Norm could have stuck around. Ned might have been able to make more of a bargain if he'd had the sprite who lost the bones in the first place and Griff... he had just sat there and said nothing. Fat lot of good that was.

'Wot we gonna do now, Boss?' asked Jenni.

'Give it a minute. If I'm right, Erick won't be able to resist coming out and offering some kind of deal. No doubt he thinks I'm a cowardly push over because I wouldn't play.'

'Awright.' Jenni started jigging from foot to foot.

'Ow long do you fink e'll be?'

'It's fine, go back in. I'll catch up with you later.'

'Fanks, Boss!' And she vamoosed back into the lair, her pockets jingling with small change.

Chapter 12

Ned was refilling his pipe, wondering whether he'd be able to get a refill of Mystic Leaf here. He usually bought it from the fae market stall back in Roshaven and even then they only had it in stock occasionally.

'Light?'

Erick struck a match on the wall of his building and offered Ned the flame. Hiding his smugness at being right, Ned puffed on his pipe gratefully and nodded his thanks. Erick lit up a cigar and they smoked in contented silence.

'I admire a man who sticks to his principles.' Erick spoke first. 'It shows great character.'

Ned said nothing. Erick came out here for a reason so Ned was going to wait for him to tell him what it was.

'You were right not to bet me. I don't have the bones you're looking for.' Erick puffed a smoke ring as Ned looked sideways at him. 'Let's say I'm a semi-honest gambler. Griff told me you were his lad and I owe him a favour, so I'm extending that to you. I have other bones, but I do not have the ones the sprite lost to me.'

Ned wondered whether Griff had mentioned he was Ned's father before or after Ned refused to gamble.

'What happened to the bones I'm looking for?' he asked instead.

'We sold them along with a job lot of semi-mystical items to the fae traders that passed through Braso Amia last week. I hear they're headed for Roshaven next, so who knows? Your luck may hold after all.' Erick put his cigar in his mouth and, hands in his pockets, wheeled around, heading back for his gaming empire.

'Bloody typical,' muttered Ned. If they'd just stayed in Roshaven, the bones would've come to them.

'Ere Boss, guess wot I just found out?' Jenni bounced out of Mannon's Lair gleefully.

'The fae traders have got our bones.'

'Ow did you know that?'

'Come on, we might get back tonight if we hurry.' Ned knocked his pipe out on the wall and strode off towards the coach stand.

Unfortunately, fate was not smiling on them. The night coach to Roshaven had already left. It irritated Ned to discover the bookings office was also closed and with no transport of their own, they would just have to come down first thing in the morning to get tickets on the early coach. There weren't even any coaches available to hire privately, which had Ned swearing under his breath when he walked into The Maiden's Blush.

Remmy instantly caught Ned's mood.

'Meester Spinks! How can I be of assistance?' The reedy tree nymph was bent to the side in an alarming manner.

'You haven't got a coach hidden around here, have you?'

Remmy shook his head, his entire body swaying with the action.

'In that case, Remmy, we need an early morning wake up call. We'll be leaving first thing on the coach to Roshaven.'

Remmy snapped upright and thrummed with energy.

'Consider it done, Meester Spinks. I shall ensure the tickets myself. Will it be all three of you travelling?' He gestured behind Ned.

Turning, Ned saw Griff had returned.

'Yes, Remmy my lad. Three seats, please,' replied Griff.

Remmy faded into the background the way good concierges do as Ned and Griff squared off to each other.

'Lost you in the Lair. You could've said where you were going.' Ned spoke first.

'Business to attend to. You know how it is, eh?'

'Not really. I'm a thief-catcher, not a gambler.'

Jenni tried to diffuse the tension.

'Anyways, we knows where to look now, don't we? Almost got wot we came for, eh?'

Ned flicked a withering glance in her direction, noticing how she had adopted Griff's speech pattern.

'I'll see you on the coach,' he said, giving neither one the opportunity to respond as he left for his room.

*****

'Wot you been up to, then?' asked Jenni, as she and Griff were left in the lobby together.

'Oh, you know, networking, buying and selling, that sort of thing. Braso Amia is a great place for connecting.'

'I saw you talking wiv Norm earlier.'

Griff maintained his smile throughout and looked indulgently down at the sprite.

'I talk to lots of people.'

'And it 'curred to me you probably 'ad a lot to talk wiv 'im about. Like 'ow the Spice Ghosts are in town and looking for 'im and stuff. Cos of corse you wouldn't be wanting 'im to do anyfink dodgy like steal any bones or anyfink.'

Jenni stared up at Griff with innocence plastered across her face.

'Ha! I can see why Ned relies on you.' Griff gestured to the communal area. 'Let's sit, shall we? I'll get the drinks in.'

Ten minutes later and they were both sat comfortably with a drink and multiple snacks. Jenni was munching on crystallised ants with relish.

'Wot's the deal then?' she asked.

'It's true that I asked Norm to help me acquire something of great value, but I had nothing to do with the theft of the bones. That was completely his own affair.'

Jenni took a slurp of her beverage.

'But you put the idea in 'is 'ead though, right? Mentioned it in passing sorta fing, yeah?'

'I can't help what I talk about. I've had many adventures – people are always asking me to tell stories.'

Jenni nodded. Stories were important.

'Wot did you tell 'im?'

Griff pulled a face and shrugged, shifting in his chair. Jenni's questioning was clearly hitting a nerve.

'Eh, you know…'

'No. I don't. And I ain't taking no more flim flam. You tell me right now wot you told 'im.' She leaned forward, jabbing her finger in his direction. 'We got the fricking Spice Ghosts bent on destroying my 'ome and I ain't 'aving it. Wot did you say?'

With a shake of his head, Griff took a swig of his beer before he started speaking.

'The Spice Ghosts are known as a myth to frighten the young. Do what you're told or the Spice Ghosts will come get you, that sort of thing, eh? They've passed a little into legend. This is not a good thing. The Spice Ghosts are a necessary part of our world. They are the guardians of the spirit realm. They use their mystical bones to communicate between realms and maintain the balance.' He sipped his drink again. 'It's an important role. Without them, there would be chaos. They appease the spirits, guide them to their peace and prevent malevolent ones from wracking their revenge on the living. They are the balance between life and death. Surely you understand the importance of balance.'

Jenni nodded. She did indeed, even more so now that she'd passed through her coming-of-age ceremony and her magic was moderated. Because she had to pay for what she used, it made her much more thoughtful in her usage and it had taken her a long time to figure out how to cast again.

'Why them, though? I fawt death sorted out stuff like that.'

'Ha! Death. He just reaps souls, cares nothing for the spirits,' replied Griff.

'Ain't they the same fing?'

Griff tugged his beard and regarded the sprite.

'A soul makes you alive. It's your very essence. Death will reap your soul, no matter who you are. But spirits, spirits are what get left behind. Energy never dies and when you live your life, you generate such life force, it has to go somewhere,' he said.

'I still don't get it. Sounds like the same fing to me,' grumbled Jenni.

'Hmm, let me see if I can explain it better, eh? Your soul is what you're born with, your spirit is what you make with your life. A bad spirit can rot your soul. A good spirit shines out a person. Your soul goes back into the fabric of the universe but your spirit remains.'

'I fink I got it. Seems like a bit of a fine line though.'

'Most things in life are, eh? Most things are.'

They both sat back and mused for a while, the

silence punctuated by the occasional crunch of ant.

'So basically, yor saying we're screwed,' said Jenni eventually.

Griff lifted his beer up and toasted her statement.

'And it's yor fault for telling Norm to steal the bones.'

'Jenni! Were you not listening? I didn't tell him to steal the bones. I just happened to tell him a tale about them and many other things.'

'Yeah, but you gotta know you can't tell people about powerful stuffs like that and not expect them to try and get a look at 'em. Plus, you knew 'e was a gambler. Gamblers are desperate people.' Jenni waved a hand around, as if to include everything around her.

Griff's face grew very serious.

'I had no idea he would take their bones. Truly. A theft of that magnitude was never my intention.'

'Yeah. Yor still a plonker.'

Griff laughed again but made no comment.

'Wot was it you wanted 'im to get for you?'

'Just some old scrolls.' Griff waved his hand dismissively. 'Nothing of any import.'

Jenni regarded Griff suspiciously, giving him her best pissed off cat glare. It had absolutely no effect, so she decided that whatever the scrolls were, they weren't anything to worry about right now.

'Well, I'm gonna call it. Early morning, I reckon. Night Griff.'

'Night,' said Griff. 'Oh, Jenni? I don't suppose I can ask you to keep my involvement with your father's decision making to yourself, can I?'

She just grinned at him and he laughed.

Chapter 13

Ned stepped down from the express coach with stiff legs. He stalked sideways to allow the others to get out and took a moment to flex some feeling back into his knees. His feet stretched across familiar cobbles. Although they hadn't been gone long, it was good to be back in his city.

The journey back had been strained. Last night Jenni had told him what she'd found out from Griff. Ned didn't think Griff was involved directly with the bone theft or that he wanted anything disastrous to happen to Roshaven. It was just an unfortunate coincidence that he'd happened to ask Norm to procure items for him, and Norm had stolen the bones as well.

Ned was not looking forward to telling Rose the news and wanted to retreat to HQ first, but as both Chief Thief-Catcher and the Empress's husband, he thought he'd better get on with reporting back.

'Jenni? Can you see if the fae traders are at the grove yet, please? If they've already arrived, don't let them leave. We need to talk to them,' he said.

'Will do, Boss.' Jenni stomped off to the small patch of green that led into the fae realm.

Ned felt a moment of pride as he watched her walk towards the grove instead of using magic to travel five minutes away and in the process burn through all the nearby foliage just to shave those five minutes. It looked like Jenni was really getting to grips with her magical restrictions.

He noticed two men collide in the street. The

bumped man was shouting at the other to watch where he was walking whilst the bumper looked dazed. Day drinker? He was about to call out to Jenni to double-check as she passed, when he noticed she'd disappeared. That had been quick. After a last check to ensure the two men were alright, he drew his attention back to what he should be doing.

'You coming?' Ned reluctantly asked Griff. It was the first time he'd spoken to him since they left Braso Amia, but he didn't wait for a reply. He was still annoyed that Griff had concealed information from him. Clearly, the former smuggler had trust issues. Griff fell in step with him as they walked to the palace.

Entry into the Imperial Palace involved a little more ceremony than it used to. Since Ned and Rose had married, the palace guards and household staff would bob a curtesy or salute him. He didn't mind so much now, but when it had first started, it had made him feel uncomfortable. The High Right had taken him to one side and explained that asking the staff to stop doing it disrupted the natural order and flow of the household. Ned had no desire to disrupt flow.

The wedding had been a beautiful day and Rose had worn that gorgeous dress. He remembered smiling so much his face hurt. The actual day had gone by in a blur, over so quickly, and Ned often found himself double checking that he was actually married.

Managing to avoid all pomp, Ned headed for the study, Griff ambling along behind. The study was the place both he and Rose felt most comfortable and least imperial, where they could talk honestly about things.

She wasn't there when he arrived, but Ned had no doubt that word would be carried. It was, at times, a little scary at how closely his movements were observed within the palace by watchers unseen.

Sure enough, Rose arrived in a cloud of her cinnamon perfume and a hopeful smile which faltered at the grim expression on the two men's faces.

'What happened?' she asked.

'Long story short, the bones are with the fae traders. They don't know what they've got, I don't think. Jenni is headed to the grove now. They left Braso Amia before us in their wagons, but we took the express back this morning and we should've beaten them.'

Rose squared her shoulders.

'We have a lead at least,' she said. 'Did you want some tea?'

'No. I'm going to drop in at HQ before I head to the grove. Make sure everything's alright,' replied Ned.

'Yes please,' replied Griff, taking a chair.

'Oh, one more thing. It turns out Griff here already knew Norm and had him in his employ to get some scrolls from the Spice Ghosts when our sticky-fingered friend stole the bones and use them as a buy-in for a high-stakes gambling game.' Ned dropped Griff squarely in it with Rose before leaning in to give her a quick hug and kiss. 'Wish me luck with the fae traders.'

Griff shot him a wry look as he left, and Ned couldn't help but grin. He knew his father would worm his way out of any serious hot water. That didn't mean that Ned wasn't still mad at him. They'd talk about things later, after they had found the bones.

Chapter 14

It relieved Jenni to see the trader wagons parked by the mushrooms. The fae traders hadn't left yet, but they were nowhere in sight. She listened for a moment and caught the low hum of chatter, so she hurried off in that direction.

The fae traders were surrounded by people clamouring to get the best deal on the hard-to-find items on display.

Jenni snagged a young faerie, who was clutching something to their chest tightly.

'Ere, do you know who's leading this year?' she asked.

Every year, someone different led the fae traders. They were a nomadic collection of fae who liked to travel where their fancy took them. Sometimes that aligned with the trade routes, and sometimes it didn't.

'The one at the back,' piped the faerie before scuttling away.

'The one at the back,' muttered Jenni, craning her neck to see who was standing at the back.

'Looking for me?' a voice came from behind her. Jenni whirled to see who it was. 'I'm Tristan, leader of the FT this year. How can I help?'

A tall elf with a shock of bright blonde hair and pointy ears that stuck out like wings stood with his hands on his hips behind her. He had a big grin on his face. Jenni narrowed her eyes at him.

'Ow did you know I wos looking for you?'

Tristan waved one hand airily.

'There's always someone looking for me. For one reason or another. You thinking of joining up?' He looked her up and down appraisingly. 'We could do with someone with magical strength like you. Bandits get bolder every year.'

'Nah, I ain't interested in that.'

'Shame.' Tristan bobbed up and down on the balls of his feet. 'What can I do you for then?'

'I'm after some bones. You got 'em off Erick at Mannon's Lair the ovver day.' Jenni tried not to put too much hope into her voice. She didn't want to drive the price up too high.

Tristan tapped one finger on his lips and began micro pacing back and forth.

'Bones. Bones. Boney bone bones. Hmmm.'

Jenni was about to lose her temper when Ned hurried over.

'Glad we haven't missed you.' He turned and gave a shallow bow to Tristan before speaking the traditional greeting. 'Happy trails, may the winds blow true and the skies stay blue. May your pockets be deep and vast and may your hearts stay light. I seek a trade. Will you come to my aid?'

Tristan clapped his hands in delight, completely ignoring Jenni.

'Oh, I haven't heard the old greeting in forever.' He suddenly became very serious and returned Ned's bow. 'Well met my friend. May your hearth stay warm and your crops grow. May happiness greet you every day and peace and prosperity walk beside you. I am willing to trade, I will come to your aid.'

The two men clasped each other's forearms to complete the formal trade request.

'What is it you are looking for?' asked Tristan,

pretending not to see Jenni despite the thunderous look on her face.

'I um… we're looking for some bones you acquired back in Braso Amia.' Ned was less successful at ignoring Jenni's face.

'I know exactly the ones you mean. I will trade you the bones for her.' Tristan pointed to Jenni and held his other hand out to Ned to seal the deal.

'I'm right 'ere,' said Jenni.

'Oh no, now, wait a minute. I can't just trade a person to you. There must be something else.' Ned cast about desperately. 'I am married to the Empress of Roshaven, you know. I'm sure we can work out alternative payment.'

'I'm literally stood right 'ere,' said Jenni again.

'I don't want her! Well, I do, but not like that. We don't trade people either, you know. What I want is her help with a little er… bandit problem we've got.' Tristan stood, mirth dancing in his eyes as he waited for Ned to shake his outstretched hand.

'Give us a minute, would ya?' Jenni asked, as she shoved Ned over to one side. 'Wot the bloody 'ell was that? I wos just about to get 'im to tell me 'ow much for the bones when you 'ad to waltz in 'ere dropping all that traditional shite. And then the pair ofs you just stand there talking about me when I'm right there.' She snorted in anger. 'Boss! I 'ad this. Now you've gone and set up a stupid, proper deal. Wiv me as the bargaining chip.'

Ned cast a worried glance at Tristan, who waggled his fingers at them in a little wave.

'I'm sorry, Jenni. I didn't know. I was rushing, trying to get here in time, and then I saw the traders were still here and I remembered the old greeting. I figured going the traditional route would get us what we wanted quickly. I didn't know it would mean trading you – so to speak.' The backs of Ned's ears had turned hot pink. 'He seems a decent enough chap. I'm sure if we explained the situation, he'd exchange the bones for some precious gems or something, instead of your help. Or perhaps we can send along some of the Palace Guards to deal with this bandit problem?'

Jenni shook her head.

'They'd be as much use as a chocolate covered fireguard. You've entered a contract now, Boss. It 'as to be seen frew. All we can do now is wangle decent terms.' She threw him a murderous glare. 'Let me do the talking from now on.'

Ned nodded meekly.

Stalking back to Tristan, Jenni looked him up and down.

'This is the deal. The only one yor gonna get. I'll come wiv you and 'elp deal with the bandits wot is giving you trouble. Then I return to Roshaven, wiv the bones. You got thirty seconds to decide.'

Ned watched as Tristan smirked, then held out his hand to Jenni.

'You got a deal.'

They shook hands, then Tristan bowed to Ned again.

'Your aid has been granted. A successful trade agreed. Go in peace,' intoned the fae.

'Go in peace.' Ned bowed back. 'What happens now?'

'Momma K has kindly agreed to let us stay here tonight, so we will leave first light. And Jenni can deal with our, er… bandit problem on the Kings Road as we travel towards Mythhorn. Once the bandits are gone, I shall pay with the bones you covet. Excuse me, I must ensure all my business transactions are as successful as this one.' The elf winked and strolled off.

'You made a right pig's ear of that,' Jenni scowled at Ned.

'Sorry. At least we have a trade. Are you alright dealing with bandits?'

'I'm gonna 'ave to be now, ain't I? Bit dodge 'ow 'e keeps saying er bandits though, innit? I fink it's gonna end up being a right palava.' Jenni looked Ned up and down. 'You'd better come wiv me.'

'Okay, strength in numbers and all that.' Ned tried to focus on the bright side of heading off to fight er bandits. Then another thought occurred to him. 'Did you get a look at the bones? Are they the right ones?'

'I ain't seen 'em yet. I dunno wot they're supposed to look like eiver. You?'

'No. Look, I'd better ask Griff if he knows. Last thing we want is to trade our help for the wrong bones.'

They both laughed, then amusement drained from their faces as they considered the possibility that Tristan might not even have the bones they needed.

'I'll nip back now and find out from Griff. You stay here, keep an eye on our boy, Tristan. He did say you weren't leaving until morning, so we've got a bit of time,' said Ned.

'Hurry back,' called Jenni as she watched her boss head for the way out of the fae realm. She had a horrible feeling about this deal.

Chapter 15

'Griff!' Ned yelled his father's name as he spied him turning the far corner of the corridor. The man peered back over his shoulder, his face breaking out into a smile when he saw who it was.

'Back so soon, lad?' called Griff as the two men walked towards each other.

'Yeah, I need to know what the bones look like,' said Ned.

'What they look like? Why? What's happened?'

'Jenni was about to get hold of them when I screwed it up with the traditional trade request. Now they're willing to trade the bones for Jenni's help, but we need to make sure the bones are the right ones. I don't know what they're supposed to look like, do you?' asked Ned.

Griff was frowning.

'How did you manage to trade Jenni's help for bones? And get her to agree to it? There's more to this tale, eh? Come on, let's go to the library.' Griff started walking again.

'Why are we going to the library? Do you know what the bones look like or not?'

Griff just beckoned Ned to follow him.

'Look, Griff, we're on a tight deadline. The fae traders are leaving in the morning with Jenni. They've said if she deals with their bandit problem, then they'll release the bones to her.'

'Ah, so you haven't traded your sprite indefinitely.' Griff chuckled.

'No, of course not.'

Griff grew serious.

'We do odd things when circumstances conspire against us, lad. Odd things indeed. Now hush, the imperial librarian likes quiet.'

Ned looked about with interest. He'd never ventured into the imperial library before. It stretched before him, curving round at the end, like a very long oval. There were bookshelves lining the wall's entire perimeter except for the door they had walked through. The shelves were at least seven feet high, and a peaceful quiet exuded throughout the space with the occasional rustle of paper. Besides that, there were rows and rows and rows of bookcases filled with books that stretched all the way to the back of the room. A thick carpet muffled their footsteps as they walked towards a desk, behind which sat an elderly lady with a large bun of snow-white hair and a pair of half-moon spectacles resting on the end of her nose.

'Madame,' said Griff quietly, sweeping an elegant bow.

The librarian held up one finger. She was writing in a ledger with the other hand. Once she'd finished, she looked up and tutted quietly.

'What do you want, Griffin?' she whispered.

'A moment of your precious time. We are looking for information on the Spice Ghosts and their bones,' replied Griff.

The librarian's eyebrows raised as she regarded him.

'Please, madame. It's a matter of urgency.' Griff pressed his hands together in prayer and bowed his head.

The librarian turned her sharp gaze onto Ned.

'Chief Thief-Catcher. Spinks, Ned. Recently married into the Family. Emotional stunted magical ability.' She reeled off the information as if she were reading off an index card only she could see. Then she smiled warmly. 'Welcome to your library. How may we serve?'

Ned dare not look at Griff, who was probably bristling or grinning at that introduction, as he thought either expression would make him laugh.

'Um, thank you, Madame… I'm sorry I don't know your name?' he asked.

'You may call us Esme.'

'Thank you, Esme.' Ned decided not to dwell on the use of the plural. Not everything in Roshaven was as it seemed. 'It's true. We are looking for information about the Spice Ghosts and their bones, specifically what they look like. The bones, not the Spice Ghosts. We've already met them. If you would be so kind as to help us, please.'

Ned waited as the librarian seemed to have frozen in thought. Finally, she spoke.

'Aisle twenty-seven. Shelf five. These titles should help.' She handed him a piece of parchment that she had definitely not been holding earlier.

'Thank you very much.' Ned wanted to ask Esme how she'd done that, but as he glanced at Griff, he was shaking his head and the librarian had already returned to her ledger.

They walked away from the desk.

'How do we know which aisle is which?' whispered Ned.

Griff pointed at the end of the first bookcase they came to. It had a small brass number four fixed to it. They walked down the length of the aisle until they came to a gap and new ones began. They soon found aisle twenty-seven shelf five. Ned looked at the parchment Esme had given him. There were four book titles written in a beautiful curly script. It took them longer to find the books, as some spines were worn with age and some books had very similar titles. There was a small alcove with a desk and two chairs nestled within the bookcases on the wall, so they took the books there and began searching.

Ned turned page after page of archaic script, not knowing what language it was, hoping to find an image that would be of some use. There was nothing in the first book, or the second. Ned watched as Griff shut his book with a shake of his head. There was only one left. It was titled *Bone Magick: Using Bone, Feather, Fang and Claw to Contact your Ancestors*.

Ned turned the book to face him and began flicking through the pages, Griff watching from across the desk. There were illustrations in this one and it was written in script he could just about decipher.

'Here!' Griff tapped the book excitedly, stopping Ned's page flicking. 'What does this say?'

Ned bent over the book and began reading aloud.

'In order to maintain the balance between the living and the spirit world, the ancient ones tasked the Valiant Ones with a sacred duty to protect the bridge from the earthly plane to the spiritual plane, connecting you to your ancestors. It is imperative that animal bones only are used. Human bones contain impure energy and shadows of intent from their former owners. Animal bones are attuned to nature and the natural balance of life. The Valiant Ones alone have the knowledge, power and skill to perform the necessary rituals required to appease the spirit realm and protect the world.'

Ned looked up.

'Do you think it's talking about the Spice Ghosts? They look more like pirates than valiant ones to me. Can they be the same thing?' he asked.

Griff tapped his lip, thinking.

'I think this book is old, eh, and things change with the flow of time. Names, places, intentions. But yes, in essence, I think our Spice Ghosts today are the valiant ones of the past.' He nodded towards the text. 'Does it say what the bones look like?'

Ned bent his head back to the book, running his finger over the text.

'Ah, here we go. The Valiant Ones have been given the following blessed bones; the deer antlers of a white stag to ease the passing between realms, the skull of a true white horse to bring luck to the realm travellers and the talon of a pure white owl to guard against evil.'

'At least now we know what we're looking for, eh?' Griff said, looking pleased.

'Yeah, but… how will we know if the bones the fae traders have are the actual blessed ones the Spice Ghosts are meant to have? I mean, can you tell if the skull of a horse came from a white one?' asked Ned.

Griff shook his head.

'Well, I need to let Rose know what's happening and then I'd better get back to Jenni, tell her what we're looking for. Maybe she'll have some ideas on how to tell if the bones are genuine or not. I just hope the traders have the right ones, otherwise we've wasted a lot of time and energy getting nowhere,' said Ned as he stood up with two of the books, ready to return them to the shelf.

'A good idea to speak to Rose before you disappear again. She wasn't too impressed at how you scarpered before, eh.' Griff spoke in a serious tone, but there was an amused twinkle in his eye, so Ned knew he wasn't really in that much trouble.

'See you later.' Ned left Griff putting the other books away and made his way out of the library. Esme didn't stir as he passed her desk, but he gave her a half-wave just in case. Closing the library door behind him was like stepping out of a cocoon. It was brighter and harsher here. He took a deep breath and wondered where he might find his wife.

Chapter 16

Ned watched Rose thinking. She was so beautiful. He pinched himself at least once a day to make sure their marriage wasn't a dream. She had listened intently as he explained where they were with the bone recovery. Now he was waiting to see what she thought about next steps.

'I agree, you'd better go with Jenni. Keep an eye on things and make sure nothing happens to her, especially as you got her in this situation,' she said finally.

Ned blinked. He had not expected her to say that.

'Are you sure?' As soon as he asked the question, Ned realised that he really wanted to do it. He felt calmer already, knowing that he was going to be part of the solution.

'Yes. You can be the official imperial representative. A reminder to the fae traders that they aren't trading with an individual. Perhaps you can persuade Momma K to add an extra layer of protection as well. She likes you.'

The backs of Ned's ears reddened. Rose caught his hand and gave it a squeeze.

'It's a straightforward transaction, right? Just some bandits? You and Jenni can easily deal with them.' She kissed him on the cheek. 'I believe in you.'

Ned pulled her into an embrace, hugging her tightly. He didn't know why but saying goodbye this time was almost painful.

'We'll be back before you know it, bones and all.' They still had two days until the Spice Ghosts were due to return.

'I know you will. Are you staying here tonight?' There was a wistfulness in Rose's voice as she asked the question.

Ned sighed.

'No, I don't think I can. I've got to check on the catchers, make sure everything is running smoothly, and then I'd better get to the Fae Grove. They said they'd leave at first light but they could mean first moonlight. You know how fae are,' he said.

'Be safe.' Rose kissed him again, and it was on slightly unsteady legs that Ned left the study.

He had almost left the palace when he remembered he lived there too and most of his belongings were in the imperial wing. He only kept an emergency set of clothes at his old house. His bits and pieces didn't take up much space in the imperial wardrobe and drawers he had been given. Back in his room, Ned eyed the Gunningtons, his good boots, but decided to stick with his old faithfuls. They had served him well on his quest in search of the rose thief. Grabbing a backpack, he stuffed it with a change of clothes and a couple of knives. He already wore his spellcaster belt and well, and he would make sure they were fully charged before he left. There were a few bottles of cure-all ointment from the druids at the thief-catcher office, so he'd grab a couple of those as well. Just in case. Bandits were bandits, after all.

It was with a jaunty whistle that Ned walked from the palace to the thief-catcher HQ. He couldn't help it. He loved Rose fiercely, but life in the palace was stifling and he'd only been living there for a few weeks. He had been firm in keeping his job and his old place. So far, so good. And now this situation felt like something he could get his teeth into and solve. A problem he could fix. Stop the bandits, get the bones, give them back to the Spice Ghosts.

Willow, Joe and Sparks were all in the office when Ned got there.

'Anything to report?' he asked.

'We've had a couple more magic stealing complaints, Boss. Nothing major, just people feeling a bit squiffy and realising they're running low on power. Whoever it is doing the skimming seems to have calmed down. Otherwise it's been very quiet. Almost like the whole city is holding its breath and waiting for the Spice Ghosts to come back. Did you get the bones?' asked Willow, the others hanging on to every word.

'No. Norm met us there, but disappeared again. The guy who had them, Erick, sold them to the fae traders before we could get them back, and the traders had already left. The entire journey was a total bust,' replied Ned.

'What are we going to do now?' asked Joe.

Ned felt a small bloom of pride for his youngest recruit.

'Jenni managed to get to the fae traders before they left, and we've agreed to a trade. She will get rid of their bandit problem and they will give her the bones. I'm going to go with her to make sure everything goes smoothly,' he said.

'Do you need us to come along as well, Boss?' asked Willow.

'No, you three stay here and keep things ticking along. If you need any extra support on a case, contact the palace. We can use the palace guards for extra manpower if we need to.'

The others murmured at that. Usually, thief-catchers and palace guards didn't get on well. Except for Fred, of course. Everyone liked Fred.

'Will you and Jenni be alright going up against bandits, Boss?' asked Willow.

'I'm sure it won't be too much of a problem. I haven't heard any reports of trouble recently on any of the trade routes, so I suspect it's a bit of a storm in a teacup.' But Ned remembered to get the ointments from the cupboard and, at the last minute, threw in a first aid kit. Just in case the bandits had archers. 'I'm sure the fae traders have some tricks of their own on how to deal with them.'

Sparks began flashing a complicated pattern. Without Jenni present, it took Ned a while to decipher it, despite Sparks being very patient and repeating the pattern more and more slowly.

'Ah, that's kind of you, Sparks. You can certainly spread the word to your friends and relations. Everything will help but like I said, I'm sure it won't be a problem.' Ned surveyed his catcher team with pride. 'Keep up the good work and we'll be back before you know it.'

Ned couldn't help grinning. This was going to be a piece of cake. He waved cheerily as he left HQ and headed for the Fae Grove. He could gain entry without Jenni or any other fae thanks to a long-standing agreement with Momma K.

'Boss! I didn't fink you were gonna make it,' cried Jenni as she saw Ned.

He immediately noticed the fae traders had packed up their wagons and were getting ready to move out.

'Let me guess,' said Ned. 'First light meant first moonlight?'

'Yeah. So, wot they look like then? Quick! Afore I 'ave to go.' Jenni cast a glance at the wagons, as if to check they hadn't already left.

'It's alright, Jenni. I'm coming with you,

remember?' Ned started walking alongside the wagon that was moving. 'I'm guessing we travel by foot.'

'You'd be right,' came a voice. Ned turned and saw Tristan smirking at him. 'What are you doing here, thief-catcher?'

'I'm here protecting the interests of the empire as a representative of Empress Rose, Long May She Rule,' replied Ned.

'Long May She Rule,' murmured Tristan, considering Ned with a thoughtful look on his face. 'Well, another fighter against the bandits can't be a bad thing.' He clapped a hand on Ned's shoulder and then strolled off, deep in conversation with another trader.

'I'm glad yor 'ere wiv me, Boss,' said Jenni.

'Me too. Now, listen, this is what the bones should look like.' And Ned bent his head down to Jenni and whispered the description he'd discovered in the imperial library.

'I don't fink we'll be able to tell if they come from white animals, Boss. That's pretty 'ard to figure out from just bone.'

'I know,' agreed Ned. 'But maybe there'll be some magical residue you could pick up that would confirm things?' Ned looked about to see whether they'd left the grove yet. It seemed like they had. The general whimsy that Momma K overlaid on the plants in her kingdom had disappeared. 'Dammit. I meant to ask Momma K for some help.'

'She can't 'elp wiv bones. Won't touch 'em. Says its nasty death magic using bones. The fing wiv bone magic is...' But before Jenni could get into it, Tristan floated back over.

'Thief-catcher, I've been talking with my second and we have little to spare freely. Can you pay your way?'

There was a glint in Tristan's eyes which put the hackles up on Ned's neck.

'Isn't getting rid of bandits for you payment enough?' he asked.

'That's Jenni's trade. Bandits for bones, remember? You can assist if things look dicey. Seems fair to let the two of you face the horde.'

Ned felt uneasy. The horde? That wasn't a comforting description for bandits. He had been thinking it would be, at most, half a dozen or so desperate men who could be easily scared off. Although, if the bandits could be easily scared off, then why hadn't the fae traders done that already?

'What exactly can you tell us about this horde? How many men are we talking about?' asked Ned.

'Let's discuss payment first, then I'll share what I know,' replied Tristan.

'Everything's a transaction with you, isn't it?' demanded Ned.

'Life is all about give and take. I just prefer to be on the side of take,' said Tristan. 'Now, payment.'

Ned scowled.

'The imperial crown will make a reasonable payment towards my inclusion in the caravan,' he said, fervently glad that Griff had coached him on how to pay for things now he was the Empress's husband.

'Define reasonable,' said Tristan with a grin.

The two men got down to haggling and in the end, Ned felt he came out more or less with his shirt still on his back. Griff and Rose had given him what seemed like a small fortune for this endeavour and he'd just signed it all over to Tristan for the privilege of travelling alongside the wagons. He'd done his best to get Tristan's price down, but at least it hadn't gone over what he had to barter. It was almost as if the fae trader knew exactly down to the last coin what Ned had to spend.

'Come on then,' said Ned. 'Tell me about these bandits.'

'I'll give you everything you need to know when we break camp. Not long now. I give you my word.' Tristan sauntered away.

'Ugh, I've got a really bad feeling about this,' said Ned, wondering whether he ought to run after the trader and demand answers. Tristan was definitely holding something back. 'Do the fae traders have any special abilities? Besides those of regular fae, I mean.'

'Wot like floating or summink?'

'No, like being able to tell how much you're worth or how much money you have. How far they can push you, that sort of thing.'

Jenni wrinkled her brow as she thought about it.

'Sounds like they might, you know. They always know exactly wot yor prepared to pay for fings. S'funny that, I never really noticed afore but now you've said it, s'obvious ain't it? Cheeky buggers.'

'If that's the case, why aren't they stinking rich and sat in a castle somewhere?'

'They're rovers, can't 'elp themselves. Gotta keep moving, never staying in one place for long. And they're gamblers too. Probably lose what they make,' said Jenni.

It was with a mixture of respect and concern that Ned regarded his travelling companions. From now on, he was not making any more deals. He had nothing left to trade.

Chapter 17

The night's travelling was uneventful. As the traders, Ned and Jenni sat round the early morning campfire to eat, Ned thought he would try again to find out more about the bandits.

'When do you normally hit bandit trouble?' he asked.

The other traders shot glances at Tristan, but nobody spoke.

'I haven't been completely honest about the bandit situation.' Tristan kept his gaze firmly on the bowl of porridge in his hands, all his earlier bravado gone. 'It's not exactly bandits. The people of Poledo refuse to let us travel through their town, the only safe way to get to the Northern Pass and through the mountain to the villages and towns beyond. Because they won't let us travel through the town, we have to go the long way around and risk being attacked by bandits if we're unlucky and damage to our wagons from the treacherous terrain if we're lucky. The bandits now know we're refused passage through Poledo and they grow ever more numerous. We risk losing more and more goods. If something isn't done soon, we'll have to abandon trade across the mountain completely. A tremendous loss on all sides.' He nodded towards Jenni. 'We thought you might be able to change the town's mind. It's time for this feud to end.'

'Why are you refused passage through Poledo? And why do you need Jenni – can't you talk to them?' asked Ned.

'We were delayed by bad weather delivering a healing tonic. A special formula from your druids, actually. Only we were too late, and it didn't work and the son of the town's chief died. It wasn't our fault, we were delayed. We weren't late on purpose. We'd never toy with the life of a child.' Tristan looked at Ned and he could see the pain the trader felt over the situation. 'As for magic, all fae have strengths in different areas – ours is with finding the items you desire to trade or precious things you've lost. Our magic won't help in this situation. We cannot bring the child back to life. We thought Jenni might erase their grief or perform a memory spell to make them forget.'

'I ain't got the juice for nuffink like that,' said Jenni sadly. 'I mighta but…' she trailed off.

'Who is the chief of Poledo? Where's the town?' The town name was semi-familiar to Ned, but he couldn't put his finger on where he'd heard it before.

'His name is Leith. Poledo is at the foot of the Northern Pass. Leith's father was Mayor but died of the same fever that took Leith's son. It swept through the town. Nasty business.'

Ned realised where he knew the name from. He remembered reading about a dangerous outbreak in Poledo in *The Daily Blag*. Travellers had been warned to stay away to prevent catching and spreading the disease.

'Are we safe travelling towards Poledo? Is the fever gone?'

Tristan nodded. 'There were travelling healers behind us who stayed and treated the rest of those afflicted. But there was nothing they could do for Leith's boy.' He put his bowl down and bowed his head. 'If I'd just pushed through the storm, we would've got there on time and maybe…'

'Hey, you don't know what would've happened. It might have helped, it might not. Fate's a tricky thing to try to guess. You can't blame yourself.' Ned glanced up and saw that the other traders had melted away, leaving just Ned and Jenni sitting with Tristan. 'What brute strength does this Leith have? What are we walking into?'

'You're still going to help?' asked Tristan in surprise.

'Yeah, corse. We made a deal and we want our bones,' said Jenni. 'But we need to know wot we're walking into.'

'Right, well, last time we came this way Leith stopped us at the town outskirts, he had big lads with him, capable of knocking you down with one blow. He had one or two archers on the rooftops and then half a dozen people armed with various weapons. They didn't look averse to using them. I'd say they're all loyal to Leith.'

Jenni tutted.

'That's a lot of people to deal wiv. I can't work miracles and yor only one man,' she said, casting a doubtful look at Ned.

'You got any fighters in your crew?' asked Ned. 'Know any defensive spells?'

'No, I told you, we don't have that kind of magic. Weapons, we have some, but it's rare we have to use them,' replied Tristan. 'Why? What are you thinking?'

'I'm thinking we arm up, get everyone looking like they're ready for a fight. Try to scare the locals a little. Me and Jenni will try to parley with Leith, see if we can get him to agree to an end to this vendetta,' said Ned.

'And if he disagrees?' asked Tristan.

'We hope luck is on our side, and he agrees. We're

not fighting a whole town.' Ned looked to Jenni for confirmation. She nodded.

Tristan didn't look too confident. In fact, he looked scared and worried. Ned hoped his face wasn't mirroring the trader. It sounded like they were heading into a troublesome situation.

Later, when Ned and Jenni were on their own, they discussed firepower.

'Wot you got wiv you, Boss?'

'I filled my well. I've got the usual stun and stop quick draw spells we use for our runners back in Roshaven. They could be useful.'

'Yeah, but they don't last long. We might need the traders to pounce on people, keep 'em down.'

'Agreed. They can tie them up, make them listen to us,' said Ned.

'You really fink parley will work? It's a helluva long shot, Boss.'

'I know, but I don't feel right going into a situation without hearing both sides of the argument. Maybe if we can get this Leith and Tristan sitting down together, speaking their piece, it will help to clear the air.'

'I 'ope yor right, Boss.' Jenni plucked a piece of grass and twined it around her fingers. 'I can only draw on wot's around anna I don't wanna take innocent lives to cast me spells.'

Ned knew she was talking about the plants and animals that were likely to suffer. Jenni's magic was limited to her ability to balance the cost. She could use the life force of living things around her to boost her magic, but at too high a price – they usually died. And Jenni wasn't that kind of practitioner.

'Unless…' but before Jenni could say anything else, Tristan whistled to get their attention.

'We're about half a mile out from Poledo. You ready?' he asked.

Ned nodded, forgetting that Jenni had been about to say something, and he walked to the head of the caravan, Jenni half a step behind. The traders made sure their weaponry was visible as they travelled closer to the settlement.

It was clear the traders had been spotted, as a large group of men waited for the wagons on the outskirts of Poledo.

Ned pulled his fist up to halt the movement of the wagons while he and Jenni walked forward a few paces.

'I invoke a parley between Tristan, leader of the fae traders and one of your own, Leith,' said Ned, his voice steady despite his trembling knees.

'Who the gods are you?' called out a voice.

'I'm Ned Spinks, Chief Thief-Catcher of Roshaven, Emperor-Consort and mediator to this parley,' replied Ned. 'Who are you?'

There was a general muttering from the men before one of them walked forward. He was as tall as Ned but stockier, with a large black beard streaked with grey.

'I'm Leith Beynon and I do not accept your parley.'

'I hope to resolve this conflict peacefully,' tried Ned with a sinking feeling that he wasn't going to get anywhere.

'Will parley bring me back my boy?' asked Leith.

Ned tried to think of something to say.

'Blocking the fae traders every time they try to pass frew ain't gonna bring 'im back neiver,' Jenni glared up at the man. 'You fink yor getting revenge, but it ain't their fault they was late. You wanna blame someone, blame Mother Nature.'

'Stay out of it, sprite,' growled Leith. He waved his

men to stand forwards with him. They were all armed and grim-faced. 'You owe us, Trader.'

The men from the village stood silent and waited for a signal from their leader.

Tristan clasped his hands together in supplication.

'Please, Leith, this has to stop. We must travel through Poledo to trade with the towns and villages on the other side of the mountain. They need our supplies and want to barter items vital to the people who live on this side. Enough is enough…'

'It will never be enough!' roared Leith.

His men took that as the signal to advance on the traders and their wagons.

'I don't fink parley worked, Boss.'

'Noticed that, did you? Can you cast an immobiliser spell? Just on Leith for now.' Ned pointed to some scrubland that looked particularly unloved, hoping that would be enough to fuel her additional magical needs.

Jenni muttered under her breath and as the scrubland further withered and utterly died, Leith became locked in a furious stance. Ned went to stand next to him.

'Listen up! We've frozen your leader. If you want him to ever move again, you'll stop. Now!'

'You can't do that!' yelled a voice and an arrow swooped towards Ned.

There was a bright flash as Jenni cast a protector spell. The effort caused the grass around the traders to wither and die, and one man staggered to his knees.

'Witchcraft!' shouted a villager, hopping about trying not to step on the now dead ground.

'I ain't no witch. I'm trying not to 'urt you.'

Ned cocked his head sideways and Jenni picked up on his idea. She flexed her hands out towards the fields.

'If you don't stop, I'll take yor crops.'

There was a lot of grumbling, but Leith's men moved away from the wagons and gathered behind their leader. Ned could see the fury in Leith's eyes.

'Jenni? Release his head, please.'

'How dare you interfere?' roared Leith. He continued shouting at Ned, descending into obscenities until he finally had to stop for breath and contented himself with glaring daggers at Ned.

'As I said, we come to parley and find a peaceful end to this animosity. Are you ready to sit down with us?' Ned tried again. Killing Leith would do nothing to improve the situation. His men were too loyal. Yet he had promised the fae traders he would resolve this problem, so he had to try again.

Leith nodded once, and some traders brought out chairs and a table while Jenni released the rest of the townsman. There were two chairs on either side, one for Leith and his second, and one for Tristan and Ned. Jenni hovered at Ned's elbow so another of Leith men copied, trying to look as menacing as possible.

'How can we reach a peaceful solution?' asked Ned, but before Leith could reply, a woman came stalking out to meet them. She was a tall, sour-faced woman with her hair scraped meticulously into a bun.

'Leith Mickael Beynon. What is the meaning of this disturbance?' she barked.

'It's no business of yours. Go back inside, woman.'

There was an indistinct murmur from the men of Poledo and instead of complying, the woman glared at the man seated next to Leith who rapidly stood and bobbed half a bow as she took his seat.

'Ma'am. My name is Ned Spinks and I've called a parley to try to reach a peaceful resolution to Leith and Tristan's dispute.'

She pierced him with a sharp gaze before she spoke.

'It's about time someone sorted out this business. What do you propose?'

'Mother…' began Leith, making Ned raise his eyebrows, but the woman held a hand up and the man stopped talking.

Jenni elbowed Ned in the ribs and when he glanced at her, she tipped her head at the surroundings. The women of Poledo had come out to join the men, who now looked shamefaced.

'The fae traders would like to continue travelling through Poledo. It's a direct route for them to the mountain pass, and their cargo is important to both sides of the pass. Having their wagons attacked and their merchandise spoiled or destroyed by being forced to go the long way around hurts everyone.'

The woman said nothing for a time, but Ned felt in his gut that he needed to just remain quiet and wait.

Finally, she spoke.

'The fae traders will pay a toll to travel through Poledo,' she began, turning her eagle-like stare onto Leith as he tried to object. 'This will go somewhat towards the pain of the loss of a child and towards ensuring our roads remain travel worthy. A win-win situation, I'm sure you'll agree.'

Ned looked at Tristan, who had leaned forwards in his chair.

'Do you accept the terms?' he asked the trader.

'How much is the toll?' Tristan asked, bending his neck in respect to the woman.

'One gold mark each time you cross,' she replied calmly.

Ned tried not to smile. One gold mark was easily made by the traders yet paid every time they passed through Poledo would soon add up and make Leith and his family feel like they were receiving something of worth.

Tristan wore a very serious face as he extended his hand out towards the woman.

'We accept your terms,' he said.

She took his hand, and they shook firmly, then she turned and looked pointedly at Leith. All the fight seemed to have evaporated out of him and he looked smaller. Ned could see the grief lines on his face now.

'Nothing will bring back my son, but I accept the terms.' He lifted his chin a little in a last act of defiance. 'If you pay ten gold coins upfront.' He held out his hand.

Tristan gripped it and the two men shook.

'I accept.'

Relieved, Ned and Jenni stood, letting the traders gather up the table and chairs and return them to their wagons.

Tristan counted out the coins and placed them in Leith's hand. The two men regarded each other, and an understanding passed between them. Leith and his cronies drifted away, but his mother remained.

'Thank you for putting these two knuckleheads together and forcing parley.' She inclined her head at Ned.

'You're welcome. I'm glad it worked.' Ned lowered his voice. 'We're very sorry for your loss.' He thought about reaching out to clasp her hands, but decided against it.

She nodded, silently thanking him for his words, and glided away, gathering up the remaining onlookers.

'You did it,' said Tristan, sounding slightly stunned.

'Thank goodness for mothers,' remarked Ned. 'Now, about our bones?'

Chapter 18

'What do you mean, you don't have the bones?' Ned looked at the three boxes of bones on the back of one of the trader wagons. 'There are so many here. How can you not have our bones?' Mentally, Ned was kicking himself for not having checked the bone boxes before making the trip.

Tristan looked sheepish.

'You never specified which bones you wanted. You just said the bones we got from Braso Amia.' He pointed to the boxes. 'These are those bones.'

Ned looked at all of them. He could recognise a few. There was a mixture of human-looking ones and animal ones. White, yellow and some brown ones. A real mishmash. He decided not to linger on why the town of Braso Amia had so many bones to trade in the first place. He wondered whether Erick had sent him on a wild goose chase on purpose.

Ned and Jenni had been through the boxes twice and whilst they'd found an owl talon, it had no mystical properties they could tell.

'Have you traded bones to anyone else before we joined you?' Ned had no idea how many people the traders had made deals with between leaving Braso Amia and getting to Roshaven.

'I don't know...' Tristan looked confused. 'I think maybe, but it's all hazy.'

Jenni peered at him.

'Wot do you remembers?'

'We were hailed. By someone on the side of the

road.' Tristan shook his head. 'Why can't I remember?'

'You've been spelled. Lemme 'ave a look. Boss?' Jenni put her hand out and Ned reluctantly handed over his power well. If she used it all, he'd have nothing in reserve. As their hands touched, he felt a sudden fizz, and his energy dipped slightly. He blinked, put it down to not having had any sleep and took back the now empty well, watching as Jenni put her hands on either side of Tristan's face, closed her eyes and screwed up her forehead in concentration. A silvery blue glow emanated from her fingers.

'It's a woman, wearing a black cloak with a big black 'ood. She's reaching out an arm. S'got greenish skin and massive nails, like claws.' Jenni leaned in towards Tristan. 'Yor going to the bone boxes now. Yep, giving 'er three bones.' She dropped her hands in disgust. 'You gave 'er our bones.'

Tristan massaged his temples. He'd grown pale.

'I know who that was. It's the Sea Witch. She must have spelled us to forget the trade.' He grew a little indignant. 'And she didn't pay.'

'Yeah, well, you know what they say. *Pay your tribute and pay it quick, or you'll be drowning in the drink.*' Jenni half-sang a few lines.

'That's just a song, Jenni. The latest one going round the taverns,' said Ned. It was one of those annoying songs that got stuck in your head. Ned hoped he didn't start humming it now. 'Why would the Sea Witch want bones?'

As soon as he asked the question, he knew the answer. These were the Spice Ghosts' mystical bones, and she was a necromancer, if the song was true. Obviously, she needed the bones for her own nefarious magical needs.

'Cos she's a necromancer, Boss. Collects souls she does. According to the song.'

'Yes, thank you, Jenni.' Ned scrubbed his hands through his hair. 'I can't believe we've been through all this to get nothing and for someone else to get our bones.' All the positive emotions he'd been feeling since the successful parley had evaporated. He would no longer be returning to Roshaven triumphantly. Instead, he would be the bearer of more bad news and he'd wasted valuable time. By the time he and Jenni got back to Roshaven, the deadline would be up with the Spice Ghosts and they had nothing to show for their investigations.

He wanted to be mad at Tristan but found he didn't have the energy. Sure, the trader had been misleading about the bandits, but Ned felt that was an embedded character flaw rather than malicious behaviour. It wasn't his fault he'd been spelled by an evil witch.

'I guess this is where we part. I take it we have fulfilled our bargain?' asked Ned.

Tristan grew solemn and clasped Ned's forearm. He returned the gesture.

'I declare the trade complete. No refunds.' There was a slight smile in Tristan's eyes as he waited for Ned to respond.

'I agree our trade complete.' Ned paused and noted the furrow of worry in Tristan's brow. 'No complaints.'

Tristan let out a relieved sigh and changed his grip to shake Ned's hand.

'Perhaps we will do business again one day.' The trader bid Ned and Jenni farewell and the wagons trundled away.

'Wot we gonna do now, Boss?'

'I guess we'll have to visit the Sea Witch, see if

she'll give up the bones. But we need to go back to Roshaven first. Tell Rose what happened and see if we can get an extension from the Spice Ghosts when they return.'

'It don't look good, do it, Boss?'

'No, but we're not done yet. Come on, we'd better start walking. Should be able to pick up a coach at the crossroads back there.' Ned jerked his chin towards the road in the distance. 'Let's go face the music.'

Chapter 19

Rose was not happy when Ned explained what had happened. Whilst she was glad to have him back, they had sat through an uncomfortable dinner as annoyed Empress warred with loving wife.

'I have to meet with the Spice Ghosts tomorrow morning. They requested first light. I don't know what I'm going to say. I can't give them what they want,' Rose said softly.

'I'll be with you. We just explain the facts. We don't have the bones and we're not harbouring the individual who stole them, but we do know where the bones are. Perhaps that will be enough and they can go to the Sea Witch themselves.'

'And Norm?'

'He's officially exiled from Roshaven. He steps one foot back and he'll be arrested. I don't think he's welcome in Momma K's realm either.'

'What makes you say that?' asked Rose.

'Jenni told me that the Sea Witch is probably the only magical being capable of taking on Momma K and maybe winning, but they've both kept themselves to their own realms. Momma K stays on land and the Sea Witch rules the waves. There's little interaction to the point that even their magic works differently.' Ned helped himself to some of Ma Bowl's sticky toffee pudding. He'd been avoiding dessert because Rose was mad at him, but now that she was talking to him, he figured he was safe to indulge.

'And with these bones?' Rose cocked an eyebrow at

the amount of custard Ned was pouring onto his pudding. He shot her a guilty smile.

'Jenni is finding out. I'm sure it's nothing to worry about.' But Ned's reassurance sounded hollow, and they both lapsed into silence.

*****

Jenni watched Momma K's impassive face for any sign of what she was thinking. It was like looking at carved ebony. She was giving nothing away. The only sign that things weren't normal was the drop in temperature in the Fae Grove. It was downright nippy. Jenni shivered as she watched icy patterns develop on the trees and flowers. Her breath plumed out in front of her.

'Er… can we knock it off for a bit?'

Momma K breathed heavily out of her nose. The temperature went from icy winter to chilly Autumn. Jenni supposed that would have to do.

'So, wot you finking?' she asked unwisely, but desperate to break the frosty silence.

Animation returned to Momma K's face as she narrowed her eyes and glared, not at Jenni, just in general.

'No good. De Sea Witch can no be trusted. Dese bones, dey powerful and in de wrong hands…' Her dreadlock chimes jangled as she shook herself. 'We must try to get em back. Offer wat we have and see. But, me doh think it will do anyting. De Sea Witch is no known fo' kindness.' Another shiver wracked the diminutive fae queen, and she seemed to realise how cold it was in the glade. She rubbed her hands together vigorously, and the atmosphere returned to a warm summer's day, complete with a buzzing bee.

'You coming tomorra? When the Spice Ghosts come back?' Jenni was hoping Momma K would say yes. She would feel more comfortable with the extra magical clout there.

Momma K shook her head.

'Me tink dey be mo' vengeful if dey see some powah displayed. Me no like meddling wid de spirit realm. It wat we have de Spice Ghosts fo'. To act as keepers and guardians. Maintain de balance. You go represent. Is enough.'

Jenni pursed her lips and waited to see if Momma K was going to add anything, but she had gone back to her introspective focus.

'Awright then. Catch you laters.'

'Daughta?' Momma K stopped Jenni in her tracks. 'Yo' magic, it mixing. Be careful wat ya doing. Slippery slopes bring bad tings.'

Jenni felt a pang of guilt. Her mother must know about the skimming. But she'd only taken a bit from that guy in Poledo in order to cast a spell for Ned and it weren't her fault that she'd skimmed a little by accident from Ned. She hadn't meant to. And as for Mannon's Lair, well that was absolutely her fault, but she couldn't help it. All those people desperate to make it big. No one had noticed losing a little here and there. She just wouldn't do it again and everything would be fine. She risked a glance at Momma K's face, but she had already turned away so Jenni quickly left through the fae portal. At least she had some partial good news to give Ned.

*****

'I'm going to go back to the library. See if there's anything that can help us with the Spice Ghosts tomorrow,' Ned said after Jenni had updated him and Rose.

'I think Griff is already there,' replied Rose. 'I haven't seen him all day.'

'If he is, I'll let him know where we stand.' Ned kissed Rose on the cheek. 'See you later.' He paused at the doorway of their study. 'You coming, Jenni?'

'Nah, libraries are too quiet for me. I'll check in at the office and make sure alls well on that front.'

Ned winced a little. He'd not had time to check in with the rest of the catchers. He'd been so wrapped up with things here at the palace.

'That's a good idea, Jenni. Tell them I'll be there tomorrow morning, after… well, after.'

She bobbed a head at Rose and walked with Ned down the corridor.

'Do you fink you'll find anyfink in there?' Jenni asked as they got to the library doors.

'You never know. It's worth a try. I'll see if there's anything on the Sea Witch, too. We might find something we can use.'

Jenni looked as doubtful as Ned knew he sounded.

'See you tomorrow. Don't be late.'

As Ned entered the library, the librarian Esme looked up and seemed almost pleased to see him.

'Young Ned. How may we help you this time?'

Ned tried to hide his grin at being called young.

'I'm looking for information on the Sea Witch. If you have any.'

Esme's gaze unfocused and her eyeballs seemed to zip along, as if they were reading something only she could see.

'Aisle thirty-two, shelf eleven. You'll find what you are looking for there.' She pointed at him. 'And tell your friend to stop eating in my library!'

Ned figured she meant Griff and made many apologies as he headed off to try to find the shelves Esme had identified for him. He found both the books he wanted and Griff close to each other.

'Esme says stop eating food in here,' Ned said by way of greeting, his arms full of books.

'Hah! Eyes everywhere, that one, eh.' He ran a hand over his moustache to shake out any stubborn crumbs. 'How did it go?'

Ned put his books down and slumped into a chair.

'Waste of time. Well... not a total waste of time. We sorted out the fae traders' problem, but it turns out they didn't have the bones we were looking for. They'd already traded them to the Sea Witch and we don't have time to go speak with her before the Spice Ghosts meeting tomorrow.' He leaned forward. 'It doesn't look good. Apparently, her and Momma K are great rivals. There's a good chance the Sea Witch will use the bones for her own gains. It may already be too late, but once we've tried to pacify the Spice Ghosts, we'll go cap in hand and see what we can do.'

'The Sea Witch is a difficult person to do business with. I should know. I've been paying her for years,' said Griff.

'So you know her? Do you think she'll give the bones back?'

Griff shook his head.

'It's unlikely, lad. Bones with that much mystical energy, she'll already have plans in place. All we can hope for is that she needs a full moon to fulfil her ritual.'

'Why? What does that have to do with anything?'

'A full moon provides an abundance of nature's energy. It's also said to weaken the veil between the realms. The perfect time to cast a spell using bone magic.'

'How do you know all this?' asked Ned, fascinated.

'I've known a witch or two in my time, eh?' replied Griff with a chuckle.

'So when's the next full moon?' Ned hoped they would have time to come up with a plan.

'Three days.'

Ned leaned back in his chair. They had a little time.

'What have you been doing in here?' he asked Griff.

'More research on the Spice Ghosts. I don't think they'll burn Roshaven to the ground. It gains them nothing, and if innocent lives are lost in the fire, they're upsetting the balance they're sworn to protect.'

'I figured the same. I thought if we could convince them we're not harbouring Norm and explain that we'd done our best to reclaim their bones, they might go visit the Sea Witch themselves. And that'll be the end of it.' Ned watched Griff's reaction to see if he'd agree with him. It didn't look good.

'The problem is, lad, the Spice Ghosts aren't exactly human. They live one foot in our realm, one in the spirit realm. They might not be able to physically go to the Sea Witch.'

'Do the books have any theories?'

'According to the texts, there is an ancient ritual for anchoring a person to a valiant one, but this is not a thing to be done lightly.' A shadow fell across Griff's face. 'There are things in the beyond that will do anything to escape and such linkage might create a weak point.'

The two of them lapsed into silence. Ned pulled one of the suggested books towards him and began reading about the Sea Witch. There might be something else they could use.

Chapter 20

Ned woke to someone shaking his arm.

'What? What is it?' He gasped as his whole body felt like he'd slept on a table, then blinking blearily around, he realised he had fallen asleep in the library. He moved his neck from side to side, trying to work out the kinks.

'We got to go if we want to be at the docks by dawn. Rose is waiting.' It was Griff, looking as fresh as a daisy and wearing clean clothes.

Ned glanced down at his crumpled attire. At least he had managed a wash and change when he and Jenni returned from the fae traders' camp. He'd do. His stomach grumbled. Griff handed him an egg roll, which Ned took gratefully, but didn't start eating until after they'd left the library. He didn't want to tempt Esme's wrath.

The others were waiting in the courtyard: Rose, Jenni, the two Highs and six palace guards, including a yawning Fred.

'No carriage?' asked Ned, as he gave his wife a quick hug.

'It's not far. I thought you might want to stretch your legs.' Rose smiled up at him briefly. 'Did you discover anything useful?'

'Not really. All the books about the Sea Witch seem to agree on one thing. She was a scorned woman who turned her back on living a normal life and poured all her rage into magic. She's immortal and spends most of her time in water form in the ocean. She can raise storms and sink ships if she feels she is not properly honoured. Griff had a working relationship with her, back when he smuggled in Fidelia, but she doesn't maintain goodwill and he hasn't sent any offerings her way for a while. Since his death.' Ned spared a glance for Griff, who was strolling along next to Jenni, engaging her in light chit chat, as if they were walking towards a pleasant get together and not a potentially devastating moment.

They arrived at the Dead Pier on the dot of dawn. The Spice Ghosts' ship was already moored, wreathed in the same crimson mist as before, with the same aromatic spices warming the air. The four representatives, Nutmeg, Clove, Ginger and Cinnamon, were walking down their gangplank towards Ned, Rose and the others.

'Here we go,' said Ned.

The Spice Ghosts arrayed themselves with Nutmeg taking the lead position again.

'You have our bones, I trust.' He scowled at them.

'No.' Rose's voice rang out. 'But we know where they are.'

'Unacceptable!' hissed Ginger, taking half a step forward, but halted her movement as Nutmeg held up his hand.

'Where?' he asked.

'The Sea Witch has them.'

There was a distinct change in the atmosphere. The smell of spice sharpened as each Spice Ghost tensed. Ginger's hand gripped the pommel of her sabre while her hair rippled out like flames.

'Easy,' cautioned Nutmeg, looking pale.

Ned was instantly on edge. The Spice Ghosts looked nervous, which didn't bode well. Why were the guardians of the spirit realm nervous about a witch?

'What of the thief?' asked Nutmeg, trying to regain

some of his earlier menace.

'We are not sheltering the thief, known as Norm the sprite. He was here but was last seen in Braso Amia.'

'Why didn't you arrest him?' The question came from Cinnamon, who loomed at the back of the Spice Ghosts.

Ned took half a step forward to answer that one.

'He was aiding us in our investigation into the location of the bones.'

'And yet you still do not have them,' remarked Cinnamon.

'We thought, now that you know where they are, you could go and retrieve them.' Ned began the sentence with confidence, but he tapered off as all four Spice Ghosts pinned him with identical glares. He took his half-step back.

Nobody else ventured to say anything. Rose glanced sideways at Griff, who shook his head ever so slightly. They waited. And the Spice Ghosts stood, immobile.

Time stretched. Seagulls wheeled overhead and there were distant shouts from the warehouse district as people arrived for work. The sky was lightening, and the sun warmed Ned's skin. He shifted his feet, wishing someone would speak.

Finally, Griff bent forward slightly, offering the Spice Ghosts a small bow. 'If I may?' he asked.

Nutmeg gave a curt nod of assent.

'We have completed our side of the deal. We have located the bones for you. For the sake of our agreement, you will not carry out your threat of mindless destruction, eh?'

There was no answer from the leader of the Spice Ghosts. Ned watched as Griff quailed momentarily then rallied.

'But you still require our aid, for you cannot remain in our plane for long, can you? You must straddle the in-between and guide the spirits within.'

'You seem to know a lot about us,' said Clove, speaking for the first time, her heady aroma washing over the Roshaven delegation.

'I have spent the night researching the myths and legends that surround the Spice Ghosts.' Griff paused as if uncertain whether he should continue. 'That is why I know you need our help. To retrieve your bones.'

'You couldn't even get the bones back in the first place. Why would we trust you now?' Ginger spat the words at Griff, her temper matching her fiery appearance.

Once more, Nutmeg raised a hand to stop Ginger from expressing herself further. She scowled at the back of his head.

'You are correct in your assumption.' Cinnamon templed his fingers 'We are not fully mortal, as we are not fully spirit. We may visit each plane for a short while, but that is all we can do: visit. If, however, one of you surrenders as an anchor, we will reconsider attacking your city.'

The other spices swivelled to stare at him, looks of shock and surprise on their faces that were mirrored by Ned and his companions.

'We've never done it before!'

'It's an ancient ritual. It might not even work.'

'It's too big a risk.'

Cinnamon waited until the other Spice Ghosts had finished before speaking again.

'As Clove said, there is an ancient ritual that speaks of anchoring a Spice Ghost to a mortal. There are risks, to both individuals and, well… we are uncertain what the impact will be.'

'If it's never been done before, is this really the time to do it?' asked Ned. 'Why can't you just gather your strength in the in-between and go visit the Sea Witch, like you're doing here? Or send a minion. You've probably got minions, right?'

'It is a matter of balance.' Cinnamon extended a finger at Jenni. 'Her blood stole the bones therefore her blood must return the bones. And we have lingered here too long.'

Ned looked more closely and noticed that the edges of the Spice Ghosts were turning transparent. They were fading away.

'You have the day to confer and put forward a mortal to act as an anchor for one of us. We would prefer the sprite, but we will accept you.' Cinnamon pointed at Ned this time. 'Return here at dusk and we shall perform the ritual.' His last words echoed as the Spice Ghosts disappeared completely. Their accompanying mist had been completely burnt away and there was only the slightest tang of spice in the air.

Chapter 21

The disappearance of the Spice Ghosts left Ned and the others in stunned silence. They walked back to the Imperial Palace, each wrapped up in their own thoughts. Even Fred kept quiet.

It wasn't until Ned, Griff, Rose, Jenni, and the Highs were gathered in the third best meeting room that they began to discuss what had just happened.

'Wot do you reckon 'bout this anchor fingy then? Sounds a bit dodge to me.' Jenni kicked the conversation off.

'I did discover mention of an ancient ritual to anchor a person to a Spice Ghost when I was researching, but there are risks involved,' replied Griff. 'Maybe too dangerous a risk, eh?'

'What I don't get is why they're so afraid of the Sea Witch.' Ned changed the focus of the conversation. 'Did you see their reaction when Rose told them who had the bones? There's something else going on there. Something they know – about the Sea Witch or the magical properties of the bones. Maybe what they can also be used for. We need to know what that is. If we agree to provide an anchor, we can't risk going in blind.'

'Fancy joining me in the library, son?' suggested Griff. 'Two heads and all that.'

'I know Momma K don't like the Sea Witch. I could go see if she'll tell us more,' offered Jenni.

'Or I could summon her here. It might encourage Momma K to actually share everything she knows,' suggested Rose. 'No offense, Jenni. Do you think she'll come?'

Jenni shrugged her shoulders.

'It's worth a go. I don't fink she'll refuse.'

While Rose ordered the High Right to send a polite summons to Momma K requesting her presence at the Imperial Palace immediately, Jenni sidled over to Ned before he could leave for the library with Griff.

'Boss? I fink mebbe I oughta try to find Norm.'

'Why's that?'

'You know he's 'ere, dontcha? Back in Roshaven.'

Ned blinked. He'd had no idea.

'How do you know? And why haven't you arrested him?' he asked sharply.

'I ain't laid eyes on 'im as such, just 'eard fings. I fawt 'e might know summink. It's gotta be worth a go, right? All hands and all that. Mebbe if we get enuff breadcrumbs we can make a loaf.'

She looked at Ned with such an earnest expression he didn't have the heart to tell her he thought Norm was as useful as a bucket with a hole in it.

'Okay, see what you can find out. But Jenni, if you find him, you arrest him. And I need you back at the Palace well before dusk so I can update you with what we find.'

'You fink there's more in those old books then?'

'Like you said, every breadcrumb will help.'

'Fanks, Boss.'

'Be safe, alright?'

She nodded and walked off to find Norm.

'What was all that about?' asked Griff, his curiosity clearly piqued.

'Just catcher business,' replied Ned. 'You ready?'

Griff nodded and the two men headed for the library while Rose prepared for a visit from Momma K.

'Chil'? Ya summon'd me?' Momma K didn't look angry, although it was hard to tell. She was giving nothing away. Her face was calm and blank.

'Thank you so much for coming. Would you like some tea?' asked Rose.

'Me take some berry infusion if ya have it.'

Rose flicked her gaze at the serving girl in the corner of her study who stood behind a large tea trolley. Luckily, berry infusion had been one option Ma Bowl had included. Once both women had hot beverages, Momma K waited for Rose to tell her why she'd been summoned. The silence stretched as Rose tried to figure out the best way to ask.

'Sometime it best ta just get it out. Say ya piece and be done wid it.'

Rose chewed her bottom lip and went for it.

'I need you to tell me everything you know about the Sea Witch and what she might do with the Spice Ghosts' bones.'

At the mention of the Sea Witch, Momma K sucked her teeth and her shoulders tensed. The hand that held her teacup gripped the china tightly. She put the cup back on the saucer with a clatter.

'Dat witch is bad news. Me advice? Stay well away. Dere nudtink but trouble fo' ya dere.'

'But why?' pressed Rose. 'Why is she bad news?'

'She speak wid da dead when de dead no want ta. She a death speaker. Corpse mover. She black to da core.'

Rose sat back, a contemplative look on her face. If the Sea Witch was a necromancer and dabbling in death magic, then that must be why the Spice Ghosts were so worried. Maybe with their bones, she had the power to upset the balance somehow. Maybe even eradicate it. But Momma K wasn't finished speaking.

'Long time ago, me and she were sista-fae. We grew in our magics togetha and played tricks on our elders like children do. We were innocent and pure. Till he came. A shifta man.' Momma K noticed Rose's sharp glance at that and shook her head, dreadlock charms chiming. 'Not dat one. Anuder. Same bad news. He poisoned her heart against me, against fae, against life in de grove and pulled her under. Under wata, under ground, under life. He showed her de darkness within and she could no resist de temptation to dabble. He put her on da path ta ruin.'

'What happened to him?'

Momma K tsked.

'Momma Gurny, who came before, she saw to him. Tore him down, made him pay for he shifter ways and de Sea Witch, as she had become, she took it hard. Blamed fae for de death of her lover, her teacher, her soul mate. He no her soul mate. He soul destroyer.'

Momma K picked up her cup and drank her tea, pensive, lost in her thoughts for a moment.

'She never forgive and she dove. Inta wata, inta death, inta sacrifice. All de tings dat doh belong ta fae. She gave up her life on land, lost her connection wid nature, turned her back on our magic. Wat she brew, is no fae.' Momma K lifted her gaze to look directly at Rose. 'We doh mix. We doh talk.'

'What about when Jenni communicated with her? When we were on the raft trying to flee Fidelia?'

Momma K narrowed her eyes.

'Dere were sacrifice fo' her?'

Rose nodded, remembering the severed head Griff had provided as payment for the Sea Witch.

'Den her bloodlust would fo'give ma daughta speak, but it good ya did no want to travel across de ocean. She would no allow dat.'

Rose shook her head in frustration.

'It doesn't make any sense. We've been in the ocean before. With the mermaids, when we crossed their territory to get to the Isle of Illusion. Why didn't she attack Jenni then? If what you say is true, that she and fae are such great enemies.'

Momma K waved her hand dismissively at Rose.

'Ya explain yaself. Mermaid territory. Dere be ancient agreement. De Sea Witch she no swim too close, mebbe she no feel Jenni den. Is ting.'

Rose sat back, her immediate questions answered.

'Me no seen her fo a long time, but me can tell you wat me remember. If it helps,' offered Momma K.

'Yes, please do. Everything will help, I think, every little thing.' And she pulled some paper forward to make notes about what Momma K said.

Chapter 22

Esme greeted them at the door of the library.

'I have activated the requested search parameters. Your results can be found in the reading nook you sullied with your snacks and beverages. If you continue to use the library as a cafeteria, I will be forced to ban you. For this lifetime at least.' With her severe bun and a pair of pince-nez glasses balanced on the end of her nose, she looked twice as intimidating as usual, although she only came up to Ned's shoulder.

She stalked away from them, back to her centre desk and Griff began walking towards the alcove they had last been working in.

'Requested search parameters?' queried Ned.

'I had some ideas on what might happen today and thought it prudent to get half a step in front of ourselves.'

'And you didn't think to let the rest of us in on your thoughts.' Ned was getting fed up with Griff's secrets and non-disclosures. 'You know, things might go a lot faster and smoother if you were upfront about things you suspect. Like the mysterious rituals you went through to fake your own death. And the different pies you seem to have fingers in.' He took a seat in the alcove but continued complaining. 'What else don't we know about you? You're meant to be an official of Roshaven loyal to the Empire, but we don't even know if you have a wife or any other children.' Ned blinked at that question. He hadn't realised he'd considered that before. 'Do you? Have other children?'

Griff smirked.

'When this is all over, I'll take you on a family road trip, eh? Introduce you to all the beautiful people in our family. But the now is important here. We need to focus and see if we can figure out what the Sea Witch is after.' Griff passed Ned a book. 'Here, this book talks about the high-level magic she might be able to work. See which spells mention bones and let's see where we get. And skim read, eh? We haven't got all day.'

'I know that,' muttered Ned, as he started scanning the pages for any bone references.

Esme had helpfully provided some paper and pen as well as a large sign that read No Snacks! Ned couldn't help but smile at that as he began jotting down notes.

He and Griff worked in silence for several hours until the twin growling of their stomachs couldn't be ignored anymore, and the pile of books had completely dwindled.

'What you got?' Ned asked.

There was a cheeky twinkle in Griff's eyes as he pulled out a half-eaten cheese and pickle sandwich, a small red apple and a few honey cakes that were stuck together.

'Esme said no food!' hissed Ned, looking over his shoulder, sure they would be caught. He inspected the contraband and noticed rather more pocket fluff than he'd prefer on his food. He shook his head at the proffered goodies. 'I meant, what have you found out?'

'I think it's probably better to share with the group than repeat information over and over, eh?'

Ned pulled his pages close to his chest.

'Yeah. I guess. I'll rustle us up some lunch from Ma Bowl then, shall I?'

'You can get a servant to do that for you, you know?

As consort to the Empress.' Griff regarded Ned with a wry smile as they left the library.

'I don't mind. Helps to keep my feet grounded,' replied Ned stiffly, wondering why he was having to defend his actions to Griff. 'I'll meet you in the meeting room.' He stalked off in the opposite direction, realising with a sinking feeling that he'd gone the wrong way and would now have to either turn back and suffer more smirking or go the extra long way round to the kitchens. He opted for the extra-long way, tired of being ridiculed.

When Ned walked into the third best meeting room with a tray of cold meat sandwiches and some honey cakes, Griff and Rose were laughing over what looked like afternoon tea. Ned pretended not to care and tried to check out the tea stand to see if there were any decent cakes left. Rose caught him looking.

'I saved you some.' She leaned back slightly and Ned saw there was an untouched plate with all his favourites.

That explained why Ma Bowl had the sandwiches made for him with such an enormous grin on her face. Ah well. Researching spells that could destroy the world was hungry work.

'The Highs will be back soon, but I don't know about Jenni.' Rose almost said it as a question and waited for Ned to fill in the blank.

'She'll be here by dusk. Catcher business.' Ned wasn't technically lying. Norm was a thief and Jenni was a thief-catcher. 'I can fill her in.'

'Okay. Well, eat up before the Highs come back. I think we've all got a lot to report back.'

Rose wasn't lying, thought Ned. He tried to swallow the now leaden piece of fruit cake in his mouth as he listened to her recount Momma K's recollections about the Sea Witch.

'She sounds like such a nasty piece of work. Why haven't we come up against her before?' he asked as he finally swallowed the last bite.

'From what I could make out, it's been a matter of non-interference. Momma K left her alone provided she didn't dabble in the fae realm, and the Sea Witch left Momma K alone provided she didn't dabble in her witchcraft,' replied Rose.

'Seems like an uneasy truce,' Ned said.

'A truce that's worked for over a hundred years.'

'Does that mean we need to add immortality to the pile?' asked Griff.

'No. She's not immortal. Just long-lived. But there is something else we need to know. Momma K was very specific about this. She said that whilst fae magic and witchcraft may look like the same thing, they draw their power very differently. The fae respect nature and maintain the balance between the living and the dead, whereas the Sea Witch's brand of witchcraft has very dark roots. It is power gained by any means necessary, regardless of the price. And it's power taken whether or not the Source likes it.'

'Hang on a minute. Jenni told me about the Source when she had her Coming-of-Age ceremony. It sounded like a powerful entity. Are you telling me it can't stop the Sea Witch from drawing on its energies?' Ned asked.

'That's what Momma K said. She said the Source is just that, the source of all magic. It doesn't only manifest on this plane and it can't stop the Sea Witch from wielding her power if she chooses to use black arts to access it.'

'But it cut Jenni's access, reduced her link to the Source. It said she had too much power and couldn't be allowed to continue to use it.' Ned shook his head. 'It makes no sense.'

'I'm only telling you what Momma K said. Maybe she knows more. I didn't ask about the Source specifically.' Rose's shoulders drooped as she spoke. 'Sorry.'

'Don't be daft, how could you have known to ask.' Ned reached out and squeezed her hand. 'This balance thing – it feels like a convenient excuse, doesn't it? It keeps being mentioned as massively important and yet when someone disrespects it, there are zero consequences.'

'There's us,' said Griff.

'Us! We don't have any power.'

'Maybe. Maybe not. But we're the ones here and we're the ones ready to stand in the way of whatever it is the Sea Witch is planning.'

Griff was interrupted with the return of the Highs and Jimmy Fingers, who helped himself to the last bit of cake Ned had had his eye on.

'Let me tell you what I found out, eh?' Griff had puffed out his chest a little, glad to be in the limelight. 'I discovered that the Sea Witch has no problem being on land. She can take both corporeal and liquid form and is able to perform magic in either.'

'I found that out too,' muttered Ned.

'That said, she hasn't been on land for at least twenty years or so. Not since she had a child.'

The interest level in the room climbed significantly.

'What child?'

'Where are they now?'

'A child?'

Griff smoothed his moustache, pleased with himself.

'The child unfortunately died – natural causes, or so

it seems. There is a spell that requires bones with mystical properties. It allows the caster to tear a hole in the realms and bring back a shade – the spirit of a dead person – in order to resurrect them. The spell destroys the bones and leaves a gaping hole in the realms.' Griff slapped his hand on the table in triumph. 'That's why the Spice Ghosts' looked so worried and that's why the Sea Witch wanted their bones. She's trying to bring her daughter back.'

Everyone else looked impressed, but Ned had a niggle.

'Then why did Norm steal the bones? You're not telling me the Sea Witch orchestrated the whole thing, are you? Getting Norm to steal the bones, lose them at a poker game, have them sold on to the fae traders so she could take them. That's… a lot.'

'I think that the Sea Witch has been waiting for an opportune moment, eh?'

Ned picked his fingers. He wished Jenni was back so he could ask her opinion, but if he was being honest, it felt like Norm had been manipulated from the start.

'If these bones have the power to create a spell like that, I don't think we'll be able to convince the Sea Witch to willingly hand them over – even if we take a Spice Ghost with us. We need to think of something of equal value we can offer her,' said Rose.

'Like what?' Ned did not know what would have the same magical value as a set of powerful bones. 'Surely we don't want her to tear open the realms?'

'No, of course not but, I have a crazy theory.' Rose's eyes were gleaming. 'I was thinking about what you said about the Source, about how it restricted Jenni's access to magic. What if we could convince the Source to return Jenni's magic plus a bit more and use that to tempt the

Sea Witch? Offer her enough power to cast the resurrection spell so that she'll give us the bones back. They won't get destroyed and the realms won't end up with a hole torn through them.'

'But what if the Sea Witch agrees – she'll want the power and we can't give that to her, can we?' asked Fingers.

'No, we won't. It's just a ruse to tempt her with power so she'll give up the bones,' replied Rose.

'But what if she tries to take the magic?' Fingers didn't sound convinced.

'Then Jenni will stop her.' Rose's belief in the sprite was absolute.

'Um… didn't Momma K say the magic was different between fae and witch?' asked Ned, deciding to ignore for now the fact that Jenni and the Sea Witch might end up battling for supremacy.

'Yes, but she said it was down to what they are using the magic for and how they're getting it,' replied Rose. 'The Sea Witch gets her power from the black arts, stealing souls and necromancy, whereas the fae get their power from nature, but all the power stems from the Source. Remember the song? *With blackened eyes and scales of green - It's a sight you'll wish you'd never seen.* Black magic corrupts whereas the fae remain good and pure and beautiful.'

Ned tried to hide his smirk at Jenni being described as good and pure and beautiful.

'I think you might be running away with fae tales a little here,' said Griff brusquely.

'And I think you forget yourself. Show your Empress some respect,' barked the High Left, who until now had been sitting quietly, taking notes. The High Right was also giving Griff the evil eye.

'My Empress, forgive me. I spoke out of turn.' Griff inclined his head towards her.

'I think it's worth looking into. Maybe Jenni can speak to the Source again, see what it thinks,' said Ned, sharing a brief smile with his wife. 'As long as we don't actually end up giving the Sea Witch more power and turning her into an even bigger threat, of course.' Both their smiles faltered.

'Did you discover anything else, sire?' The High Right asked Ned, who looked momentarily confused. He wasn't quite used to being addressed with such respect.

'Err… just more of the same, really. The Sea Witch is a powerful necromancer and the Spice Ghosts maintain the balance between the realms.' The backs of Ned's ears were burning. 'But it looks like we have a plan now, at least. Going to see the Source and having someone agree to be an anchor for the Spice Ghosts. I don't think Jenni should do that though.'

'Me either,' said Rose. 'If I'm right about the Source and the temptation of more power being the only thing we can trade for the bones, then tethering a Spice Ghost to Jenni as well isn't going to be a good idea. We don't want to put all our eggs in one basket, so to speak.'

Something else had been niggling at Ned.

'What if the Source pinched Jenni's magic on purpose, knowing that we would need some extra firepower in the future?' he asked. 'What if it knew we'd be going up against the Sea Witch and that we'd have to come and ask for help?'

'How do you mean, lad?' Griff looked confused. He wasn't the only one.

'I mean that if the Source had never restricted Jenni's magic in the first place, then we would have walked into this fight without a second thought. She's the most powerful fae I've ever met – or at least, she was.' There were nods of agreement from the others. 'But what if the Source knew Jenni's power would not be enough and that we'd need more in order to win? A cosmic entity can't just meddle in the lives of people. There are rules, according to the Great God Unami, anyway.' Ned had spoken to the God briefly after rescuing all the priest's animals from his brother's clutches. What felt like a lifetime ago. 'What if the Source is waiting for us to come and request help so it can return Jenni's magic, and maybe a bit more, as a trap for the Sea Witch?'

There was a long silence from the others.

'It's a pretty long game, considering none of us even knew we were playing it, eh?' said Griff, eventually.

'That's cosmic entities for you. Time is not linear, it's more wibbly-wobbly. Or so I've been told,' replied Rose with half a smile. 'We need to get Jenni to go speak to the Source again. Where is she?'

Ned sidestepped the question with one of his own.

'Don't worry, she'll be here. Are you sure about this?'

'Yes,' said Rose. 'And I also think Norm was the long game for the Sea Witch. She must have set him up months, if not years ago, to get onto the Spice Ghost ship as crew and be in a position to steal the bones in the first place. She probably didn't expect him to lose them in a poker game, or maybe she counted on it. On that and the greed of Erick and the roaming nature of the fae traders.'

'There are a lot of ifs, buts and maybes in there,' remarked Griff. 'But I have to admit, there's a smidge of truth about the whole thing. Complicated coincidences are often nothing of the kind.'

Chapter 23

Jenni had been to nearly all the usual haunts the dodgier visitors to Roshaven frequent and so far she'd come up empty. No sign of Norm and no one had admitted to seeing him, either. She trudged back to The Noose, thinking she'd check in with Willow, Joe and Sparks just on the off chance. When she walked into the pub, she saw him at once. Sat on a bar stool, hands wrapped round a mug of ale. Hardly daring to breathe, she went to sit next to him.

'Awright?'

Jenni had to give him credit. The only sign that she'd scared the life out of him was the slight sloshing of the ale.

'Jenni, love. I didn't expect to see you here.' Norm took a long drink.

'Yor kidding, right? It's 'eadquarters. Basically the only place yor sure to find me.'

'Headquarters? But Thief Catcher HQ is over on Justice Heights, isn't it?'

'Not for at least ten years. It got moved afta it got burnt down again.'

Norm's shoulders hunched a little.

'You going to arrest me then?'

'I fink we need to 'ave a little chat, yeah. But we can 'ave it 'ere or I can take you to the palace. Up to you.' Jenni wanted Norm to talk, so if that meant doing it at the bar of The Noose, then so be it.

'What do you want to talk about?' Norm sipped at his ale.

'Wot are you doing 'ere? You was free and clear. Why come back to Roshaven?'

'Can't a father just want to spend time with his daughter?'

Jenni looked at him.

'Okay, so maybe not.' He tipped back the rest of his drink and smacked his lips. 'How did you know I was even in the city? Have you got tabs on me?'

'Nah. I felt it. We're blood, right? So I knows you was 'ere. Just like I knows when Momma K comes out the fae realm. Only works on youse two though, so must be a daughter fing or summink.' She shrugged. 'But don't panic. The Network knows who you is and they'll keep tabs on yer wherevers you go in the city.'

'The network?' Norm queried.

'Yeah, the Network. You don't need to know who it is. Just that they're watching.' Jenni figured if Norm didn't know the Network meant the beggars of Roshaven, then that was one up for the thief-catchers.

'How's your magic?' Norm changed the subject and Jenni felt the familiar ripple of guilt. It was her turn to be on the back foot.

'S'alright.'

'Have you been skimming lately? I heard a fainting bug made its way through Mannon's Lair. That's a lot of people to all feel giddy at the same time.'

Jenni tensed.

'It weren't my fault. There was so much in there. I couldn't 'elp it.'

'How did you do it? Skim a whole room like that? Mannon's Lair is cavernous. I'm very impressed.'

Jenni squirmed on her stool. She wasn't sure if she was happy about impressing Norm or not.

'I just did wot you told me to. Extend and skim, no

dipping. S'easy.'

They both sipped their drinks quietly.

'You trust this Ned fella?'

That question caught Jenni off guard.

'Corse. E's me boss. E's awright and that.'

'And you live with him? Or lived with him before he married the Empress.'

'Oi. It's me meant to be asking you, not the ovver way round. Me and Ned ain't no beeswax of yors.' Jenni was feeling thoroughly discombobulated now, and she didn't like it. 'Why you working for the Sea Witch? Wot's she got on you?' She watched Norm flinch as she said Sea Witch.

Norm hunched over his empty drink further.

'She's not a good person to get mixed up with. Keep your nose out and stay away from her.'

'Ha! Fat chance of that. She put the Spice Ghosts on yor tail cos she got you to steal their bones for 'er. She's probably mad as anyfink cos you lost the bones at poker when you shoulda took 'em to 'er.' Jenni had a sudden epiphany. 'That's why yor 'ere ain't it? Yor 'iding from the Sea Witch cos you don't know.'

'Look, it seemed like a good idea at the time. Without the bones, she can't touch me here. Especially with the Spice Ghosts anchored in Roshaven. I'm safe here.' Norm downed the last of his drink. 'What don't I know?'

Jenni flicked a coin over at Reg, the barman, to pay for Norm's drink.

'You've lucked out, mate. The Sea Witch 'as got the magic bones, and she's fixing to use 'em. You'd better come wiv me.'

All the colour drained out of Norm's face at hearing Jenni's words. She half pulled him off the bar stool and shooed him out the door of The Noose toward the Imperial Palace. He went with her, in too much shock to resist.

There were still a couple of hours until dusk and the Spice Ghosts' deadline, when Jenni and Norm met up with Ned and the others in the third-best meeting room.

'Jenni? You found Norm. Did you… arrest him?' Rose peered at Jenni's dad to see if he was cuffed or not.

'E ain't going nowhere. 'E came 'ere to 'ide cos he fawt the bones were still at Braso Amia. Bit of a shock to find out they ain't.'

Ned noticed Jenn's grin didn't quite meet her eyes, but her words seemed to revive Norm. He suddenly moved and grabbed Ned's arms.

'You gotta protect me! She'll kill me for double crossing her. Sanctuary!' he shouted.

Ned shook him off brusquely.

'We ain't gonna do nuffink for you unless you tell us everyfink wot you knows about the Sea Witch. Every crumb.' Jenni poked her dad in the chest, forcing him backwards to sit in a chair.

The others arrayed themselves around Norm, so he was caught in their gazes and had nowhere to run to. They wanted some answers.

'There's not much to tell really, she's the Sea Witch. The person lives up to the legend,' said Norm.

'Explain it to us as if we didn't know the legend,' prompted Ned, taking the lead on the questioning.

'Okay, um… well, she lives in the ocean, being the Sea Witch and all. But keeps away from the mermaids. They don't like each other, and whilst she has power, it's derived, whereas the mermaids sea magic is instinctual. They are one with the water. The Sea Witch is more… taker of the water. Does that make sense?'

Ned nodded and motioned for Norm to continue.

'She used to be a woman who walked on land and breathed air and so forth. But her dabbling in the darker magics gave her the power to change her form and live under water. She can bend the weather to do her bidding, forcing ships to sink at sea if proper tribute isn't paid. The tribute usually being human sacrifices, which is why most ships leave port with a condemned criminal on board if they can manage it.' Norm half smiled but quailed under the stares of his audience. 'Um, what else, what else?'

Ned shifted in his seat.

'Why don't you tell us how she came to hire you?'

'Ah, funny story. There was a mix up in Oxharbour and somehow they thought I was a condemned criminal when really it had just been a misunderstanding on preferred ownership. But before I could plead my case, I found myself trussed up on a ship headed for who knows where with me as their tribute.'

'And you talked your way out of that?' asked Griff, looking impressed despite himself.

'Not exactly. I didn't manage to not get thrown overboard, but I had made friends with the ship's lad and he loosened my bonds for me. Gave me the chance to wriggle free and swim for it.'

'And the Sea Witch never got you?' asked Jenni. 'You part merman?'

'I wouldn't say never. We definitely met and… gurgle, gurgle,' Norm had to stop talking because he was choking and water was running out of his mouth.

'Stop! Stop trying to tell us!' shouted Griff, leaping up. 'It's a curse. She's cursed him from telling us. I've seen this before.'

Norm continued to cough and splutter for a while

after the water stopped pouring out of his mouth and one of the Highs signalled for a servant to come quickly and mop up the mess.

'Can you maybe write it down for us?' asked Rose.

Norm shook his head.

'I can't write. Never learned.' He wiped his mouth with the back of his hand, looking shaken. 'Do you think that will happen again?'

'As long as you don't try to tell us about the deal you made with the Sea Witch, you should be alright.' Griff was pacing again. 'We're in a bind, eh? Could be this deal is important, could be it's nothing at all.' He considered Norm. 'I reckoned he'd drown before we found out. Probably best not to risk it?'

His half question stunned the others for a moment.

'No. No, we can't risk killing him just to find out about the deal he made.' Ned glanced at Jenni. 'It wouldn't be right. Norm, can you tell us anything?'

Norm looked at Jenni and another gurgle swept out of him, bringing with it another sploosh of water. While the others watched as the servant cleaned up the water again, Ned was staring at Jenni.

'Wot?'

'Are you alright?' He gestured at Norm and the damp floor. 'This is a lot to process. Your Dad making some kind of deal with the Sea Witch that he can't talk about. Just wanted to make sure you're doing okay.'

'Yeah, well, we knew 'e were up to summink, didn't we? Cos the Spice Ghosts were gunning for me when I didn't do nuffink. He's probably sold me soul or summink.' Jenni looked at Ned's horrified face. 'Aww, I'm joking, Boss. He ain't sold me soul. Don't worry.' She patted his knee. 'Lemme see if I can do anyfink.'

'But Jenni, have you even got the power to break a

curse like this? Maybe we should get Momma K to come and have a go.' Ned watched the sprite as she opened her mouth to argue, cast a panicked look at Norm, and then closed her mouth again. What was all that about? he wondered.

'I've sent a message to Momma K,' said Rose. 'I'm sure she won't be long.'

Ned marvelled at how easy it was to get things done when you had staff that did what they were told, questioning nothing. Then he felt bad because at the end of the day, he wouldn't change his thief-catchers for anything.

Momma K arrived in a whirl of sparkly smoke. An unusually theatrical appearance that she had never used before. Ned thought it was in order to impress and possibly intimidate Norm.

'Wat he doin' here? Me doh want him. Pass ye own judgements.' Momma K's dreadlocks clicked loudly as she vibrated angrily.

'Thank you for coming so quickly, Momma K. We believe Norm has been cursed by the Sea Witch and we wondered if there was anything you could do?' asked Rose.

Momma K sucked her teeth.

'Wat happened?'

'When we asked him about the deal he made with the Sea Witch, water started gurgling out of his mouth, threatening to choke and drown him,' explained Rose.

'Standard. Me prefer ta seal mouths completely, dat way dey can never spill der secrets.'

Ned shivered. Sometimes Momma K scared the absolute wotsits out of him.

'Jenni, attend.' Momma K ordered her daughter to observe. 'Dis is how me break a curse. Me doh get many to crack dese days.'

Momma K muttered something unintelligible to Ned and begin to glow as she sent out silver threads from her fingers into the sides of Norm's head. The sprite gasped and his eyes shot open super wide, back arched and hands curled into fists. Ned winced despite himself.

There was a moment when Momma K frowned and began muttering faster before droplets of water appeared on Norm's skin. One by one, they floated upwards, linking with each other, creating larger and larger globules of water until an impressively sized sphere of water hung above Norm's head. Momma K clicked her fingers, and the sphere imploded, drenching Norm from head to toe.

'Wat deal did ya make wid de witch?' she demanded.

'I-I-I offered my services. To skim for her,' replied Norm in a feeble voice. He was soaked to the skin and looked to Ned as if he'd sunk into himself.

'Skimming magic? Wat ya skim dat for?' asked Momma K, the disgust clear in her voice.

'Not magic.' Norm lifted his head and looked at Jenni directly in the eye. 'Souls.'

There was a collective gasp from the riveted audience.

'Ya can't skim souls. Ya don't have de power.'

'I, er… found out that if you dip and twist, then…' Norm trailed off under the glare from Momma K and went back to shrinking into himself.

Ned glanced at Jenni and saw she'd turned white. Obviously finding out her father was a soul skimmer had shocked her to the core.

'We knew the Sea Witch collected souls. Stands to reason she'd employ others to do the same, widen her net, eh?' Griff crooked a finger at one of the palace guards standing watch. 'Take him to one of the spelled cells. Make sure he's comfortable.'

Nobody made a move to stop the guard. There was a tense silence.

'Will ya give he to de Spice Ghosts?' Momma K was the first to speak.

'Not necessarily,' replied Rose, and Ned thought he saw a flash of relief pass through Momma K's eyes. 'But we need to get ready to meet them at the Dead Pier. Momma K, we want to send Jenni to the Source. We think maybe it can help us tempt the Sea Witch to give up the bones.'

Momma K turned a calculating look at Jenni, who looked thoughtful at the suggestion.

'It worth a try. Me daughta got potential.' She gave Rose a small bow. 'Good luck wid de Ghosts.' And she popped away.

'Wot you gonna do wiv 'im?' asked Jenni once Momma K had gone.

'I don't know yet. But I think keeping him here for now is probably a good idea.' She glanced at Ned before continuing. 'Jenni, as you heard, we want you to go speak to the Source. We think if we can tempt the Sea Witch with more power, we'll be able to get the bones back. We need you to ask the Source to give you your magic back.'

'Wot if it says no?'

'We don't think it will and if nothing else, perhaps it can arm you with enough power to stop the Sea Witch.'

'I see. Make me a weapon. I like it.' Jenni puffed out her chest. 'Yeah, corse I can ask. Afta we seen the Spice Ghosts though, yeah?'

Rose nodded.

'Hang on. If I'm gonna go see the Source, who's gonna be the anchor?' asked Jenni.

'Me. I'll do it,' Ned spoke up quickly before anyone else could volunteer. 'They said they'd have me as an alternative and it makes sense. I'm Chief Thief-Catcher. This is my city to look after, so if I'm tethered to a Spice Ghost then it's on me to make sure nothing goes wrong.'

'Are you sure? We could find someone else…' Rose was looking at Ned with a sorrowful face.

'Who would we ask?' Ned gestured at the few people in the room. 'I'm the obvious choice and you know it.' He glanced out the window. 'We'd better go or we'll be late.'

The High Right ordered half a dozen palace guards to accompany the Empress to the docks with instructions for the imperial carriage to follow, guessing correctly that Rose, Ned, Jenni, and Griff would want to walk the short distance.

Chapter 24

Only one Spice Ghost waited for them on the Dead Pier. Clove.

'Who has agreed to be my tether?' She wasted no time.

'I have.' Ned stepped forward, unsure exactly what was expected of him. Now that he stood closer to Clove than before, he could see she had an odd quality about her. Like she wasn't all there and not as solid as a real person would be. It was hard to tell, though, and Ned's brain kept telling him it was just a trick of the light.

Clove held out her hand, so Ned held out his too. She clasped her arm with his and muttered an incantation under her breath, too quietly for Ned to hear her words. Her arm solidified against his, making Ned gasp. There was a rush of heat throughout his body and the aromatic smell of cloves momentarily overpowered his senses, making his eyes water and his tongue burn. Just as quickly as it appeared, it was gone and Clove dropped his arm.

'That's it?' he asked, glad that he appeared to be all in one piece.

'It is done. Where you go, I go and where I wish to go, you will take me.'

There was no doubt in Clove's voice that Ned would do exactly as she asked and to be honest, Ned didn't feel like testing the link right now.

'Please, come back to the palace. Have some dinner with us as we plan our next move,' invited Rose.

'I'm afraid there is little time to lose. The full moon

is two short nights hence and we must get our bones back before she uses up their essence in her magics.' Clove started walking down the Pier towards the city and as she got twenty paces in front of Ned, he felt a strong desire to follow her.

Instead, he ground his boots into the deck.

'Wait! Stop, please. We have questions and a possible incentive to offer the Sea Witch, but we need tonight. Besides, we don't even know where the Sea Witch is.' Ned glanced back at the water behind him. 'And we don't want to be travelling in the opposite direction, do we?'

Clove stopped walking, for which Ned was immensely grateful. His entire body was trying to dash after her.

'Your waters are mer-protected. We'll never find the Sea Witch here. We need to travel to the next closest coastal shore. Shady Cove I believe?'

'That's right,' said Griff. 'It's no more than a day's walk from here. We can leave at first light tomorrow. But Ned's right. We have questions and surely sharing information will be to the benefit of both sides, eh?'

Clove regarded Griff for a long time before acquiescing with the smallest of nods. She still strode off, but this time it was in the palace's direction, and Ned had to scramble to keep up with her.

'Miss Clove? How do you know where to go?' he asked as the others trotted behind.

'Just Clove is fine. And this is not my first visit to Roshaven, although changes have been made.' She flicked her gaze towards Rose. 'Good changes.'

Despite having hundreds of questions tumbling in his head, Ned decided to go for one of a more delicate nature.

'Clove? Um... the, er... tether... seems to be quite short and er, what happens with privacy, that sort of thing?'

A small smile appeared on Clove's face.

'The tether is fuelled by intent. If you, or I, bend our will with purpose towards achieving our goal, then the tether will shorten, enabling both parties to travel with speed in the same direction. However, without intent, the tether relaxes, offering some privacy. Don't worry Catcher, you won't have to pee next to me.'

Ned was relieved, although that hadn't been his initial worry. He had been concerned about where exactly he was going to be expected to sleep tonight. A bed roll on the road with your travelling companions was fine but sleeping in the same bedchamber as another woman in your wife's palace was a whole other can of worms.

On their arrival in the Imperial Palace courtyard, the Highs sprang into action, organising the room next to Ned and Rose's into guest chambers for Clove and sending instructions down to Ma Bowl to rustle up travelling provisions as well as a hearty meal tonight.

They returned to the third-best meeting room, as there were too many of them to meet in the cosier study, and Clove glanced round with interest.

'Some things have stayed the same,' she commented on the decorative nature of the palace.

The Highs puffed out their chest with pride.

Once again, Clove wasted no time as they took seats around the table.

'Now that I am tethered to this plane, you will accompany me to Shady Cove and we will retrieve my bones,' she said matter of fact.

'We don't think the Sea Witch will want to give

them up,' replied Rose. 'We think she's going to use them in a spell to break through to the spirit realm and bring back the shade of her daughter so she can return her to the living.'

Clove's face tightened, and she clasped her hands together, the knuckles turning white at the tight grip.

'We agree.' Clove released her hands and pressed them on the table. 'This spell will destroy the bones and without them, we cannot work our magic and preserve the balance. If she tears a hole in the veil, we cannot fix it without our bones.'

Ned had been watching the Spice Ghost closely and realised that under her initial bravado, she was scared.

'We have a plan to get the bones back,' he said. 'We're going to offer something the Sea Witch won't be able to refuse.'

'What incentive do you think will work with the Sea Witch?' asked Clove, the scowl on her face mirroring the disbelief in her voice.

'Power.' Rose spoke up, taking the reins of the conversation. 'We are sending a representative to speak with the Source, tonight, to request access to more magic in order to tempt the Sea Witch.'

'Access to fae power is something the Sea Witch has long craved. This could work – her greed will make her less cautious.' Clove's shoulders relaxed a little. 'I'm assuming you are not planning to just hand it over? The consequences could be catastrophic.'

Rose sat back in her chair. 'No. Of course not. It's meant as an enormous temptation.'

'And the fae making the offer?' asked Clove, her gaze lingering on Jenni.

'Yeah, that's right. It'll be me.'

'And what if the Sea Witch tries to take this power?

How are you going to stop her?'

Rose answered for Jenni.

'We think the fae power will fight back against the darkness of the Sea Witch. If it comes down to it, they'll fight for supremacy and with any luck the fae power will wipe her out.'

'We do?' Ned didn't mean to speak out, but he hadn't realised that was part of the plan. He wasn't sure he liked the idea of putting Jenni in that much danger.

'Gotcha,' Jenni sounded impressed. 'I fink that might work, you know. Fae magic don't like sharing, don't work often. Cept with you, Boss. But I reckon you gotta bit o' fae in you somewhere.'

Ned blinked, doubly shocked, and looked at his father for confirmation. But Griff just winked at him.

'What was your plan?' Rose asked Clove.

Ned saw she couldn't entirely keep the smugness out of her voice at being the one who had thought of magically destroying the Sea Witch.

'Steal them,' replied Clove flatly. She turned to look at Ned. 'I assume you know some good thieves in your line of work.'

'Fingers,' said Ned and Rose together.

Rose directed the High Right to summon Fingers immediately, and while they waited, Ned took Jenni to one side.

'Do you want me to come with you? To see the Source, I mean.'

'I don't fink she'd let ya.' Jenni nodded over at Clove, who was being regaled with one of Griff's tall tales. 'Sides, I'll be awright. Me and the Source got on last time, I fink it'll be up for 'elping.'

'What if it says no?'

'Then we got Fingers, ain't we?' Jenni sounded

confident, which helped boost Ned's a little. Fingers was an excellent thief or had been until he'd taken up the official role of Lower Circle. He now looked after all of Roshaven's imports and exports, a job he was well suited to.

'Okay, you'd better go now and come straight back here when you're done. Good luck.' Ned watched as Jenni hurried out of the room and hoped things went as straightforward as Jenni thought they would. His thoughts were interrupted by the arrival of dinner, and his stomach growled in appreciation.

Chapter 25

Jenni marched into the fae realm with determination. Momma K was going to open the sacred connection and let her talk to the Source, and that was all there was to say.

Only Momma K wasn't on her preferred toadstool. Or in the lemon grove. Or the strawberry fields. Jenni snagged a passing fairy.

'Where's Momma K?'

'Out.' The fairy tutted at being asked, then looked and saw who was doing the asking. 'She's out on an errand. Said she might not be back until tomorrow, but she didn't say where.' The fairy fluttered her wings, wanting to leave and get on with her pressing business, but Jenni had hold of her arm.

'Wot about the Elders? Where they at?'

'I don't know. But you can probably find Amos at the University.' The fairy fluttered harder. 'Can I go now?'

Jenni let go, and the fairy sped away. It had always struck Jenni as odd that the fae realm had a university, considering most fae could just use magic if they wanted something or needed to fix something. Still, it was a good place to look for the large black dog, Amos, as he taught and worked there.

She stomped across the fairy bridge so hard that she heard the river troll who lived underneath panicking.

'Noooo, not those goats on the loose again! That's it. I'm packing all my belongings and leaving for the River Whine. It's annoying sharing a body of water with Piss-

Eyed Nelle but that'll be better than goats.'

Good riddance thought Jenni. *I never liked her anyway.*

Jenni's grim humour didn't stop there. She barely noticed that the sky was turning more purple than blue or that the temperature was dropping slightly. She was on a mission. The smell of marzipan echoed in her footsteps, a warning sign for other fae to take cover.

When she got to the University, Jenni marched up to the front desk.

'Oi, you can't bring that in here,' yelled one of the pixie administrators on the front desk, bustling around to confront her.

'Wot?' Jenni turned back and noticed the effect she was having. A small black cloud was following her and crackling gold energy in her wake. She tested her internal power levels, but they seemed untouched. Clearly her surroundings were reacting to her state of mind, like they did to Momma K. Only with no queen in residence, the grove was resonating with the next best thing.

'Bloody 'ell.' Jenni really didn't need Momma K hearing about this. She would not be pleased that the realm was reacting to Jenni, especially after Jenni had walked away from succession to the crown. 'Look, I need to speak to Amos toot suite, so just tell me where he is and I'll be out of yor 'air.'

'He's teaching in 4B,' began the pixie, but Jenni was already striding towards the stairs, intent on finding Amos. 'You can't just walk into a lecture!' The pixie yelled after her, but it made no difference.

Jenni paused for breath on the second floor. There seemed to be an awful lot of steps between floors. The black cloud crackled as if it were encouraging her onwards. She glared at it, then carried on stomping up the stairs. On reaching the fourth floor, Jenni entered the hallway to discover there were only two doors available, 4A and 4B. Both had a handy circular window in them. Out of curiosity, Jenni glanced into 4A but saw only darkness. Peering into 4B, she saw a row of seats filled with lots of students arranged in a semi-circle around a stage. The stage was at the bottom of a slope and the chairs went up in rows. She could make out Amos on the stage, so without hesitation, she opened the door.

Hundreds of heads swivelled to see who was late to Dr Amos's lecture. There was a bout of frenzied whispering.

'Yes, yes. Hurry up and take your seat. You've missed the first half and will have to rely on another student to catch you up,' said Amos wearily.

'I ain't 'ere for that. I wanna talk to the Source,' said Jenni as she walked down to the stage.

It went silent as every student focused their attention on Jenni and Amos.

The large dog was flustered.

'I can't just take you to the Source. There's the matter of protocol.' He leaned closer to Jenni. 'And you've already had your coming-of-age ceremony. It's most unorthodox to request a second audience.' He lowered his voice further. 'Do you have Momma K's permission?'

'She ain't 'ere. And I ain't got time to waste. I need to see the Source, now. LOD.'

LOD was short for life or death and only used by fae in dire chain letters when urgent help was desperately required.

'Class dismissed!' barked Amos, much to the disappointment of his students. There was a great deal of whispering and conjecture as the student body clattered out of the lecture theatre, discussing what disaster could cause LOD.

'You know, it would've been less disruptive to go ask QuiQuo the imp.' Amos glowered at Jenni as he put his own papers away in his bag.

'I don't know where 'e is. You was the closest one to me. You gonna let me in then or wot?'

'What exactly is this life or death situation?'

'The Sea Witch 'as got the Spice Ghosts' bones and we don't know zactly wot she's planning to do, but it'll probably be tearing down the veil tween the spirit world and ours, upsetting the balance. And we gots to stop 'er and we fink the Source can 'elp. On account of the balance.'

Amos was nodding along and shot Jenni a sharp look when she mentioned the balance.

'And what, you think the Source will offer the Sea Witch an alternative power source?' His tail wagged slowly as he considered the idea. 'It might work. But it could also tear the Sea Witch apart. She's not fae anymore, you know.'

'Yeah, I do. How do you know?'

The dog let out a small whine and picked up its now full briefcase.

'Come on, I'll take you to the sacred grove but I warn you, the Source might not be there.'

'Whaddya mean, it might not be there. That's where it is, ain't it?'

'The Source is a cosmic entity and doesn't exactly exist on our plane permanently. It's fascinating really…' Amos launched into describing the current theory on cosmic entities that he and his peers were working on at the university. Luckily, he enjoyed the sound of his own voice enough to not notice Jenni wasn't listening, as she had perfected the art of making interested noises while thinking about something else.

Amos led Jenni into a small clearing which revealed itself to contain the entrance to the sacred grove. The clearing conveniently happened to be just outside the university grounds.

'It weren't 'ere afore.'

'Well, no. As I was saying, entities shift through space and time. You can't expect them to stay in the same place.'

'Ow do you know where it is?'

'Resonance. We Elders are tuned into the sacred grove's resonance. Now, let me concentrate.' Amos closed his eyes and began muttering incantations under his breath.

A stone archway appeared from nowhere. It was black, and the stone was etched with a multitude of magical symbols. There was an air of severity about the archway in its harsh construction, as if it had been hacked into shape. Jenni recognised it from her coming-of-age ceremony. The stone hummed like a warning alarm. It both repelled her and lured her towards it.

Chapter 26

'Hello Jenni. It's so nice to see you again.'

It took Jenni a moment to reorient herself now that she was non corporeal and bathed in the Source.

'Weren't you pink afore?'

The surrounding colour was purple with flashes of gold pulsing through, although it was difficult to hold on to the concept of being surrounded by colour when your body had disappeared. Jenni's brain tried briefly to hold on to some kind of comprehension, then decided to just go with the flow.

'I am whatever you project me to be. My true form is not something you can easily grasp. But you're not here to talk about my manifestation. You want something from me.'

'Yeah. Um.' Now that she was in the Source, Jenni felt somewhat overwhelmed to ask such a powerful entity for help.

'Do you not remember that I can read your thoughts?'

Jenni winced. She had completely forgotten. Her stomach clenched as she thought about the skimming she had been doing. Would the Source punish her for that? She tried desperately not to think about it.

'Er… you already know why I'm 'ere then, right? Can you 'elp?'

The colour purple disappeared and Jenni was left with the sensation of floating in nothing, being nothing, utterly without form or purpose or cognitive ability. There was a feeling of expansion so strong that Jenni thought she would be smeared across the universe before her entire sense of self was suddenly compressed so tightly that if she had any breath, it would've been utterly crushed out of her lungs. Then the purple glow returned, this time with silver flecks that danced about like manic glow bugs.

'Wot were that?' gasped Jenni. Although being insubstantially suspended within the Source of all magic, she didn't actually have breath.

'That was what will happen if the Sea Witch wins. Her path is heading towards nothing. If she is not stopped, then she will summon the void and it will be the end to our universe as we know it.'

'Wot was all that expanding and crushing?'

'That would be the birth of a new universe. The balance you understand. What is destroyed will be re-created.'

Jenni thought for a moment.

'If the universe is just gonna grow again, does it matter if we don't stop the Sea Witch?'

There was an undercurrent of fondness washing through Jenni's awareness as the Source replied.

'I like this permutation. This universe is full of magic and wonder. The next… your world could just be a cold lump of rock in the vast emptiness of space. The harsh reality is that LIFE continues, regardless. It is the way.'

There was something about the way the Source said life that got Jenni asking more questions.

'You don't mean life life, do you? You mean like the carrying on of general fings like stars and stuff, right? Not like fae and people and our world and that.'

The Source radiated approval at Jenni.

'So if we wanna keep our life, our version going, we

gotta stop the Sea Witch.' Jenni had momentarily forgotten that she was supposed to be asking for a magical assist. 'Why ain't you just stepped in and squished 'er like a bug or summink?'

'The Source is outside free will and cannot interfere.'

'So you can't 'elp.'

'Can't interfere, can help. Help can always be given if it is asked for. By the right person.'

Dread overcame Jenni, and she felt sure that if she had her body, she would've come over cold with goose bumps.

'I dunno if I'm the right person but I'm 'ere to ask for 'elp. We fawt if you could offer the Sea Witch that extra power wot you took from me when I 'ad me ceremony, then mebbe that would be enuff to stop 'er from doing the bone magic. We finks using the bones will rip open the realms. But if we tempt 'er wiv lots of magic, then she'll giv us the bones instead. Obvs we ain't gonna acktually giv 'er the magic but even if she tries to take it - cos it's different from wot she's been using - she'll blow up or summink. Mebbe.'

Jenni waited, mentally crossing her fingers and toes that they'd been right and that the Source would agree to help. The Source was taking a long time to reply. Jenni's heart sank. So much for that idea.

'The Source is willing to return your magic to you, so you can offer the temptation. You are the most powerful fae in your realm. It is up to you to stop her.'

'Yeah?' Jenni's mood soared, and miniature fireworks started exploding in the ether.

'It's down to you. Use your strength wisely, but be wary, young Jenni. Don't let the Sea Witch take your power. She is tricksy and false. She may ask you to walk the realms for her. It's difficult, but it can be done. Look for the edges and will yourself through.' The Source radiated warmth. 'Go forth with sensitivity and hold love in your heart. Be sure to guard yourself against loss. Fortify yourself with family.' The Source paused and, for the first time, sounded unsure. 'The future before you is cloudy. The path before you is obscured and much can go wrong. You have ventured down the wrong path – you know this. Taking power from others, no matter the reason, will only lead you to disaster.'

Jenni's stomach swirled. The Source knew about the skimming.

'Stay steadfast and true. We're counting on you.'

The Source's last words faded into darkness as Jenni was whisked back through the arch and became aware of having an actual body again. Amos was speaking.

'Now let me concentrate.'

'Did you...' Amos scratched his ear. 'Have you been in and come back again already?'

Jenni didn't answer. Instead, she crackled and silver and gold sparks rippled over her entire body, shooting sparkly black stars out of her fingertips. When she looked at Amos, her eyes glowed brightly.

Amos took a step back.

'Jenni?'

The sprite shook her head, and the crackling stopped. Her eyes went back to their usual blue and she wobbled slightly.

'Are you okay? What happened?' Amos sounded concerned, but he didn't come any closer to her.

'Yeah. The Source gave me back me power. And mebbe a bit extra.' She looked down at her hands, which weren't shooting stars anymore, but still she turned them over, a wondrous look on her face. 'It feels so much more than before. I ain't sure…'

'Not sure about what?' prompted Amos as Jenni stopped talking.

'Fanks Amos, I gotta go.' And she popped, winking out of sight, leaving the guardian of the source feeling rather uneasy.

Chapter 27

Jenni appeared in the third best meeting room at the same time as pudding. It was treacle tart, one of Ned's favourites, but it lay forgotten on his plate as his brain slowly registered that Jenni had just popped into the room.

'How...' he began to ask but was interrupted by the arrival of Jimmy Fingers. Ned glanced to see if Rose or Clove had noticed the sprite popping in, but they were both focused on the Lower Circle. Only Griff seemed to have noticed, and he had a big grin on his face. 'Did you see that?' Ned had to ask. He needed someone else to verify what he'd just seen. Griff winked.

'Fingers, do sit down. We need your particular expertise. Treacle tart?' Rose offered the last slice that Ned had had his eye on, despite the fact that he hadn't finished what was on his plate. There was always room for two slices of Ma Bowl's treacle tart.

'Wot about me?'

'Jenni! Where did you come from?' Rose looked at the door and then back to the sprite.

'I popped, awright? And I want some tart.' She clicked her fingers and a whole tart appeared on the table, looking shinier and stickier than anything Ma Bowl had ever created. Jenni helped herself to a sizeable chunk and was busy making yummy noises, oblivious to the startled looks everyone else in the room was giving her.

'How did you do it though?' asked Ned.

'I'll tell you in a bit. I'm starving.'

Jenni ignored him, too intent on eating. Ned figured he may as well wait until she'd finished eating before asking her again, which meant he could finish his own pudding. He kept casting comparative glances across from his Ma Bowl special to Jenni's creation, and in the end, he had to give in to temptation and snag a bit to taste. It wasn't as tasty as it looked. It tasted like something was missing, but Ned couldn't put his finger on what it was.

Finally, everyone had finished eating. Sticky fingers were wiped, and plates were cleared as Rose tried to get down to business.

'Fingers, this is Clove, one of the Spice Ghosts. She has a plan to steal the bones back from the Sea Witch. We know the witch has to come to shore to perform her ritual in two nights' time under the light of the full moon. We also know the whereabouts of the Sea Witch is likely to be Sandy Cove. What we need from you is your specific skill set. Clove?' Rose gestured for the Spice Ghost to fill in the blanks.

'The ritual the Sea Witch needs to perform requires a few days of preparation and meditation. This will be the best time to steal the bones when her attention is elsewhere. There may still be wards, traps, and possibly guards for us to get past. We will need a fighter, a mage and a thief in order to be successful.' Clove cocked her head to one side. 'We may also need a sage and a healer. We must be fully prepared for what will come.'

'You make it sound like a quest,' commented Ned.

'Of course it's a quest.' Clove gave him a withering look. 'How else do you expect to win the day without the right company?'

Ned could feel the backs of his ears reddening under her scrutiny. Rose came to his rescue.

'Well, we have the thief and the fighter,' she said. Ned's chest puffed out a little. 'I am skilled with knives, hand to hand combat and archery.' He quickly deflated.

'Should you be putting yourself in danger like that, love?' asked Ned, sitting back when Rose shot him a sharp look.

'The safety of my empire rests on the successful completion of this mission,' she said. 'Besides, the Highs have agreed that my participation is essential.'

Ned glanced at the Highs, both of whom looked pale and wan as if they'd lost a huge argument and were now facing up to the consequences, but before he could say anything else Jenni spoke.

'I can be yor mage fingy.'

'Yes, about that. I'm guessing the Source agreed to our plan, Jenni?' asked Rose, taking the words out of Ned's mouth. He was beginning to feel a bit like a spare part.

'Yeah. It knew wot was going on and gave me back me juice. Anna bit extra, I fink.' She crackled again, causing the others to gasp in surprise. 'It feels...' Once again, Jenni broke off and shrugged, a few golden sparks falling off her shoulders.

Ned watched Jenni as her new power pulsed. To him, it almost looked like there was too much for her to contain.

'I can be your sage or wise one – plus I have met the Sea Witch before. She may lower her defences when confronted by a familiar face,' offered Griff.

Ned's eyes narrowed. He hadn't had the chance yet to properly grill his father about the relationship he had with the Sea Witch. In fact, everything seemed to be moving too fast.

'I will be healer,' said Clove.

'What about me?' Ned's question came out much more sorrowful than he had intended. Rose patted his hand.

'You're a fighter and an integral part of the team. You're the glue. You hold us all together,' she said with a smile.

Ned muttered a reply. Glue. He was sticky sticky glue. Integral my hat. He resolved there and then to be the best damn glue they'd ever seen. This quest would be a success.

Chapter 28

The next morning, Ned discovered that being the glue turned out to be a lot less like an integral part of the team and a lot more like a messenger slash babysitter for the major players. After Ned had sent two palace staff to find out where Fingers had disappeared to, helped Rose pack a light bag six times, attempted to pin Jenni down to talk about her magic, and told Ma Bowl repeatedly that they did not have space for her kitchen on wheels, nor were they taking ice to keep ingredients cool, he felt like he'd rather be anything other than glue.

Eventually, though, he shepherded everyone into the courtyard, ready to move out on their highly important quest.

'Are we not riding?' asked Clove, peering about for stealthy steeds.

'No, it's not that far to Shady Cove and the horses will only get spooked by the magical confrontation. I don't want to explain to the Stablemaster that we lost half a dozen of his best horses.' Ned shuddered. The Stablemaster was a man with zero sense of humour and seemed to care only for his equines.

'We could take the carriage. There would be more room for luggage then?' suggested Rose hopefully.

'No! We are not taking the carriage, which requires horses, and we do not need more baggage. What you can carry on your backs is quite enough,' snapped Ned. He hadn't meant to snap and instantly regretted his harsh tone, especially as his wife looked at him with hurt in her eyes. 'What I mean to say is, it's a short trip and we need to keep our wits about us and not worry about carrying heavy bags.' He attempted a joke. 'Besides, if our plan fails, then it's the end of the world anyway and you can't take luggage there, eh?'

Griff was the only one who reacted, giving Ned a small smile of support.

'I could just pop us all there in a jiffy. Save all this buggering about,' said Jenni. 'Just saying.'

'No, I think you should save all your magic for the Sea Witch,' replied Ned.

'But it wouldn't take much and poof! We'd be there already.'

'No, Jenni. You need to conserve your magic for what it's meant for, not to pop all of us down the road. We've got time.'

Ned was relieved when Fingers finally sauntered into the courtyard.

'Jimmy! Where have you been? Come on, we're ready to go.' Ned surveyed the others, but there was no objection. 'Let's move out.'

Ned strode out the gates with purpose. His second-best boots were on his feet, pipe and tobacco in his pocket, spellcasters belt filled to bursting and he had a tight grip on the best fake confidence he could muster. He faltered slightly as he realised he didn't know which way to go.

'Left or right, Jenni. Which way to Shady Cove?'

'Left.'

Ned advanced forwards with Jenni at his shoulder. Clove, Rose and Griff chatted behind him while Fingers brought up the rear, whistling a jaunty tune as if they were just going out for a walk in the countryside and not about to steal magical relics from a powerful fae who could potentially destroy them all.

Once out of Roshaven, the group fell into a looser gathering, less strung out and more conversational as Fingers asked question after question to Clove, debunking Spice Ghost myth and legend.

'So you're more like gatekeepers than anything else, right?' Fingers asked.

'Basically, yes. Except the gate we guard just happens to be the one between the spiritual and physical realm.'

'But you got access to magic and the like?'

'Yes, and no. There are spells that go hand in hand with being a Spice Ghost, such as the enchantment for the ship and, of course, accessing the realms. But conjuring and casting, they depend on the innate magical ability of each ghost.'

Ned was listening and felt Clove was definitely holding something back. There was an air of evasiveness about her, but he supposed it could be because she just wasn't used to being quizzed.

'Why Clove? Is there importance to the name?'

'The name is more of a title. There are certain spices one expects to see – Clove, Nutmeg, Cinnamon and Ginger. But I am not the first Clove, nor will I be the last.'

'But you get something out of being a Spice Ghost, right?' The mini question-and-answer session had drawn everyone back together, so now five pairs of eyes were firmly riveted on Clove.

'Spice Ghosts are respected throughout the world and our ship can travel faster than any other upon the waves,' replied Clove, again radiating a certain amount of evasiveness.

Jimmy rethought his question.

'How long have you been a Spice Ghost?'

Clove pierced him with a dark look.

'Four hundred and twenty-three years.' She then turned to Ned. 'Are we intending to travel the entire distance today?'

Ned was trying not to look too shocked at the fact that a quadricentenarian stood in front of him.

'Um… I thought we might camp about a mile out from the beach. Give us time to rest and prepare for what's coming.' He looked around at the others for support. There were general nods and shrugs of if-you-say-so. 'We'll probably get there around tea-time.'

Clove nodded and increased her pace slightly, pushing her hood up and wrapping her arms within her cloak. It was clear she wanted to be left alone. Ned found he could walk about five paces behind her easily enough before a weird pulling sensation occurred. The tether wasn't letting them get too far apart at the moment. He guessed she must be focused on keeping them together.

'Fine figure of a woman,' said Fingers, whistling softly. 'Four hundred years. Bet she's got some tales to tell.'

'I wouldn't push your luck,' replied Ned. 'Why were you asking so many questions?'

'I'm curious. Aren't you? The Spice Ghosts. I always thought they were a folktale told to little kids when they were naughty to keep them in line. I never actually thought I would meet them or even get to go on an adventure with one.' He grinned at Ned. 'Besides, if you don't ask, you'll never know. Right?' He smoothed his hair down and strode off to walk beside Clove again.

'He's a brave lad.' It was Griff.

Ned nodded and looked back to see Jenni and Rose a few paces behind, chatting about something that was making them laugh. He smiled to see his two favourite people getting on so well.

'I love this part,' said Griff.

'Sorry?'

'The bit before things get real. Where hope is riding high and you have a plan. Before you get tired and beaten and defeated. When you actually think you can win the day.'

'Are you saying we can't win?' Ned peered at Griff, checking to see if he was trying to be funny, but he had a serious look on his face.

'This is when we can achieve anything. Tomorrow, after negotiations fail and the Sea Witch has begun her assault on us... well, that's when we learn our mettle, eh?'

Ned felt quite certain that his mettle was doing just fine.

'You think negotiations will fail?'

Griff assessed Ned frankly.

'You don't?'

Ned opened his mouth, thought about it for a moment, and then closed it again. He scratched his ear.

'She might be willing to trade bones for power.'

'Aye, she might, if she's not too far gone.' Griff snagged some tall grass from the roadside and began peeling it apart.

'Too far gone? What do you mean?' Ned checked to see if anyone else was listening to their conversation, but Fingers was still talking one-sidedly to Clove while Rose and Jenni were out of earshot.

'A powerful magical being is looking to rip a hole between the physical and spiritual world, and now she has the bones to do it. I'm just not sure she'll give that up. The power from the Source will make her more powerful. It's true. But is it enough of a temptation? I don't know.'

'So we're doomed before we start then?' Ned could no longer ignore the gnawing pit of worry in his stomach.

'We have a chance. A slight chance. We must cling to that and let hope lift our hearts, eh?' replied Griff.

Ned nodded. Yep. Definitely doomed.

Chapter 29

They had made camp for the evening. Ned was watching his father cooking. That was something he had never thought he would see. He did not know Griff could even cook, and it smelt wonderful. Ned's stomach rumbled appreciatively.

'Bit different from last time, isn't it?' Rose came and sat down next to him.

'Hmm?'

'You know, when we camped out the night before facing down Joe's dad.'

'Oh yeah.' Ned grinned. 'We were brewing up that potion to coat all those daggers in.'

'And I used it for my arrow tips, too. Good job really.'

Ned remembered Rose firing that arrow, finishing off the evil sorcerer and breaking his spells.

'We're quite the team.' He kissed her hand as she snuggled closer to him.

'This doesn't feel quite the same,' said Rose in a small voice.

'True. But we have a plan, of sorts.'

'Do you think the Sea Witch will give up the bones?' asked Rose.

Ned puffed out his cheeks and didn't answer.

Rose sighed. 'Me either.'

The pair fell into silence and Ned watched the others around the campfire. Fingers was still peppering Clove with questions, but now they were about the different places she'd visited rather than her mystical powers and she seemed much more inclined to answer those. Jenni was setting magical alarms around the camp.

'Jenni looks the happiest I've seen her in a while,' commented Rose as Jenni's protection spell sparkled in the air and sank down in a dome around them.

'She's got her magic back.'

'She seems different with it, don't you think?' asked Rose.

Ned considered the question. He hadn't really thought about it, but now Rose mentioned it Jenni was acting more cavalier than usual, trying to use her extra magical abilities for everything. If he hadn't stopped her this morning, she would've had popped them all immediately to the beach. Who knows if that would have drained some of her extra power away? Ned knew Jenni had found it tough to balance her magic, especially just after her coming-of-age ceremony, but she'd seemed to have got to grips with her situation. Yeah, she was grumpy about having less magic, but Jenni could be grumpy about things. The more Ned thought about it, the more he realised that actually Jenni had been in a bad mood for months. And resentful of other magic users. He hadn't noticed that before. He glanced in her direction and saw she was conjuring her own food and drink. There was a gleam in her eyes that Ned wasn't entirely sure was just the campfire reflection. Realising that he had said nothing for a while, he patted Rose's hand and decided to go chat to Jenni, see how she was doing.

Griff chose that moment to serve his culinary creation, and Ned's stomach took over from his brain. Food first, chat later.

'What is this?' asked Ned, around a mouthful of what he hoped was rabbit.

'Rabbit stew. More or less, eh?' replied Griff, with a twinkle in his eye.

Ned's hunger overrode his brain's hesitation, and he finished his bowl, going back for seconds. Everyone was quiet as they all concentrated on eating and it was with reluctance that empty bowls were finally pushed to one side.

'I suppose we ought to talk about the plan for tomorrow,' began Ned.

'This is wot I fink. I go in, ask for the bones back and when she says nah, I zap 'er.'

'Just like that?' asked Fingers.

Jenni clicked her fingers, making a large blue flash appear with a loud bang that made everyone jump.

'Just like that,' she replied smugly.

It took a moment for everyone's vision to readjust, and Ned shook his head to get rid of the ringing in his ears.

'Perhaps a little more diplomacy? If I were to approach the Sea Witch as Empress of Roshaven, she might give us a fair audience and consider our offer,' suggested Rose.

'No offence,' said Clove. 'But the Sea Witch is unlikely to be impressed by the ruler of a two-bit town. I will go in with the full might of the Spice Ghosts behind me. She will be cowed into returning the bones, or else.' As she was speaking, Clove seemed to grow taller, looming over the campfire. Her voice deepened and there was a definite air of menace about her.

Ned had bridled at the thinly veiled barb directed at his city and wife, but Rose caught his arm, a small smile on her face.

'Roshaven has a big heart, but we are a small nation. It's okay,' she whispered.

'Perhaps I should talk to her first. After all, we are acquainted, eh?' Griff puffed out his chest. 'I've been bargaining with the Sea Witch for years. We have a rapport.'

'I'm not sure chucking dead bodies into the ocean for her is exactly a rapport,' replied Ned, still nettled by Clove's comment about Roshaven.

A brief silence settled over the group.

'Why don't I go?' offered Fingers. 'Being the Lower Circle, I am a representative of Roshaven, bringing the weight of the Empire with me. I too have made offerings to the Sea Witch in the past and can claim association with Griff. I have no magic, so I am unthreatening.' Fingers held out his hands and gave a small bow. 'I can present the trade – power for bones and request that the Sea Witch meet us under parley.' He looked around at the others. 'I'm probably the least threatening person here and I reckon she's probably a bit stressed getting ready to rip apart the realms. A show of power might not be the best plan.'

Ned had to give it to Fingers. It was a solid idea.

'Jimmy,' said Rose. 'Are you sure you want to put yourself in to the jaws of danger like that? If you go alone, you will be without protection. I wouldn't want anything to happen to you. You're a much-valued member of my court.' Rose was in full Empress mode now.

'My Empress, Long May You Rule.' Fingers dipped his head in her direction.

'Then let's put it to a vote,' said Rose. 'All those in favour of sending Jimmy in first, raise your hand.'

Rose immediately lifted her hand into the air, closely followed by Ned. Griff rubbed his chin thoughtfully, then gave a small shrug and lifted his hand as well.

Clove regarded Fingers with narrowed eyes before gracefully raising her hand. All eyes swivelled to Jenni, who was sitting, arms crossed, a grumpy expression on her face.

'I fink yor all a bunch of idiots. Power's wots gonna get this done, not some fancy talking or wotever.'

'Jenni!' Ned was surprised at her reaction. It wasn't like her to be like this.

'I ain't finished,' she snapped at Ned. 'Youse all agree, so fine. We'll do it this way, but you ain't going in with nuffink, Fingers. I'll do you a protection spell, full strength. And then when she laffs at yor offer of parley, I can pull you out of there if needs be.'

Ned was partially relieved that Jenni had agreed to go along with the plan and that she was offering to protect Fingers, but he was a little stung at being snapped at. Jenni never snapped at him.

'Then it's agreed. Jimmy will request parley with the Sea Witch in order to offer our trade of power for bones. I suggest we all try to get some rest.' Rose stood and said her good nights, prompting the others to do the same.

'I'll take first watch,' offered Ned.

'I got this, Boss. We're fully protected,' said Jenni.

'Then I'll just sit up for a bit till the fire goes out,' he replied.

'Suit yourself.' Jenni stalked over to the opposite side of the camp, lay down on her bed roll and turned her back to the rest of them.

Chapter 30

Ned was woken by his wife giving him a kiss and pushing a hot cup of tea into his hands. He stretched his body, trying to work out the kinks from sleeping upright against a tree.

'Thanks. How come nobody relieved me?' Ned was disappointed that no one had stepped up to take the second watch and annoyed that he'd fallen asleep.

'I slept through, must be all the fresh air.' Rose sat down next to him. 'You didn't have to take watch, you know. Jenni's protections seem pretty powerful. Above and beyond her usual.'

Ned slurped his tea. It needed biscuits.

'Where is Jenni?'

Rose glanced around.

'Not sure.' She leaned closer to him. 'Have you noticed she's been a bit…?'

'Yeah. I'm sure it's just everything with her dad and then taking on the Source. It's bound to mess with your head.' Ned tapped his own. 'Look at me, I'm still struggling with mine.' He looked across the campsite but could only see Fingers and Clove sipping their own hot cups of tea. 'Where is Griff?'

'I don't know.' Rose held her own empty mug in her hands. 'Want a refill?'

'Yeah, okay. I'll get it.' Ned took her mug and stood up to go to the campfire and get the kettle but halted. There was no fire lit. Instead, there was a silver tea tray sitting incongruously on a flat-topped rock, holding a milk jug and a teapot wearing a jaunty, knitted bright pink cosy. 'Erm…'

'Jenni made the tea,' said Rose by way of explanation.

'Should she be wasting the Source's power on things like that? What if she needs to save it all up for the Sea Witch?' Ned felt the side of the teapot. It was still hot, so he poured the tea. Milk in first for him, milk second for Rose. Ned felt that milk in first made a highly superior beverage but had given up trying to convince others who often visibly recoiled when they found out how he made his tea. He took satisfaction from time to time making other people cups of tea his way without telling them and smirking at the compliments he got for his tea making.

Griff and Jenni wandered back into the campsite clearing.

'If that's what you think, who am I, eh?' said Griff, obviously finishing up their conversation.

'Who wants brekkie?' asked Jenni, ignoring the question. She snapped her fingers and a small table appeared complete with a red and white check tablecloth. On the table was a bowl of fruit, some bread and cheese, cold sausages and Ned's favourite cinnamon twists.

'Where did you get this from?' he asked, concerned that Jenni was stealing somehow.

'I wishes for it and I gets it. S'called magic, Boss.' Jenni snagged a twist for herself. 'Not that you'd know,' she murmured quietly.

Not quietly enough as Ned still heard her. That was a bit of a low blow. True, he had issues with his magic. It had a mind of its own, came and went when it liked and only ever really worked in million to one chances when Rose's life was on the line. Ned's ears reddened, and he decided to pretend he hadn't heard her barb, helping himself instead to some fruit and cinnamon twists.

'Is magical food the same as regular?' asked Fingers around a mouthful of bread and cheese.

'Ow do you mean?' Jenni scowled at him. 'Food's food, ain't it?'

'I just wondered if it filled you up the same is all.'

Clove eyed Jenni. 'Everything created from magic is created from the same energy that it would normally have been created. Instead of the energy coming from the sun to grow the plant and the energy from the baker to mix the ingredients and bake the item, magic shortcuts the process and creates the item out of raw energy. So yes, it will have the same effect as the real thing. Provided the magic user is not creating an illusion.' She snagged a cinnamon twist for herself and bit into it with relish.

'How come you need to eat?' asked Fingers, who clearly hadn't finished questioning the Spice Ghost.

'I am tethered.' Clove gestured to Ned. 'Bound to the physical world, so now I must nourish myself as I did when I was fully human.'

'So not really a ghost then?'

Clove looked at Fingers flatly. She shimmered and became transparent. Her eyes darkened while her hair waved around her head as if in a gentle breeze. Holding her arms out to the side, she floated above the ground. Ned was closest to her, and he felt the cold emanating from her. Sure enough, his breath billowed out like dragon smoke.

As smoothly as she'd transformed to shade, Clove returned to her previous physical appearance, leaving Jimmy's jaw hanging open. Ned had to admit, it had been an impressive transformation. Jenni forestalled any more questions by getting down to business.

'Right, so I got a protection spell for you all. Word to the wise, it ain't gonna be infallible cos I dunno wot she's gonna frow at us. But it'll keep you mostly safe pending on what she attacks us wiv.'

'What do you need us to do?' asked Ned.

'Nuffink. It's already done.'

Ned blinked. For Jenni to cast a spell like that without anyone's permission was unusual. There were social guidelines when it came to the use of magic. And polite casters always asked permission first. Furthermore, he hadn't felt a thing. Had she really done it? Ned didn't know why there was the prickle of doubt in his mind, but there it was, chaffing away. Jenni picked up on his doubt.

She threw a fireball at him.

'Argh!' yelled Ned, diving to the floor too late and feeling the flames engulf him. His brain caught up with his body and realised nothing was burning, nothing hurt. 'Jenni! What was that?' Ned barked as he stood up and dusted his knees.

'You didn't believe me. Now you do. Simples.'

Ned huffed. When this was over, he and Jenni would be having serious words.

'Are we completely invulnerable now?' asked Fingers, holding out his arms and turning his hands over, looking at them.

'Nah. It's a lotta magic to cover youse all so it'll only last few hours but it should 'old up to anyfink wot she frows at us. C'mon on, we'd better get going.' Jenni clicked her fingers, and the campfire was out with everything put away neatly.

'Jenni? You've not forgotten the plan, have you?'

asked Rose gently.

'Yeah, yeah. I know. Fingers goes in first asking for parley. Let's get on with it, yeah?'

No one really had anything to say to that, so they moved out.

The Sea Witch's beach was about half a mile away. The sun was shining, the sky blue and if it weren't for the fact that they were about to walk into the jaws of a powerful evil, Ned could almost fancy he was on holiday. He'd heard about holidays. Stretches of time you spent how you liked with pleasant weather, minimal clothing and drinks with umbrellas in them. Ned wasn't sure why you'd want a drink with an umbrella if you had pleasant weather, but apparently that was one of the most important factors.

'Can we trust the sprite?' Clove was walking next to Ned. The others had stretched out a little along the path, with Jenni walking up front next to Fingers.

'How do you mean?' replied Ned, although he had a bad feeling that he knew what she meant.

'She seems a little power drunk. She does know that eventually she will have to give up this power? Holding on to so much magic will ultimately corrupt anyone who tries to contain it. Only the Source can do that.'

'She's just giddy. Got her mojo back, is all. Jenni's coming-of-age ceremony was unexpected, and the Source put a big restriction on her connection to the magic, forcing her to work within the balance.' Ned wasn't sure why he was telling Clove Jenni's history, but he was certainly trying to convince himself as he spoke. 'It was a hard thing to master, but she did it, balancing her power and making sure she took from sources that could replenish rather than people, and so on.'

'And she hasn't minded that restriction?' asked

Clove. 'Or been tempted to skim?'

Ned opened his mouth to say no but stopped. Jenni had struggled and moaned and whinged and been angry. But he'd always just put it down to general grumpiness or busy days or lack of food. As for the skimming… he had thought Norm had been the only culprit, but then there was Jenni's reaction when her dad admitted to the skimming and that time he'd felt a little peculiar. And the fainting illness in Braso Amia. And those blokes going all funny in the street that time.

'Excuse me,' he said softly, hastening his pace to catch up with Rose, who was walking with Griff.

'How worried are we about Jenni?' he whispered loud enough for them both to hear him, but not anyone else.

Rose looked up at the sprite and then sideways at Griff, who was stroking his goatee.

'Very.'

Other than being worried about Jenni, there wasn't time to be anything else. Ned could almost hear the clock ticking in his ear, counting down the magical protection he was currently wearing. They had reached the sand dunes of Shady Cove beach. It was time.

'You good with what to do?' Ned asked Fingers.

The man was bouncing on the balls of his feet, winding his neck around as if preparing to step into the ring.

'Yep. Request parley. Mention Griff and a trade. Don't ask about the bones directly.' Fingers puffed the air out of his cheeks and looked Ned dead in the eye. 'I've got this.'

'Wait! You need a flag.' Rose was rummaging in her backpack. There was a sharp ripping side, and she proffered him some white silk.

Ned wondered what item of clothing that had come from. Then the backs of his ears reddened.

'Good luck, Jimmy,' he said, echoed by the others.

'If it all starts going pear-shaped, just yell the safe word and I'll be there,' said Jenni.

'Okay, great.' Fingers thought for a moment. 'What's the safe word?'

'Help usually works well,' remarked Ned. 'And we'll all be there for you.' He cast a sideways glance at Jenni.

'Wot about knickers? S'fun word and if you yell that at the top of yor voice, it'll probably give you a few seconds. The Sea Witch ain't gonna know wot yor on about.'

Fingers laughed.

'Okay, knickers it is. See you soon.' He threw a nod and a wink at them all before striding purposefully over the dune towards the Sea Witch's lair.

*****

The beach was pristine. White sands sprinkled with pretty shells and clear turquoise waters ebbing and flowing dreamily, white surf sparkling in the sunshine. There was no one around, no sign of people at all. Fingers left apologetic footprints in the sand as he searched for a lair. He wasn't sure exactly what he had been expecting – skeletal remains, lots of seaweed and possibly killer crabs. The idyllic seashore was a surprise.

To his left, the beach stretched away in an enticing curve. To his right, the sands petered out to rocks that grew to boulders and eventually cliffs. There was a shadowy recess just before the boulders took over. Fingers squinted. It could be the mouth of a cave. He set off to investigate.

As he drew closer to the opening, the temperature dropped. The loom of the cliff cut off the sun's warmth and here the rocks were slick with green algae and there was definitely scuttle. Doesn't mean they're killer crabs, Fingers told himself. Could be anything. That line of thought didn't help, so he tried to focus on the cave opening itself. It was dark and gloomy, full of odd-shaped shadows and patches of darkness, forcing him to walk closer and closer to get a decent look.

A voice stopped him.

'Leave.'

The voice sounded like sea foam on a pebble shore. Like dark kelp forests harbouring hidden wickedness. Like the cold, dark depths of the never-ending ocean abyss and he was falling, alone, into nothingness.

Jenni's protection spell bungeed him back into the here and now, making his heart race and his skin tingle. He took another step.

Something rustled in the darkest corner of the cave. A salty wet tang hung in the air and menace emanated in ripples.

'Go away.'

'P-p-p-parley?' Fingers forced the words out, remembering belatedly about the white silk he held, which he now waved with a leaden arm.

Some of the menace in the cave fell away and there was more than a hint of surprise in the hidden voice.

'Parley? Why do you want to parley with me?'

Fingers mind went blank. His fear of killer crabs had notched up a level as he noticed the floor in front of him was undulating its way towards him with hundreds of pincers clicking and clacking.

'Er…'

Menace returned and brought threat with it. The air was almost too thick to breathe, and Fingers took half a scared step backwards.

'Who sent you?' The voice spoke again, spiked with irritation, and Fingers knew he needed to pull it together before the crabs pulled him apart.

'Griff sent me,' he squeaked as the foremost crabs began scuttling around his boots.

'Away with you! Shoo!' The Sea Witch emerged from the shadows, waving the crabs away, who reluctantly moved aside.

Fingers forgot to breathe.

The Sea Witch might have looked almost human once, but that would have been long ago. Rusty red hair floated around her face, as if she were submerged in water. Something moved against the ripple and Fingers shuddered as he recognised tentacles and saw fish skeletons in amongst the hair and seaweed. Her skin was green-grey and mottled, giving the impression of large fish scales. But they didn't glint in the light, rather, they were dull and lifeless.

She wore a tunic that looked to be fashioned from a discarded sail – it was torn and dingy, cinched in at the waist by rope. Her arms were bare, and a webbed hand clutched a wicked-looking harpoon. Fingers gulped as he met the Sea Witch's gaze. Her eyes were completely black, and she had slits for a nose with large, pointy ears that splayed out either side of her face. She seemed amused at his gaze, for she grinned lazily, revealing razor sharp, white, pointed teeth.

'What does that conniving thief want with me?' asked the Sea Witch. 'And why send you to parley? Lost his nerve, has he?'

Fingers felt lost. He couldn't remember exactly why

Griff hadn't come with him and he couldn't help but notice there were now three crabs on his left foot and two on his right, all of them waving their pincers manically.

'I accept your parley. We will meet in one hour on the beach, by the blue rock.' The Sea Witch receded back into her cave. Her voice echoed out once more. 'Tell Griff he owes me.'

Almost as quickly as they had appeared, the crabs melted back into the nooks and crannies they'd emerged from. Except for one. It stood on Fingers' boot, eye stalks bobbing and weaving, its pincer poised to inflict maximum pain to any phalange it could reach.

'Sorry,' whispered Fingers as he jerked his boot quickly, dislodging the crab before he turned and fled, terrified at being chased by the crabs.

His breakneck arrival back to the others had them all baring arms and girding their loins, ready to fight the hideous horde of sea devils that must chase him. When they saw nothing was following Fingers, weapons were sheathed.

'What happened?' asked Ned.

Fingers checked over his shoulder to make sure he hadn't been pursued, then let out a shaky laugh.

'Crabs!' he explained to a none the wiser audience.

Chapter 31

Once Fingers had calmed down from his crab experience, he explained the Sea Witch's terms to the others.

'We're to meet her at the blue rock on the beach in an hour. Well, less than an hour now. In fact, we probably ought to get out there, as I have no idea where the blue rock is. I can't say I noticed one.'

'It's a blue rock, can't be that hard to find, right?' asked Ned, grabbing his backpack, ready to move out.

'I know where it is. We've met there before,' said Griff, and once more Ned wished he had the time to find out more about his dad's escapades. 'We'd better move. It's the other end of the beach to her cave. We don't want to be late.'

The group scrambled over the dunes and started plodding along the beach. No-one had thought to bring suitable beach footwear. However, Ned was feeling smug that his boots were holding up to the challenge. Who knew city street stompers would work just as well on sand? He eyed the surf distrustfully. Salt damage would do his almost leather boots no favours at all.

Rose had thrown caution to the wind and took her shoes off, walking in the water with quiet glee. Ned knew she got little down time as Empress and couldn't help grinning as he watched her. There was almost an air of blissful holidayness among them.

'Oi, snap out of it. Don't let the beach lure you in. We're 'ere for one fing and one fing only,' yelled Jenni, breaking the honeymoon feeling.

'The sprite is right. The idyllic setting will lure you into a false sense of security if you let it. Don't forget why we are here. It will soon be the full moon, we cannot fail.' Clove glared at Rose and Ned, who stared guiltily back.

Fingers was on high crab alert and Griff was striding with purpose, the only one who knew where he was going.

'Over here,' he called, gesturing to the others.

Sure enough, there in the sand was a blue rock. Only that wasn't what held everyone's attention. Instead, it was the golden dragon sleeping on top of the rock that stopped them in their tracks.

'Fingers, did the Sea Witch mention anything about a dragon?' hissed Ned.

'No – she just said that Griff owed her. Sorry, I should have said that before.' Fingers glanced at Griff. 'What else do you owe her for?'

Griff ran his hand over his goatee. Ned knew him well enough to know this was his 'buying-time' gesture. Whatever he was about to say would be an approximation of the truth.

'I'm sure it's the price for this parley, eh?'

Ned was instantly on edge. Well, probably along the edge a bit and hanging over a deep ravine with razor sharp rocks considering the larger than he'd like golden dragon occupying most of his *run, danger* brain. Griff sounded unsure. Griff never sounded unsure.

'E's bootiful,' breathed Jenni, who had moved closer than Ned thought wise to look at the dragon. 'It's just like the one I seed in Roshaven. The one you fawt I was making up.'

'Jenni, I wouldn't get too close. Jenni!' Ned's words had no impact on the sprite. She was almost close enough to touch the dragon now. 'Don't touch it! You don't know where it's been.'

Ned inwardly cursed at himself, trying to ignore the raised eyebrows from Fingers and Rose. Where the dragon had been was hardly the major problem here. That there was a dragon at all was the issue.

Clove walked boldly over to the beast and began tickling it under the chin. The dragon started purring. Immediately, Rose and Jenni joined Clove and began cooing.

'Are we sure that's safe? Tickling a dragon?' Ned shot a pleading glance at Fingers to back him up, but he was too busy peering about looking for ninja crabs.

'It's just a sea dragon, a young one at that. Completely harmless,' replied Clove without bothering to look in Ned's direction.

Griff clapped a hand on his son's shoulder.

'Babies and cute animals – irresistible to the fairer sex, my lad, especially when joined together. You'll find out soon enough, eh?'

Ned stared at Griff's back as he strode to join the women. Babies?

His incoherent thoughts were interrupted by the arrival of the Sea Witch. The blue rock was located on the sand, but while they'd been standing there, admiring the young dragon, the tide – assisted by the Sea Witch - had quietly crept up on them and the sea was tickling Ned's boots. The Sea Witch stood firmly planted within the water. She wore the sail cloth tunic as described by Fingers, together with a hooded cloak that looked to be woven from seaweed. Her distinctive features were hidden in the hood's gloom. Ned was both disappointed and relieved not to have to look her in the eye.

The women were still cooing over the dragon when

the Sea Witch lifted a grey-green scaly hand and clicked her fingers. The clicking was echoed by the phalanx of crabs that now surrounded her. Fingers moaned softly. The golden dragon preened for a moment before undulating off the rock and darting to the side of the Sea Witch.

'You called for parley. State your business,' she rasped.

'Good to see you again,' began Griff.

'Not you.' The Sea Witch's bony finger stabbed in his direction before wheeling around and coming to a stop in front of Ned. 'You speak for them.'

'Er...' Ned was caught unawares. He cleared his throat and felt rather than saw Rose move to come stand at his side. He took a deep breath, grateful for the support, and tried to remember all the details he was supposed to mention. 'We've come to request a trade,' he began, but faltered at the intake of breath from his wife. Apparently, that wasn't how he was supposed to start.

It seemed, however, that the Sea Witch was perfectly happy with getting straight to the point.

'No trade,' she replied.

'But you haven't even heard what we're prepared to offer you,' protested Ned, taking half a step forward.

'I don't need to. You've brought a Spice Ghost with you and a third-rate fae humming with borrowed power. You seek to trade fae trickery for mystical bones. I reject your trade.'

'Oi, fish-face! I ain't fird rate. And it ain't no trick — I got Source power for you. The good stuff.' Jenni did the weird flex she did when showing off her power and a bright light engulfed her entire being, causing everyone to shield their gaze.

Once the light had died down and Ned could see again he was unnerved to discover the Sea Witch, and the tide, had moved even closer to them. She now stood directly before Jenni, looking down at the sprite, her hood hiding her face.

He cast a look round at the others and saw that Fingers had retreated to the top of the blue rock in an effort to get as far away from the crabs as possible. Griff and Clove stood together on one side of Jenni whilst Ned and Rose were on the other, but the Sea Witch seemed utterly oblivious to the crustaceans.

'It is done. You have five minutes.' The Sea Witch retreated with the tide and her crabs, the sea dragon left gambolling in the surf.

It happened so fast that by the time Ned looked between Jenni and the retreating Sea Witch, the witch had completely disappeared.

'What's done? What just happened? Jenni?' Ned fired off questions as the others joined him in clustering around the sprite.

'She spoke in me 'ead. Said she'd give back the bones if I went wiv 'er. Said she could use me.'

'But we're not doing that, right? Right?' Ned appealed to the others but was met with mostly stony faces.

'We cannot allow the Sea Witch to rip a hole in the realms. If Jenni has to go with her to stop her, then so be it,' said Clove. 'This way, perhaps the Sea Witch can be stopped once and for all. If you're up for the task, of course.'

Jenni's eyes glowed back at her in response.

'But, but…' Ned was confused. What had he missed?

'Are you sure you want to do this, Jenni? We can

find another way to stop her,' offered Rose, her face full of sympathy.

'Yeah, I got this. Go in, get the bones out to ya and then makes sure I stops 'er afore she does the spell. The Source said it would be up to me, this must be wot it meant.'

'But you're not going to actually do the power trade... are you?' Ned felt like he was half a week behind everyone else.

'Nah. It's my power. It ain't for the likes of 'er. I'm using it. I'll use it to stop 'er and save the world innit.' Jenni seemed unfazed. If anything, she was verging on the edge of cocky. 'Anyways, I ain't got long so I'll sees you all later, yeah?' And she popped away, leaving a salty tang behind her.

'Wait, Jenni!' Ned took half a step towards the sea but had no idea where he was going. He cast back desperately. 'Fingers! Show me the cave. I can't let Jenni do this.'

Fingers paled and his hand shook as he pointed down the other end of the beach, but before Ned could march off in that direction, Griff caught his arm.

'Ned, lad. Let Jenni do this, eh? The Source chose her for a reason.'

'But we're worried about her, aren't we? We don't think she can do this, and I never got the chance to check she was alright.' His voice broke a little. 'What if she's not okay?'

Chapter 32

'You gonna give the bones back, right?' Jenni cast a suspicious glare at the Sea Witch's back.

'In good time. Show me what you have.' The Sea Witch sat back on a seaweed encrusted throne-like chair, carved into the cave wall and decorated with barnacles, starfish and whelks.

'Eh?'

'Your magic. Show me that it's worth having.'

Jenni was momentarily stumped. She wasn't sure how far her magic would go now she had the Source's power with her. How did she show the extent of that power? She concentrated on one of the smaller crabs scuttling on the floor in front of the Sea Witch and doubled it in size. It tottered and waved a pincer.

'Is that it?' The Sea Witch looked less than impressed.

The crab rose in the air and began slowly rotating, growing bigger and bigger. It was now the size of a small dog and turning blue.

'Parlour tricks for charlatans.'

The crab descended back to the floor of the cave with a definite click clack of its claws. It bulged and grew larger still, now easily as tall as Jenni. Hair sprouted around its eye stalks and a natty bow tie appeared.

'I say! What-ho, chaps. Splendid morning, eh?' The crab took a stylish bowler hat off its carapace and bowed in the direction of the Sea Witch. Or at least bowed as much as a crab can bow.

The Sea Witch clapped her hands. There was a loud cracking noise, and the crab was back to its former smallish size and reddish colour. With an air of reluctance, it sidled backwards, returning to its cast.

'Is that really the best you can do? I thought you had power to give me?'

Jenni bridled.

'Wot do you want me to do? Most like I can do it but wiv no structions that's all wot jumped in me 'ead.' She went on in a smaller voice. 'I fawt a talking blue crab would be funny.'

'Can you travel through?' The Sea Witch leaned forwards, her black eyes fixed on Jenni. 'Can you go to the spirit realm?'

'I ain't never tried afore but… yeah, why not?'

'Prove it. Cross the realms and find my daughter.' The Sea Witch held out a silver locket. 'Use this to orient yourself, and when you find Avery, ask them to finish this sentence. I love you more than… The answer is dolphins. That's how you will know you have the right girl. Tell her I am going to bring her back.'

Jenni blinked. On the one hand, they'd all been right and the Sea Witch was looking to resurrect her daughter, but on the other hand, she hadn't expected sentimentality. Or dolphins.

'Awright, 'ow long have I got? To prepare and that.'

The Sea Witch sat back on her throne.

'Until midnight tonight. If you don't have the power I need, then I shall grind the precious Spice Ghost bones to dust and use them to tear a way through the realms.' She grinned toothily at Jenni.

'You sure you don't want me to just bring 'er back wiv me? Then you can giv us the bones and everyone's 'appy.'

'Don't be a fool. Crossing the realms is only one part of the ritual. You have not prepared your body to bring a shade back. It will destroy you.' The Sea Witch narrowed her eyes. 'I want you to prove you have the power I need. Tick Tock.'

Jenni wasn't entirely sure how exactly she was going to travel the realms. She'd never done it before. Momma K probably had, but she wasn't here, and Jenni didn't think the Sea Witch would let her call her mum. Jenni tried to remember what the Source had said about the realms, something about overlay or edges. She needed to find the edge and then will herself through. Somehow.

The Sea Witch was watching Jenni with hooded eyes, not moving a muscle yet radiating impatience. Jenni started biting her fingernails. How was she going to find the edge of her reality?

She flinched as something nudged the back of her legs. Looking down, she saw the golden sea dragon. It was winding itself around her legs like a cat would. Jenni did not consider herself to be a cat person. Cats were so selfish. But the dragon was humming and watching its golden scales flash around her legs was hypnotic. Jenni began swaying to the rhythm of the dragon, and the atmosphere grew thick. Her body felt like it was moving slower than her consciousness, always catching her up to her but never quite getting there.

The cave was dimming around them, yet the sea dragon was glowing brighter and brighter. The hair on Jenni's arms stood up and her breath caught in her throat, pressure building in her chest as if she were being sat on. As it continued to rise, the light grew so bright Jenni could barely see. Her ears popped, and she blinked. The brightness had gone. Jenni stood in the same cave, only it was different. It was like her eyes had a filter on them, making everything look greeny-blue. Rapid movement caught her eye, and she danced a few steps in surprise before she realised that the hundreds of spectral shapes at her feet were ghost crabs scuttling across the floor. In fact, all the sea life in the cave had a ghostly glow about it, apart from the sea dragon. It remained bright and golden, pulsing with energy.

Jenni looked down at her own hands. They were translucent grey with bright silvery blue and golden lines pulsing through them. It was the Source's magic mixed with her own, clearly running on the same wavelength as the power used by the sea dragon, existing here in this space, on this plane. As it faded, Jenni felt slightly better knowing the Source was with her, in a roundabout way.

'We're 'ere then.' To her ears, Jenni's voice sounded the same as always, which continued to help make her feel better about having been transported to the spirit realm and not really knowing if she died in the process. 'Am I dead?'

The sea dragon rippled in amusement and shook its head.

'S'pose that's summink.' She looked down at her body again. 'Why ain't I all 'ere?'

This time, the sea dragon cocked its head onto one side.

'Cos it's the spirit realm and you gotta be a spirit to be 'ere. Right, gotcha.' Jenni watched the spectral crabs for a short while. 'Awright then Slinky, I gots anuvver question for ya. 'Ow comes you ain't transported 'er greenness over 'ere afore?'

The sea dragon's ears fell flat against its head, and it arched its back. If it had been a cat, it would have been hissing.

'Kay, you don't like 'er. I gets that. But 'ow comes she ain't made you bring 'er with her mojo and wotnot?'

The sea dragon lidded its eyes and curled around itself, feigning disinterest. But it kept peeking at Jenni to see if she was watching or not.

'Yor trying to tell me summink, ain't ya?' Jenni puffed her cheeks, trying to figure it out. 'Soz Slinky, you gotta give me a bit more than that.' As she spoke, the magic within her surged and the tip of Jenni's finger glowed blue.

The sea dragon watched with interest and uncurled itself, a forked tongue flicking out to investigate. As tongue met finger, the sea dragon wiggled in excitement and a gold halo built around its head, which it pushed towards Jenni's finger.

It is so nice to talk to someone!

'Eh? Zat you Slinky?'

My name is… unpronounceable in your tongue. So I guess, yes, this is me.

'Wot we doing right now?'

This is a magic meld. I must say there's an awful lot of power surging through you, young sprite.

'Ere, I'm seventy-four, fank you very much.'

And I am almost five thousand year's next birthday. I like cake, by the way.

'Noted.' Jenni was impressed. 'So tell us then, 'ow comes she ain't made you bring 'er 'ere?'

I am amongst the last of my kind. The Sea Witch believes I am the very last. In order to keep the rest of my clan safe, I pretend to be under her thrall and perform small magical acts upon request.

Jenni raised an eyebrow at that.

Yes, well, perhaps request is a rather nice way of putting it.

'Ow many of youse are left now? If you don't mind me asking, corse.'

Enough to survive if we keep safe. I can't tell you any more, you understand.

Jenni nodded thoughtfully.

'Could I 'ave got 'ere on me own? Did I 'ave the juice for it?'

I believe so, but it was my understanding that you need all your magic in order to stop the Sea Witch. I thought me bringing you here would help.

'Yeah, it's great. Fanks, Slinky. 'Ere, you got any tips on 'ow to stop 'er from tearing through the realms and that?'

I would say the answer is within you, young sprite. The choices you make could have a huge effect on life as we know it. Just remember, at your core, you know how to do the right thing.

'You don't even know me.'

I can read your soul.

A shudder of green sparks ran down Jenni's body. The sea serpent kinked its body as far away from it as possible.

That does not belong to you.

The tone was bordering on accusatory. Jenni flushed. It must be the remnants of the power she'd been skimming after Norm had shown her how. Her skin tingled a little at the memory of that first rush. She didn't know exactly how many other people she'd skimmed, but she wouldn't do it anymore. Once she got out of here and back to Roshaven and her life, with all her magic. Hopefully.

'I got anovver question.' Jenni decided not to dwell on the stolen power. 'Ain't the Sea Witch gonna know you can travel realms now you've brung me 'ere?'

You can tell her you did it on your own.

'But you disappeared before 'er eyes!'

Did I? The sea serpent radiated humour. *I left a simulacrum which will curl up and go to sleep. I sleep a lot. It's a useful state of mind for getting things done.*

'Oh, right.' Jenni was feeling a tug towards the core of the sea serpents' power. She did her best to ignore it. 'Wot we gonna do 'ere then – 'ow do we find this person?'

You could just call their name.

Jenni broke the connection with some relief at having the temptation of skimming a highly magical creature removed from right in front of her. She looked around at the cave and decided that calling for a dead person would be better coming from the beach, so she stomped outside.

But they weren't on the beach anymore.

Chapter 33

Instead of the sand, sea and crabs Jenni was expecting, she stood in greyness. Grey floors, walls and ceilings surrounded her, but it wasn't a room - more like a grey space. The lack of colour was disconcerting, and Jenni felt abruptly nervous, as if she were about to audition for her life or something.

'Wot 'appened to the beach an stuff, Slinky?'

The sea dragon shrugged sinuously.

'I guess this is wot the spirit realm looks like then. S'not all that, is it?' Jenni looked around again in case she'd missed anything, but the greyness remained. 'Right then. Wot we gotta do again? Oh, yeah.' Jenni put her hands around her mouth and yelled out, 'Avery! Avery! Here Avery Avery Avery. I gotta message for you.'

She waited. And waited. The sea dragon curled up on her toes and hid its head within its coils. Soft purrs began and heat radiated through Jenni's feet.

A little girl came running towards Jenni. She was about four years old and had auburn hair in two bunches. A cuteness that was not matched by the serious expression on her face.

'I'm Avery.'

'Are you now?' Jenni looked down at the child. 'I don't fink yor the one I want, but wot do I know. Can you finish this sentence for me? I love you more than…'

'Umm… lollipops? Are you my mummy?'

'No, love. I'm just looking for someone called Avery. Do you…' But before Jenni could ask the little girl if she knew anyone else with the same name, she'd turned and run off the way she'd come, fading into the distance. Jenni felt a small twinge of sadness that she hadn't been the poor little things mum but tried to console herself with the thought that eventually the kid would be reunited with her parent, wouldn't she? That train of thought was threatening to unravel some deep and meaningful thinking, the type Jenni avoided at all costs, so instead, she opened her mouth and shouted Avery again.

This time the click clack of high heels proceeded a smartly dressed woman with green hair. Jenni thought she might be in luck here, with the Sea Witch being greeny-grey skinned and all.

'Awright,' Jenni gave the spirit a nod. 'Can you answer this question for me? I love you more than…'

In answer, the woman gave Jenni a card. It had the name Siobhan O'Keefe and beneath that, in shiny green writing, Jade Purveyor.

'You ain't related to the Sea Witch, are you?' Jenni passed the card back, but the woman didn't take it. Instead, she shook her head, gave a small bow and click clacked back the way she'd come. Jenni looked at the card again. She didn't think she'd ever need to purvey jade, but you never knew about these things, so she tucked it in her pocket.

'This is getting silly now, ain't it?' She looked down at the sleeping sea dragon. 'Fat lot of good you are. Awright, let's try again then, shall we? Avery!'

This time, an old man shuffled into view. He and Jenni had a lovely chat about beetle cheesecake. It turned out he was one of the original beetle ranchers, back when it was a more popular dish and the beetles enjoyed free ranging. But he wasn't related to the Sea

Witch, so they said a fond goodbye and Jenni tucked some cheesecake making tips into her pocket. At this rate, she was going to run out-of-pocket space. Before she had a chance to call out again, a teenager appeared.

'All that shouting is dangerous, you know,' she said. She stood taller than Jenni, but that wasn't hard. She was dressed all in black with a severe black bob and a very pale face Jenni thought wasn't entirely down to being dead and a spirit and everything.

'I'm just trying to find the right Avery. I guess the spirit realm is full of lots of different Averys.' Jenni hadn't really thought about that before, although now she did, it was obvious.

'It's infinitely vast,' replied the teenager in withering tones. 'How else can it hold the souls of the dead?'

'Awright, awright.'

The teenager leaned against a wall that wasn't there before and inspected her fingernails, painted black, of course.

'Ow'd you do that?' Jenni pointed to the wall.

The teenager shrugged.

'All spirits can build their own dreamscape. Anything they like. It's usually contained within their own private sphere, but you can visit. If you want. You don't really think you're standing on something, do you?' The teenager smirked. 'You don't really think that's air you're breathing, do you?'

Jenni's rational brain fought for control as her lungs screamed for oxygen. Luckily, Jenni's legs stayed well out of the tussle and she remained standing on her fake grey floor as she took a shaky fake breath. She decided to let her lungs pretend they were breathing air and to keep going. The teenager's smirk was getting on her nerves.

'You shouldn't shout like that, either. You'll attract the bad ones.' Despite her nonchalant tone, Jenni noticed how still the spirit was holding itself, like it was ready to dart away at the first sign of danger.

'Bad ones?' asked Jenni, wriggling her toes, trying to wake up the sea dragon in case they needed to make a quick getaway.

'Not all spirits are good, just like not all people are good.' The teenager scowled at the sprite. 'And not all spirits are happy here. They yearn to break free and wreak havoc on the living world. You, being a fleshie, are the perfect vessel.' The teenager loomed, gathering darkness around her, making herself look scarier.

'I ain't gonna let that 'appen. I'm looking for someone. Do you…' But before Jenni could ask her question, the teenager interrupted again.

'Yeah, I know. I heard you.' She stood up from the wall and it vanished, as did the looming shadows. 'There's actually someone here who wants to see you.' She turned and walked a few steps before stopping and sighing loudly. 'Are you coming or what?'

The sea dragon quickly unwound itself and slinked after the girl, leaving Jenni muttering and stomping to catch up.

'Who wants to see me?'

A red door appeared, and the teenager opened it outwards for Jenni and the sea serpent. Slinky went scampering straight in, but Jenni paused, feeling like she was about to get ambushed.

'How do I know you ain't taking me to the bad ones?' she asked, peering up at the teenager.

'You don't.' The girl huffed impatiently and swung the door a little wider indicating that Jenni needed to hold it open as she followed the sea dragon inside.

Jenni dithered for a moment, then figured whatever was happening inside the door was likely to be far more interesting than the greyness without, so she headed in.

A twinkly eyed, rotund sprite sat in a large floral squishy armchair in the middle of a front room that could only be described as chintzy. Lace doilies covered every surface and there were pot flowers, pot animals and pot houses acting as dust gatherers on every nest of coffee tables, with display cabinets filled by porcelain dolls in pretty dresses. The carpet was floral; the curtains were floral and there were bunches of flowers dotted around in mis-matched vases and jugs. The smell of cake baking wafted through the air and there was a tea tray with three cups on the low table next to the armchair. The delicate china cups and saucers were also floral, and the teapot was wearing a bright pink knitted tea cosy.

The sea dragon had flowed up the armchair and was curled contentedly on the lap of the sprite who had put her knitting to one side in order to scratch its ears. The teenager was sitting cross-legged in another armchair to the left, still feigning indifference, but Jenni could feel the girl watching her.

'Awright Jenni, love? I'm yor Nan June, chuffed to bits to finally meet you. Come 'ere, let's be looking at you.'

Chapter 34

Jenni found herself sat in a squishy armchair with a cup of tea and a slice of the best beetle cheesecake she'd ever had. The teenager had gone back to picking her nails and the sea dragon was slurping from her Nan's saucer.

'You me Dad's mum then, yeah?'

'That's right, love. I seed you got the accent. Bin 'anded down for generations. Always fawt it were a bit rum yor Dad never 'ad it.'

'Wot should I call you?'

'You can call me Nan June if you like. Bin watching you, down there. We're so proud of you. You did so good in yor coming-of-age ceremony and a catcher! Fancy that, eh? Wot a life.'

Jenni glowed a little. She couldn't help it. It had been a while since anyone had said they were proud of her. Momma K was still smarting over Jenni's decision to remain a catcher.

'I only just met me dad. Norm. The ovver day.'

Nan June sniffed.

'Yor best off keeping away from 'im luv. I don't mean to speak bad of people, but yor father ain't the brightest spark. You don't let 'im drag you into any funny business, you 'ear? That's 'ow we lost yor Uncle Stu. Terrible business that, terrible.'

Both Jenni and the teenager leaned forward with interest.

'Uncle Stu? I didn't even know I 'ad a nuncle. Wot was 'e like?'

Nan June's face wreathed in smiling crinkles.

'Oh 'e was a good lad. Always ready to 'elp anyone, always 'ad a kind word for everyone. And a good-looking lad, an'all. Brushed up smart. Yor Boss knew 'im a bit, young Spinks. 'Elped 'im out of a tight spot back in the day. Was a tragedy when it 'appened. A real tragedy.' She took a large slurp of her tea. 'Need a top up, love?'

Both the teenager and Jenni shook their heads, eager to hear the next part of the story. Jenni was especially intrigued to find out more about how Ned knew her uncle. She would definitely be asking him about that when she got home. Nan June wiggled into her chair, getting extra comfy. Jenni could see she was enjoying being the centre of attention.

'Magic didn't come easy to yor dad, and he never liked school much. Said all the letters and numbers looked like chicken scratches in the dirt, but we wanted both boys to have good learning. S'important.' She looked fiercely at Jenni, who squirmed slightly. Whilst she'd never had a problem with letters and numbers, Jenni had never really enjoyed school and had scarpered out as quickly as she could. 'Some sprites just ain't good at magic. Peoples fink if yor fae you can cast and wotnot but it ain't that simple and for yor dad, the magic just didn't flow.'

Nan June took another slurp of her tea and waggled her fingers at the tea tray. A plate of sliced fruit cake appeared, and she helped herself to one, gesturing for the girls to do the same. Jenni shook her head, but the teenager slinked over to get one. The sea dragon opened one eye and extended a paw, scooping up his own slice to enjoy.

'Wot you 'ave to understand is, it were a different time. Momma K weren't in charge yet and there was fierce competition between fae and families. Right fierce.'

Nan June paused to eat and Jenni was trying to think just how far back they were talking if Momma K wasn't in charge. She'd never really thought about what it might have been like before.

'Norm, yor dad, was flunking, and we called in a tutor to 'elp 'im out. Well, he elped 'im alright, but it weren't zactly wot we 'ad 'oped. 'E taught 'im 'ow to skim magics off ovvers and use it for hisself. It ain't no good taking someone else's magic, less they give it you freely corse, ovverwise bad fings 'appen. Very bad fings.'

Nan June lapsed into silence, obviously caught up in her memories.

Jenni, on the other hand, felt the familiar wash of guilt flood through her. She thought back to what her dad had told her. Skimming mopped up spare magic, the bits that people weren't using. He'd told her it was harmless, taking the spare that people wouldn't notice. It didn't hurt anyone as long as you just skimmed and never dipped. Jenni had been so desperate to have more magic at her disposal she'd dismissed the unease and given it a go, skimming a little here and there. People like Ned topped up regularly anyway so they wouldn't even notice. And it was just spare magic going to waste. Really, where was the harm?

Jenni looked up to see Nan June watching her with shrewd eyes and she picked up her teacup to hide her discomfort.

'Don't get me wrong, I love my son. Corse I do. E's me son. But…' Nan June let out an enormous sigh. 'I dunno. Summink 'appened. 'E grew wrong, and it didn't seem to matter wot we said, 'e wos the way 'e wos and that were that. And the power skimming, that seemed to be the last brick in the bad wall. 'Is bruvver tried wiv 'im. Got 'im a job at the docks and that. But all the while, Norm were skimming. A bit 'ere, bit there and oftentimes from 'is own bruvver. Skimming is a slippery slope. You start doing it too much and you can't 'elp yorself. In the end it were that skimming wot killed Stu.' Nan June lapsed into silence.

Jenni watched the grandparent she barely knew get swept up in memories. The teenager was dunking biscuits into her tea. Jenni looked around. She didn't have any biscuits. Glancing back at the teenager, she saw her smirk. Jenni tried using her magic, but nothing happened. Clearly, magic didn't work the same in the spirit realm. Then Jenni remembered. The dreamscape let you create whatever you wanted. She concentrated and a plate of biscuits wobbled into being in front of her. It took a moment for them to fully coalesce, but eventually the selection solidified enough for Jenni to pick one up and eat it. It wasn't quite right, but it was better than nothing at all, and the appearance of her own plate of biscuits had wiped the smirk off the teenager's face. Totally worth it.

Nan June started talking again.

'It were a busy day on the docks. Lots of shipments coming in and the Sea Witch was annoyed. Too much coming and going, not enough froing. They say she was down several payments. They say the mermaids saved too many sailors wot fell overboard. They say it were the moon affecting the tides. They say a lot of crap. Wot it boiled down to wos the Sea Witch was a greedy arse and just wanted souls.' Nan June fixed Jenni with her beady gaze again. 'That's 'ow she gets 'er power. From souls. And yor dad had some kind of argy bargy with Stu.

Fings got a little 'eated, apparently. I dunno. I wasn't there. But push came to shove and Stu ended up in the drink. Would've bin awright if 'e 'ad all 'is power. Could've spelled hisself out of there in a jiffy. But 'e didn't cos e'd bin skimmed. And the Sea Witch took 'im as tribute. Didn't take much to put two and two togevver once we 'eard wot 'ad 'appened. Yor Grandaddy never really recovered from it.'

Jenni let out a breath she hadn't realised she'd been holding.

'What 'appened to Norm?' she asked.

'Yor Dad? 'E ran off like a coward. Left us to pick up the pieces. I 'ear 'e's working for the Sea Witch now, is that right?'

Jenni nodded. She was feeling very uncomfortable. She didn't like being tarred with the same brush as a man she barely knew and she was feeling grubby from the skimming. Both because she'd been doing it, and also because the power high had worn off and she was feeling antsy.

'Did you know, every time you skim someone's power, you lose a little of yor soul? Bet 'e never told you that, did 'e?' Nan June managed to look both worried and triumphant at the same time. 'And once you've lost yor soul, you can dip down and take someone else's instead.'

Now that was news to Jenni. She hadn't known that skimming made you lose your soul, but it made so much sense. Things clicked into place. Why Norm was able to hide so well – he didn't have a soul. And why the Spice Ghosts thought Jenni was their thief. She still had her soul. Jenni clenched her fists. She'd been so stupid to listen to him encouraging her to skim – was he siphoning off her soul as well? She touched her chest. How much did she have left?

Nan June broke Jenni's thoughts as she touched her arm gently. Jenni flinched. She hadn't been aware of the old woman moving.

'Yor soul is safe for now, love. But you got some big decisions in front of you and it's fragile. Very fragile. Be careful and trust in those wot you love.' Her nan leaned forward and kissed Jenni on the forehead. It felt very much like one of Momma K's protective kisses and Jenni felt tears prick the back of her eyes. Suddenly, she felt very homesick.

'Fank goodness we 'ave the Spice Ghosts. That's all I can say.' Nan June was back in her armchair, a cheerful grin on her face. 'They'll keep that Sea Witch out of the spirit realm. She can't 'ave us.'

Jenni had a horrible feeling.

'Yeah, about that.'

Chapter 35

No-one had spoken for at least ten minutes. Jenni was feeling like she wanted to cry. She never cried. The teenager had frozen in spot and seemed to be doing her best to melt into the armchair. Indeed, unless Jenni looked directly at her, she couldn't see the girl in her periphery anymore.

Nan June, on the other hand, she was looking more corporeal than ever. She finally spoke.

'You mean to say that yor good for nuffink father stole the bloody bones from the sodding Spice Ghosts, lost 'em in a poker game to some Charley-boy wot sold 'em to fae traders who didn't know wot they 'ad and give 'em away to the Sea Witch for nuffink?'

'More or less, yeah.'

'And yor 'ere cos yor lot tried to trade power for bones, but the Sea Witch wanted you to prove you 'ad it and give someone a message first.'

'Yeah.'

Nan June cogitated for a short while longer.

'Which one?'

Jenni was confused.

'Which one wot?'

Nan June huffed.

'Which Spice Ghost you got wiv you?'

'Oh, Clove. She's awright.'

Nan June helped herself to a lemon sherbet and did not offer one to Jenni. Or the teenager.

'Least it ain't Paprika. E's a rum un.'

Jenni's attention was caught by the teenager shifting

in her chair. If she didn't know better, Jenni would have said the girl was hanging on her every word.

'We didn't see no Paprika. Wot is 'e, a mate of the sea witch or summink?'

'Pfft. Mates. That's one word for it. Lovers more like. United in their love of the sea, for a time at least. Then she got herself knocked up, and that were that. Only she weren't 'appy bout it and 'e fawt she shouldda been more cepting and stuff. She had a proper bee in 'er bonnet.'

Jenni was lost. There were too many shes.

'Wot are you talking about, Nan?'

'She's talking about the relationship Paprika and the Sea Witch had before the Sea Witch got pregnant.' The teenager spoke, surprising both sprites. 'Paprika retired from the Spice Ghosts and raised the child after the Sea Witch abandoned it.'

'It weren't just the child wot broke 'em. The Sea Witch is fickle, ever-shifting and tinged wiv madness. Right gone in the 'ead she is.' Nan June sipped at her tea. 'Nasty business all round, but the child was loved by her father.'

'Till he died at sea,' muttered the teenager.

'It's you. Yor the child! Yor the Avery I'm looking for.' Jenni glared at the girl. 'Why didn't you say anyfing? I gots a message for you.'

'So.'

'Whaddya mean so? 'Ere answer this. I love you more than…'

'I'm not answering you.' And she faded away.

Jenni gaped at the empty chair.

'Wot am I supposed to do now?'

'You can go after 'er easy enough. I'll show you 'ow to track 'er essence, but first I gotta question for you.

Somefink's bin bovvering me about you. 'Ow come yor so powerful? I fawt you'd 'ad it all locked up at yor coming-of-age?'

'I did, but the Source gave me its power so I could trade it for the bones and save the world.' Jenni replied despondently. So far, the plan wasn't going very well.

Nan June cackled.

'You ain't got the Source's power. That's way too much for one person to 'old. Wot's the actual plan?'

'I have too.' Jenni bristled. She didn't like being called a liar.

'Prove it.' Nan June's eyes glinted as she threw down the challenge. 'Show me your colours.'

'Wot?'

'Wot do you mean, wot? Show me the colour of yor magic. Don't they teach you nuffink no more? Yor a sprite, you should know wot colour yor magic looks like. If you've got the Source in there as well, you'll 'ave some extra golden bits.'

Jenni knew her Nan was being careful in not telling her exactly what her colours would look like, so she couldn't fake it. She thought about when she first arrived in the spirit realm and how things had glowed under her skin, so she concentrated on that feeling and tried to bring that back. First came her fae blue and silver. Then there were golden ribbons and sparkly black stars from the Source. It was quite a display. Then came different shades of orange, red, green and a purple that made Jenni think of Ned. She realised these extra shades resulted from the skimming she'd done. She thought it looked pretty.

There was a sharp intake of breath from Nan June.

'You got too many colours, even if you 'av got the Source power an'all.' The old woman rounded on her granddaughter. 'You bin skimming? You bin listening to that waste of space of a father of yors?'

Jenni flinched back, not used to having small old people shouting at her.

''Ere leave off, awright. 'Ow was I supposed to know? E's me dad, ain't 'e?'

'Fat lot of good 'e is. Didn't yor muvver warn you?'

Jenni recalled Momma K's warning.

'No trust him. No one inch. No one second. No believe. Look afta ya heart.'

She shifted uncomfortably. She didn't feel like admitting that to her Nan.

'All this extra sloshing around. S'not good for you. It's gonna bend you the wrong way. Make you fink you can do stuffs wot you can't. Wot you shouldn't. The Source wos right to put a block on you. I fawt so at the time. You 'ad too much and wos too young for it. That magic is gonna corrupt you, you gotta get rid of that extra power. As soon as you can.'

Jenni had been getting angrier and angrier at the crone's words. Her stolen power was roiling under her skin and the Source's boost was making her tingle all over.

'Why would I do that?' Jenni's voice was low and menacing, but it grew louder as she continued speaking. 'I'm out there, 'elping people. I'm saving the world. Wot are you doing? Stuck 'ere, doing nuffink.' She gestured angrily at her Nan, who was now sitting right back in her armchair, as far away from Jenni as she could get. The rest of the room had faded away, leaving only Jenni's Nan in her chair. 'You don't know me. I ain't never met you afore. You don't know my life. You ain't bin in my shoes.' She leaned forward and jabbed a finger in her Nan's face. 'I don't gotta listen to this.' She clicked her fingers imperiously at the sea dragon. 'Get us out of 'ere.'

They stood back in the grey. The teenager had returned.

'Are you alright?' asked the teenager eventually after several long minutes of watching Jenni fume.

'Wot's it to you?' snapped Jenni.

The sea dragon hissed at her and went to go sit with the teenager. There was more awkward silence. The teenager finally spoke.

'You can tell my mother I'm not interested in anything she has to say. I'm happy where I am. I'm okay, I'm experiencing the natural order of things.' She waved a hand and created a rainbow. 'I like it here.'

'It were you all along,' replied Jenni flatly. She felt doubly annoyed with herself now. She should've figured that out. 'Look, all respect and that but I don't fink yor mum is gonna like that.' She thought quickly. 'Can you at least come back wiv me to tell 'er yorself?'

'No. I've moved on. She needs to as well.' The teenager softened slightly. 'You ought to listen to your Nan, you know.' She looked past Jenni's right shoulder. 'Your aura is infected. It's only going to get worse unless you get rid of that extra power.'

'Wot do you know? Yor just a dead girl who don't wanna see 'er mum.' Jenni knew she was being rude and hurtful but she didn't care. For the first time since her coming-of-age ceremony, she had felt like herself again. She had magic at her fingertips again. This was what she needed to live, to breathe, to be. Power crackling through her, able to cast at will for anything she wanted. 'You don't know wot it's like. 'Aving power taken away from you for no good reason. 'Aving to pull on ovver life just to cast simple spells.' Jenni turned away from the scrutiny of the teenager. 'I killed a cat. It were an accident. I just wanted to pop down the road, but I didn't 'ave the juice no more, so I pulled energy from around me. And just like that, it were dead. But I didn't mean it.'

There was more silence. The sea dragon returned to Jenni's side and wound itself around her legs a few times. It made her feel slightly better.

'You know yor mum wants to raise you, right? That's wot she's bin collecting all this power for. So she can break the veil and bring you back.'

The teenager shuddered.

'I don't want to be raised. It's my afterlife. I don't have to do what she wants anymore.'

While they had been talking, the grey had been growing darker and darker.

'You should go. It's not good for mortals to stay too long in the spirit realm. The others have noticed you're here.' The teenager shot a fearful glance over her shoulder. 'Your way back is closing.'

Jenni looked down at the sea dragon, whose golden glow was definitely dimmer. She reached down to stroke him and the dragon began humming again. Jenni felt the same hypnotic tug as before as she watched the golden scales flash around her legs. She began swaying to the rhythm of the dragon and the atmosphere grew thick. Her body felt like it was moving slower than her consciousness, always catching her up to her but never quite getting there.

She lifted a hand in farewell to Avery, who gave her a small wave before fading away.

'Ere Slinky, you'd better go get the ovvers if you wanna get these bones away from the Sea Witch. I'll keep 'er busy. She ain't gonna be 'appy about Avery.'

The grey was dimming around them, yet Jenni thought she saw the sea dragon nod its agreement as it glowed brighter and brighter. The hair on Jenni's arms stood up and her breath caught in her throat, pressure building in her chest as if she were being sat on. As it continued to rise, the light grew so bright Jenni could barely see. Her ears popped, and she blinked. The brightness had gone. Jenni stood back in the Sea Witch's cave.

Chapter 36

Ned had been pacing back and forth so much in the sand he had created a little gulley. His mind was in overdrive worrying about Jenni, and his body was trying to keep up. The others were sitting by the blue rock. It had taken lots of coaxing to cajole Fingers down from the top of the rock and he was still looking around for crabs.

Rose had handed out provisions and Ned knew she had done her best to occupy everyone's thoughts with small talk, but he could not sit still. He needed to do something, anything.

'She should be back by now.'

'We don't know what it was the Sea Witch wanted her for. It might not have been a quick in and out thing,' replied Rose gently.

'What if she needs help?' That was his biggest fear. That Jenni might need him and he'd not be there.

'There isn't much you can do that she can't already, lad.' Griff tried to put Ned at ease. 'She's a very capable sprite.'

'She might be waiting for backup. Thief-catchers always work together.'

'This is a matter of magic, not law enforcement. There is nothing for you to offer.' Clove's response was particularly sharp, which made Ned wince inwardly and realise that this was the third time he had voiced his concerns.

'But…' Ned was about to start again when he was interrupted by Fingers.

'What's that?' Fingers had half scrambled up the

rock again, clearly not fully convinced all the crabs had disappeared.

'What? What?' Ned squinted in the distance. He could see a dust devil coming from the direction of the Sea Witch's cave. A golden shape was undulating across the sand and moving towards them at speed.

'Looks shiny,' called down Fingers. He looked at Ned for reassurance. 'So probably not a crab, right?'

'Not unless Jenni covered one with gems,' Ned replied, which gave everyone pause.

'Not a crab!' The relief in Fingers' voice was palpable. 'It looks like… yes, it's that sea dragon. The one that was with the Sea Witch earlier.'

Ned's heart sank. If the sea dragon was coming back, then did that mean Jenni had won or lost? She had told him that she kept seeing a mini dragon around Roshaven, but he hadn't believed her. Thought she was just messing about, some sprite mischief or something. What if the sea dragon had been trying to warn them about the Sea Witch? It was too late now for recriminations. He had to hope the sea dragon was coming with good news.

The group on the sand held a collective breath as the sea dragon swept in. Ned noticed Fingers checking especially for any crab additions.

'What is it? What happened? Is Jenni alright?' Ned fired questions at the creature, not caring that it didn't speak. Ned's finger itched. As he looked down, he saw a very faint purple haze coalescing around the tip of his index finger. The sea dragon flicked out its forked tongue to touch it and a halo of gold light travelled down from the sea dragon's head towards Ned's finger.

Jenni has proven her power to the Sea Witch. She wants you to come and collect the bones while she deals with the monster.

'I knew it! I told you, didn't I? She needs our help.' Ned let the relief wash through him, but it did not entirely sweep away the worry. The blank looks from everyone else reminded him they hadn't heard the message from the sea serpent. 'Er, what do I call you?' He asked the beast.

Jenni calls me Slinky. There was an air of intense satisfaction around the sea dragon.

'Right.' Ned turned to the others. 'Slinky says Jenni needs our help. She's proven her power to the Sea Witch, so while she's busy pretending to trade that power, we've got to sneak in and get the bones.' Ned cast a quick look at the sea dragon to make sure it wasn't disagreeing with him. He had embellished slightly, but the sea dragon was looking as grave as a cute looking dragonesque creature can and nodding slowly in agreement.

Their camp had been packed up and Ned watched as Rose stood, backpack on, ready to head out to the caves, radiating confidence. He wished he felt like that. He was worried about what they might find.

'Ready?' Ned waited impatiently for nods before striding out across the sand, the sea dragon slinking in and around his feet, careful not to trip him up.

It didn't take them long to cross the sand. Everyone wanted to get there as quickly as possible. Everyone except for Fingers, who was bringing up the rear a few paces back. Ned noticed his reluctance.

'Fingers, you stay here. Keep an eye out for any unexpected arrivals. Rose, you're with me. We'll head right once we've entered the cave. Griff, Clove, wait a few minutes then come in and head left. If we're lucky, we'll all get in without the Sea Witch noticing. If not, the first team should be able to keep her busy.'

While Ned had been speaking, the sea dragon had slinked back into the cave.

There were grim faces before him, but no-one objected. Taking a deep breath, Ned headed into the cave with Rose just behind him.

Chapter 37

'What did she say? Did you find my daughter's shade?' asked the Sea Witch.

Jenni shook her head to get her bearings. She felt like she'd been flushed inside out and then back again, which was probably pretty close to what had actually happened travelling between realms. She checked her body quickly to make sure it wasn't transparent anymore. It wasn't, but she felt the pull of all the different magics under her skin and there was a multi-coloured ripple across it.

'She ain't interested,' Jenni yelled back, forgetting for a moment who she was talking to. Then she remembered and moderated her tone. 'She doesn't want to be resurrected.'

Jenni's power kept crackling and random multi-coloured sparks began shooting out of her fingers.

'Why doesn't she want to come back? Did you give her my message? Are you sure it was the right Avery?'

'Yeah, I'm sure!' snapped Jenni. She was still feeling cross after the last conversation with her Nan and she wasn't in the mood for having her abilities questioned. Again. The riled-up power stretched beneath her skin and for a moment Jenni felt light-headed.

'You will go back and make her,' ordered the Sea Witch imperiously.

'No, I ain't. You want 'er so bad, you go,' retorted Jenni, forgetting for a moment that that was exactly what they were trying to avoid.

The sea dragon slinked round a rock, but the

movement caught the Sea Witch's eye. 'Why did you steal my sea dragon when you crossed over?'

'I…' Jenni was about to deny it but remembered what the sea serpent had said about hiding its power.

The Sea Witch began pacing crossly, the dragon already forgotten.

'I need your power to cross the veil, then I will have enough to bring Avery's soul back and return her to the living. You can have your pathetic bones – just give me the power.'

The Sea Witch stepped in close to Jenni. They were almost nose to nose except Jenni stood at least a foot shorter.

'Give me the power. Otherwise I will destroy your friends and family, starting with the thief-catcher you seem to revere so much.' Her voice was icy and her black stare pinned Jenni in place.

But Jenni's magic plus the Source and the stolen top ups began boiling, churning, whipping through her body, desperate to be released. She began speaking quietly.

'You ain't gonna do nuffink to my family. I'm more powerful than you and you knows it.'

Jenni took a step forward, forcing the Sea Witch to back off. She tried to take another step and her foot wouldn't move. She looked down and saw she was trapped in a fae ring. Ancient fae glyphs were carved on the floor.

'You didn't really think you could beat me, did you?' The Sea Witch gloated. 'You fae always think you're better than everyone else.'

'Whaddya mean *you fae*. Didn't you used to be one of us?' Jenni couldn't move her feet, but she was sending out tendrils of magic all around the ring to see if she could find any weakness.

The Sea Witch looked at Jenni darkly.

'I left the fae realm behind long before you came into existence,' she said with a touch of bitterness.

'Oh yeah, I member now. Momma K told us about 'ow she 'ad a bestie wot went off the rails. Fell in love wiv a shifter and turned 'er back on the fae. Stealing magic and souls. Becoming summink twisted and evil.'

The Sea Witch stiffened.

'What do you know about love? You're nothing but a limpet holding on for dear life while the real power is wielded around you.'

Jenni felt the chink.

'You know nothing of my life or the sacrifices I've made. Nothing!' The Sea Witch took a step forward, careful not to stand too close to Jenni. 'Maybe after you've spent a century trapped in there, you'll learn some manners.'

'I ain't gonna be in 'ere for a century.'

The Sea Witch cackled.

'I've trapped you. You cannot escape. Not even you, with all that stolen power, can break a fae trap.'

Jenni stepped calmly out of the ring. The Sea Witch staggered back, shock written all over her face. The stone floor cracked where Jenni had stood, startling all the crabs and even making the sea dragon scurry for a better hiding place.

'No! It's impossible. How did you…?'

Jenni flexed her power and all the ancient glyphs melted away, leaving polished stone.

'It's all about who you are, you know? If you wos a bit nicer, mebbe yor daughter would wanna come back to life. But you're not and she don't. Mebbe if you wos a bit kinder, the sea dragon woulda took you cross the realms hisself. But you're not so 'e won't. Mebbe if you

'adn't freatened my family, I'da let you go. But you did,
so I ain't.' She cracked her knuckles and threw a trap
spell at the Sea Witch.

The Sea Witch leapt out of the way at the last
moment with a howl of frustrated rage. She began
chanting, throwing hexes at Jenni as she ran towards the
rocky gloom at the back of the cave. Jenni dodged the
spells easily and fought back with a few of her own.
They crashed into the rocks the Sea Witch was now
hiding behind and fizzled.

The crabs were boiling, desperately trying to get out
of the cave and nipping anything and everything that got
in their way, including each other. The sea dragon was
dodging them as best as it could, but when one gave a
particularly painful nip to its tail, it roared and
shimmered, taking itself elsewhere.

The Sea Witch watched in dismay.

'Yeah, all this time, old Slinky coulda taken you
cross the realms.' Jenni sniggered and released a few
more spells. She was enjoying herself. But she had
miscalculated the Sea Witch. She hadn't just run to hide
behind some rocks. She'd bought herself time to cast
more complicated magic.

The fight became tense, with both sides flinging
increasingly deadly spells at each other. Jenni barely
parried a low-flying paralyser and her toes tingled madly
with pins and needles. She threw a screaming fireball
back that singed the Sea Witch's seaweed hair, filling
the air with an acrid smell.

Jenni's magic was singing to be released. All of it.
Every scrap she'd borrowed. Everything the Source had
given her, plus her own innate power.

'You will not defeat me!' screamed the Sea Witch,
firing off another bout of deadly hexes. 'When I get out

of here, I'm going to raze your precious little town to the ground and use your beloved thief-catcher as bait for my crab traps.'

Jenni's blood boiled and her magic snapped, flying out of her at the same time as the Sea Witch poured all her saved soul power into her nastiest spell. The two torrents of power collided with a massive boom.

Chapter 38

The two spells colliding created a swirling vortex of power. Ned's ears popped loudly. Muted green, mud brown and grey whirled together with blue, silver, gold, sparkly black and flecks of orange and purple. Ned felt a deep pull towards the purple splodges.

'That's my magic,' he murmured to himself, confused why his magic was fighting the Sea Witch's.

The brighter swirls seemed to win against the darker ones as they whipped around, faster and faster. The vortex spun around so fast, small pebbles from the cave floor got sucked into it. Then one crab and another lost their footing and were swept into the magical tempest, clacking their pincers in desperation.

'Nooooo!' shouted the Sea Witch as Jenni leaned forwards.

Ned felt suddenly light-headed as his knees gave way. Rose slumped to the floor with him. Ned noticed more purple splotches tinged with pink appearing in the power flow from Jenni. She'd skimmed them.

'We have to get out of here,' he said. But Rose couldn't seem to hear him as she shook her head in a daze. She was clearly struggling to focus on anything at all. Ned pushed himself to his feet and hauled her up, holding onto the cave wall for balance. He waved his arms at Clove and Griff to get their attention, but as he did so he saw a rusty brown cloud with lilac stars sprinkled in amongst it pass from them into Jenni's power surge. Ned saw Griff clock what was happening and speak urgently to Clove. But he was too far away for

Ned to hear what he was saying.

Strength was returning to Ned's limbs, and he helped a disorientated Rose back track to the opening of the cave, meeting Clove and Griff at the opening.

'She's skimming!' Griff exclaimed.

'I know, but I don't think she's doing it on purpose. Get her out of here.' Ned thrust his wife into Griff's arms.

'What are you planning to do?' asked Clove.

'See if I can't find your damn bones,' replied Ned.

'You go back in there and you run the risk of having all your power drained. It's madness.' Clove was watching Ned with a critical eye.

'Having magic doesn't define me.' For the first time Ned realised he really didn't care about having magic or not and that if he lost his magic, it didn't matter. He could still help Jenni. He gave them a gentle shove to start them moving clear of the cave and take Rose to safety. She was coming around, so he quickly moved back into the cave before she could realise what he was doing.

This time, Ned kept his back pressed against the wall to keep as far away from the magical vortex as possible. He also did his best to hold on to his own power. It was usually hard work to grab hold of it in order to use it, so instead of trying to get it, he focused on pushing it down and away. Ned moved away from Jenni, closer to the Sea Witch. He was hoping if he could distract the Sea Witch for a moment, however small, it would be enough for Jenni to gain the advantage.

The extra power Jenni had skimmed certainly seemed to work to her advantage. The Sea Witch was bending backwards, doing her best to force Jenni's magic away and avoid touching the vortex, which was slowly inching closer and closer to her.

Ned looked around and saw a rock trembling in the path before him. It was being pulled by the magic but was dug too deep into the wet sandy floor to come free. If he could loosen it, that might be the distraction Jenni needed to win the fight. He crouched down and began digging sand out from around the rock. It didn't take long to free it. The rock shot out of the ground, its sharp edges grazing Ned's hands as it flew towards the duelling couple. It whipped past the Sea Witch's face, causing her to flinch, her focus ever so slightly shaken.

It was enough.

Jenni let out an anguished howl and pushed her magic forwards.

The vortex teetered over towards the Sea Witch and sucked her in. She vanished instantly. The swirling magic took on a darker tinge before it spun tighter and tighter, getting more and more compact but looking no less deadly.

'Jenni!' Ned shouted a warning, but it was too late. The vortex slammed into the sprite, throwing her across the cave as the power was completely absorbed by her slight frame.

Ned scrambled across the cave as fast as he could. Jenni lay unmoving on the floor. She was cold to the touch. Her skin was flickering with strange pulses of energy. They were moving so fast Ned couldn't tell if it was her usual sprite energy, the Source's power or something else entirely.

'Jenni? Please, don't die. I need you. Roshaven needs you. You're the best thief-catcher I ever saw.' Tears were running down Ned's face, dripping onto Jenni. 'Wake up. Please.'

Jenni's eyes snapped open. They were completely

black.

Chapter 39

'Jenni? Are you alright?' Ned had leaned back when Jenni had opened her eyes. Gone were her blue eyes that he was used to. Now they matched those of the vanquished Sea Witch.

'I'm good. Wot 'appened?' Jenni sat up quickly and began looking around the cave. Ned followed her gaze. There was nothing much to see as far as he could tell. Most of the seaweed had been singed during the magical fight, and the crabs had disappeared completely. 'I can see everyfing. It looks amazeballs.'

Ned felt slightly bemused, but at least she still sounded like Jenni, even if her eyes were wrong. Then she flexed her fingers, and the entire cave flexed with her.

'Woah! Wot were that?' Excitement grew in Jenni's voice. 'Did you see that, Boss? I made the cave flex. Wonder wot else I can do.' She pointed to the cave floor and thousands of grains of sand floated half a metre into air wavering to a stop. They began swirling around in complex patterns until a small dust devil grew larger and larger.

'Er, Jenni!' Ned had to raise his voice over the sand dance.

'Wot? Oh right, sorry.' She lowered her hand, and the sand fell back to the ground. 'Do you wanna drink?' Without waiting for an answer, Jenni clicked her fingers and a small table appeared with a bottle of scumble and two tumblers. 'Oh, where are me manners? 'Ere you go.' Two stools popped into existence. 'Nah, I reckon we deserve better than that.' The stools popped out and two throne like wooden chairs took their place. 'Bit o' comfort needed.' Another click and the chairs were cushioned. Jenni took a seat and poured herself a generous measure. 'Not 'aving one, Boss? Oh right, 'ang on.'

And before Ned could reply, Jenni had clicked ice cubes into the two tumblers. Ned half fell, half sat into the chair, grateful for the cushions, and poured himself a drink. He needed to steady his nerves. Besides, it would be rude not to.

'Where is the Sea Witch?' he asked.

'Dunno.' Jenni focused for a minute. 'I can't read 'er person but I fink I gots 'er magic. Won that fight, didn't I?'

Jenni didn't seem remotely bothered, just rather pleased with herself.

'But, your eyes…'

'Wot about 'em?' Jenni conjured a hand-held mirror and took a look. 'Bloody 'ell! That's a fing an'all, innit?' She peered into the glass, turning this way and that, admiring her uniquely coloured eyes. 'Bit of awright though, ain't they?'

'Um, I'm not so sure. I think your eyes turning black because you absorbed all the bad juju from a dangerous Sea Witch might not be something you want to be happy about.' Ned hadn't meant to be so abrupt, but all the worry he'd been nursing about what was happening between Jenni and the Sea Witch had boiled over.

Jenni regarded Ned coolly as she took another sip of her scumble.

'I saved the world, right? 'Ere - take the bones back to the Spice Ghosts. Job jobbed.' She waved her hand and the three bones originally stolen flew through the air from some hidden recess in the cave.

Ned just about caught them. As he stood up to do so, his chair vanished along with the table, the scumble and the glasses. He held the bones in his arms, uncertain what was going to happen next.

'I'll just take these out to Clove then, shall I? You coming?' he asked.

Next thing he knew, he stood outside the cave, where the others were. Ned felt a little miffed at being magicked without being asked. Jenni was certainly throwing her power around.

The others were all scrambling off the sand, coming towards him and Jenni, but stopped when they noticed her eyes. Clove was the first to react. She held out her arms imperiously for the bones and Ned handed them over.

With the bones off his hands, Ned's concern for Jenni rose a notch. She wasn't acting like herself.

'Jenni, are you alright? What happened?' Rose asked, taking half a step forward.

Ned was relieved that it was a half-step closer to him and not exactly closer to Jenni.

'I won, didn't I? Knew I would.' Jenni shrugged her shoulders and magic crackled off her like static. 'You want summink? I'm starving.' She pointed at the empty sand in front of her and a table appeared, laden with all her favourite foods, including, of course, a very large beetle cheesecake.

'Err, I'm okay, thanks.' Rose cast a worried glance at Ned and inclined her head slightly, asking him to move away from Jenni and her feast.

Griff took Rose's hint to distract the sprite and moved closer to the food, helping himself to the most innocuous food item. His action emboldened Fingers to drift closer as well. Ned eyed Jenni to make sure her attention was fully on the two of them before he bent his head to listen to Rose's whispers.

'Why does she have black eyes?'

'I don't know. Her and the Sea Witch were fighting as I got there. Jenni got the advantage and blasted her. There was this massive vortex and then vamoose! She was gone. Jenni got thrown back. Smacked the ground with an almighty thwack.' Ned leaned in even closer to his wife. 'Honestly? I thought I'd lost her. She was cold and not moving. And then… then she just woke up. Her eyes snapped open, all black like that. Startled me something chronic.' Ned let out a deep breath.

'Have you been drinking?' accused Rose, looking aghast.

'A tot of scumble. Jenni conjured it. Seemed rude not to.' Ned shrugged helplessly as Rose turned back to the feast table.

Clove had joined now and was closely inspecting what looked like a pile of honey cakes.

'They ain't gonna sprout legs, you know.' Jenni grinned at the Spice Ghost and then caught Ned's eye, beckoning him over. 'I got some cinnamon twists for youse an'all. Knows there yor favourites.'

Ned's feet took over and led him back to the table. Everyone was tucking in to something and no-one seemed to be experiencing any side effects. What harm could it really do? Jenni used to pop things in and out all the time before she had her magic curtailed by the Source.

Six chairs appeared dotted around the table, and they all took a seat. Ned thought it was all a little surreal, sitting down to eat on the beach with the surf lapping nearby, after having won the day.

'You sure you're up to all this?' Griff asked.

Everyone kept quiet, waiting to hear Jenni's response.

'Why wouldn't I be?'

'Well, just wondering if you're feeling any side effects after everything. Given the colour of your eyes and that. Your skin is looking a little… scaly.'

Ned held his breath at Griff being so forward. He peered at Jenni, noticing the grey-green scales that had appeared on the sides of her face and the tops of her hands. Her usually blonde hair now had a definite red tinge to it. He was surprised he hadn't noticed it before.

'Yeah, maybe you should take it easy, Jenni. Until we can get you back to the Source and get all this extra power sorted out,' he said, instantly regretting having spoken up as she swung her black-eyed gaze upon him.

'There's nothing to sort out. I'm fine.'

One of the table legs flickered, causing food to roll off the end and fall onto the ground. Jenni huffed and clicked her fingers, making the table and the feast disappear. They were all left sitting on chairs, looking rather foolish.

'Jenni! Your nose…' Rose put a hand to her own and Ned stared at his friend in disbelief.

Gone was her snub little sprite nose. Instead, she had two slits – just like the Sea Witch.

'I really think you should stop doing any more magic. You are literally changing before our eyes.' Ned stood up, hands out. 'Please, Jenni. Let us take you back to the Source.'

'No.'

The word was quiet, yet it rocked through the group. Jenni was eye level with Ned, which was impossible given that she usually stood at least a foot shorter than him. He glanced down and saw that she was levitating.

'Jenni, please.' He begged. 'I really don't think you should be doing more magic.'

'What do you know?' replied Jenni.

The air behind her got darker as it crackled with tiny branches of lightning. A wind sprang up out of nowhere and buffeted Ned and the others. They had all stood up now, and the chairs were gone. The sea reacted to Jenni's darkness and began getting choppier and choppier. More and more clouds gathered with thunderous rolls.

'You know nothing. You don't have the faintest idea what power feels like. You have no comprehension of what I can do.' Jenni's hands curled inwards and balls of green energy sparked into life.

'Jenni! Please, don't…' Ned put out a hand to stop her from whatever it was she was going to do. His best mate was being consumed by evil magic, putting his wife and friends in danger, and there was nothing he could do.

Darkness cloaked them like thick fog. Ned knew he was still on the beach because he could feel the sand shifting beneath his feet and hear the water lapping at the shore. As the darkness slowly dissipated, Ned did a quick head count. They were all there except for Jenni. She had disappeared. He could only hope she wouldn't hurt anyone before he could find her again.

Chapter 40

Clove was the first to speak.

'I must return to my ship now that the bones have been successfully recovered. If we leave now, we can be back in Roshaven by this evening.'

'Successfully! You'd call that a success, would you? I'd call it a bloody nightmare.' Ned was angry and scared. Angry with the Spice Ghosts for losing the bones in the first place, angry at Jenni for risking everything to get them back and angry at himself for letting her do it. He was scared that he might never see her again.

'Either way, my quest is complete.' Clove spoke with resolute calm, and Ned knew that he would have to take her back to Roshaven and her ship so he could get rid of the tether. She was right, it was barely midday and if they hurried, they would get back by early evening.

He held his tongue and fumed while everyone got ready to leave the beach. It didn't take long. After all, it had been Ned who'd insisted they pack light.

The journey back to Roshaven was subdued. Nobody apart from Rose approached Ned, not even Griff.

'Are you alright?' she asked softly.

'Did you hear her voice? At the end – after she'd absorbed all that power?' Ned observed his wife.

'What about it?'

Ned's shoulders dropped. Rose hadn't noticed.

'Her accent was gone. It wasn't Jenni speaking. Not really.'

Rose rubbed his arm.

'Maybe she's in there deep down. Absorbing all that magic must have had an effect on her.' She tried to console him.

'But what if she's not there at all because the Sea Witch has taken her over? Or what if she is in there and she can't break free?' He glared down the road at Clove, his anger fixating on the Spice Ghost and her bones.

'I'm sure we'll find Jenni.' Griff braved the conversation.

Ned refused to acknowledge him, but the backs of his ears went red. He wasn't sure at all.

'Once you're untethered, we can come up with a plan to help Jenni. If that's what she wants, eh?'

'If that's what she wants? Of course that's what she wants – she doesn't want to be abandoned by all her family and friends. And she doesn't want to spend the rest of her life chasing souls at the bottom of the ocean.' Ned took a breath. 'She doesn't even like water.' He looked at Rose, eyes half filled with angry tears.

'We'll come up with a plan, I promise. We won't abandon Jenni.' She gave him a reassuring smile. 'We need to get back to Roshaven so you can get rid of this tether.' The unspoken thought was left hanging in the air.

If Ned got rid of the tether, then Roshaven would be rid of the Spice Ghosts and things could go back to semi-normal.

Griff changed the subject.

'You know we're being followed, right?' He jerked his head over his shoulder. Both Ned and Jenni looked back.

In the distance there was a slow-moving golden shape.

'Is that?' Ned peered, trying to get a better look. 'It's

the sea dragon from the beach. Should we wait for it?'
The others shrugged. 'I'm going to wait for it. It might
know where Jenni has gone.'

He called ahead to the others, calling a halt to their
journey back, then paced impatiently back and forth as
he waited for the sea dragon to catch up. Clearly it
wasn't used to travelling on foot, as the golden speck
seemed to slow down and pause more and more often.
But eventually, the sea dragon cautiously approached
them.

Its colour was diminished and its paws were dusty.
A long pink tongue lolled out of its mouth and its long
eyebrows drooped.

'Need a lift?' Ned asked, offering an arm which the
sea dragon clambered gratefully onto.

'Do you know what happened in the cave? With the
giant burst of energy?' asked Ned. He tried to conjure up
his magic so he could talk to the creature again with no
luck, but apparently once a connection had been
established, they could talk to each other anyway.

*The Sea Witch has been defeated. That much I do
know. But all her energies, her soul magic, that has been
absorbed by the young sprite. I fear a war is happening
right now within her. It is uncertain who will win.*

'But do you know where Jenni's gone? Can you help
me find her?'

*I can read her energy signature. You are already
heading in the right direction.*

'She's definitely gone home,' Ned said with
certainty. 'Come on, let's get moving.' He strode to the
front of the company, the golden sea dragon coiled
around his neck, and marched confidently towards
Roshaven. He would find Jenni and they'd sort out the
destructive energy she'd absorbed, bring her back to

normal.

When Ned and the others entered Roshaven, it felt normal to him. It smelt the same, looked the same, sounded the same. But he just knew, deep in his bones, that the city wasn't quite right.

Sparks was the first thief-catcher to find them on the streets and report in. He was flashing so fast in Ned's face that there was no way Ned could translate. Out of habit, Ned looked for Jenni to help him out, then remembered she wasn't with them. It was like a blow to the stomach.

'He says weird things have been happening,' said Fingers helpfully. 'Apparently they've been keeping a log of them back at your HQ, but Sparks can have it brought over to the palace if you want to go there first.'

Ned stared at Fingers. He'd forgotten the man could speak bug.

'We have to see her off,' Ned said, heading for the Dead Pier without delay. He wanted to hurry to HQ and find out what had been happening, but first he would return Clove to her ship and see the Spice Ghosts out of his city.

The others had to hurry to keep up, but Ned didn't care. The more time he spent on the streets, the weirder things felt. He hadn't seen a beggar for at least five minutes.

The Dead Pier was empty. That was unusual. There was always something going on there. It was, after all, a nexus of power. A good place for priests and other religious figureheads to recharge belief. It was a popular site to remember your dead, especially as one of their bones was likely to be lashed on the bridge somewhere. It was also a meeting point for the city's youth. Despite continual signage to the latter, they would still dare each other to jump off at the Drop Off and risk an encounter with a mermaid. But Ned didn't have time to worry about any of that. His focus was on the ghostly masts of the ship moored alongside the Dead Pier.

'Right.' Ned shivered in the mist. It felt like he'd taken off a cardigan and the extra warmth he hadn't realised he was holding onto was now dissipating into the air. He rubbed his arms and stamped his feet. 'We all good here now?'

'Thank you for your help,' replied Clove. The other Spice Ghosts had joined her on the pier and the bones had been passed along, each ghost confirming for themselves the right bones had been returned.

'She hasn't… what I mean is…' Ned struggled to find the right words. If he asked the question it would make it a reality and he didn't want to think of Jenni ripping through realms.

'The realms remain intact. Disaster has been averted.' Clove sounded reassuring, but her demeanour remained serious. 'However, the sprite has the power to inflict serious damage if left unchecked.'

'Well, she won't be. I plan to check on her right away. At least, I'm going to make sure she doesn't do anything stupid.' Ned felt relieved that Jenni had left the realms alone, but it made him nervous as to what it was she had been up to.

Clove turned her attention away from Ned, focusing on Rose instead.

'We can stay, if you would like,' she said, making the suggestion yet hinting at much more.

Ned watched Rose dart a look at him.

'Perhaps you will consider being our guests for a short while longer,' offered the Empress of Roshaven.

Ned knew his wife was only being diplomatic, and it

made sense to keep a group of powerful people close by in case it all went wrong with Jenni, but at the same time he felt hurt. Jenni was his responsibility. He didn't need any assistance talking to his best friend and helping her with whatever problem she had.

'Can we get rid of this tether please?' Ned held out his arm. Clove clasped arms with him and again there was a rush of heat as their limbs touched. Once more the strong powerful smell of cloves momentarily overpowered his senses, making his eyes water and his tongue burn. Clove's arm felt less corporeal and as Ned risked a glance, he saw her body return to her previous half in, half out state. He let go.

'Right, well, now that that's sorted, I'm headed to HQ,' Ned said brightly, eager to be away from everyone.

'Keep us in the loop, please?' Rose put a hand on Ned's arm, her face wrinkled with worry and concern. 'And don't approach Jenni without backup, okay?'

'Of course.' Ned gave her a bright smile, nodded to the others and strode off, Sparks flashing in his wake. He had no intention of calling in the cavalry. So far as he could tell, Jenni had done nothing wrong. Yet.

Thief-Catcher HQ wasn't that far away. Ned breathed in the smoky, slightly stinky aroma of The Noose as he marched up the backstairs to get to the offices above the inn. It felt like he'd come home.

'Boss! You're back.' Willow greeted him with a bloom and a smile while Joe bobbed his head and puffed his chest out. 'Oh! What's that?'

Ned had been admiring the huge, towering piles of filing, which had been reduced by at least two-thirds.

'What's what? Oh, this? This is a sea dragon. His name is Slinky.' Ned carefully unwound the creature from his neck and settled him into his office chair. The sea dragon observed the other catchers with bright eyes.

'Well done on the filing, Joe. Good to see you, Willow. Now, tell me what these odd occurrences have been?' asked Ned, taking his customary perch on his desk.

He listened as the thief catchers filled him in on the strange reports that had swamped the office in the last few hours. A swarm of beetles all congregating on Justice Heights. Unusual crab activity. Unexpected flooding but with sea water not fresh.

'And the most unusual thing of all is the kelp forest that has sprung up out of nowhere at the bottom of Justice Heights hill.' Willow wrung her hands. 'I didn't even know kelp could exist out of seawater but it's there, sprung up within the last half hour or so and whilst there aren't any fish out of water, there have been numerous crab sightings.' She puffed out her cheeks, several leaves falling to the floor as she did. 'What's going on, Boss? Why do we have a sea dragon?'

'It's Jenni. She fought the Sea Witch, and won, but she absorbed the Sea Witch's dark energy and she's fighting for control.' Ned didn't know if that was the whole truth or not, but it was the truth he'd decided to believe. His Jenni was still in there and there was no way she was going to give up without a fight, of that he was certain. He just needed to get close enough and remind her of who she really was. 'The sea dragon is, er… our new mascot?' He glanced at the creature with a slight shrug of his shoulders. Slinky radiated acceptance and pleasure.

'What do you need us to do?' asked Joe, taking half a curious step towards the sea dragon.

Ned felt a swell of pride at his catchers for taking the situation in their stride.

'Just hold the fort here and keep everyone away from the kelp forest. Look after Slinky. Hopefully, I won't be long.'

'Good luck, Boss,' murmured Willow as Sparks flashed his support and Joe gave Ned a thumbs up.

He was about to leave the office when he heard a familiar clattering on the stairwell.

'Oh no, not now.'

It was Fred, the palace guard.

'Look, if the Empress sent you with some urgent missive, then it's just going to have to wait. Or deliver it to my catchers. They'll be happy to deal with whatever civilian unrest is occurring.'

'Oh no, Mr Spinks, sir. I've not come from the palace. Well, I have because that's where I was, but they've not sent me along. This is all me. I've come to offer my help.' The young lad beamed earnestly at Ned.

'I'm sorry, Fred. I really don't have time for this.' Ned clapped a hand on the guard's shoulder and headed out of the office, down the stairs.

He could tell from the clanking that Fred was following him, so he decided to just ignore him and hope that he'd fall behind and leave him be. No such luck.

'Mr Spinks, sir, please – I can help, I know I can. I know our Malcolm says I'm always getting in the way and such like, but this is one time I think me being in the way and that is an advantage.'

'What?' Ned didn't slow his pace, but he couldn't help but respond to what Fred said. Mostly because he had absolutely no idea what he was talking about.

'I can keep people away. From the kelp forest, I mean. I am, after all, a rising star in the Empress's guard. No one works as hard as me, no one tries as much as me, and no one has ever bounced back as much as me.

Our Malcolm says I must have a bit of rubber in my soul on account of never being knocked down.'

Despite the haste in which Ned was hurrying towards Justice Heights, Fred caught up with him easily and tugged on his sleeve.

'Please, Mr Spinks, sir. I can help. I know I can.'

'Fine. Keep everyone out of the kelp forest.'

They had arrived and truth be told, Ned felt adamant that nobody in their right mind would want to set one foot inside the giant seaweed forest that had sprung up in front of Justice Heights hill. It looked dark, dank, and smelled of the salty ocean. Ned wished he'd thought to bring Sparks along with him.

Wordlessly Fred passed Ned a light. It was one of the small portable palace lights that the guards carried when they were on night watch. A marvellous invention which allowed the carrier to keep a small light with them at all times.

'Always be prepared, Mr Spinks, sir.' Fred gave him a lopsided grin, then turned and adopted a defensive stance on the cobbles in front of the kelp.

Ned shook his head ruefully as he entered the unnatural sea forest. He might have to keep a closer eye on young Fred. He was looking more and more like catcher material.

Chapter 41

Ned had been right - it was dark and dank in the kelp forest, and it smelt salty. It also scuttled. Clearly Jenni had adopted the Sea Witch's fondness for crabs, along with her scary eyes and power.

Continual use of black magic had burnt the Sea Witch's soul away and her dark arts were fuelled by stealing the souls of others. Ned had to make sure Jenni hadn't put her soul at risk.

He entered deeper and deeper into the kelp forest, only shuddering slightly when a kelp tendril touched his skin. He'd never been a fan of seaweed.

There seemed to be a silverly light up ahead, slightly to the left, so he veered in that direction and came out in a small clearing.

Jenni sat cross legged, floating in mid-air, her forefinger and thumb pinched together like one of the visiting yogis they'd seen a few years ago. Around her span multi-coloured sparks. With a pang, he recognised his own purple.

'Jenni? Are you doing alright?'

Her black eyes snapped open.

'Spinks. What can I do you for?'

Ned tried not to gulp. Jenni had never called him by his surname before. Her voice didn't sound the same and her hair had now turned fully red, just like the Sea Witch's had been.

'I er… I came to see how you are, after everything.' Ned winced a little. It wasn't his strongest opening but maybe Jenni would talk to him.

She smirked at him. Her face looking more Sea Witch than Jenni. There was a sudden blur in the magical powers swirling around her, and a large bolt of silver went through her.

'Boss? I ain't sure wot's going on. There's a lot of stuff and…'

Jenni shook her head, dislodging the magic, forcing back into the swirl. Two black eyes turned to regard Ned.

'Jenni doesn't need you anymore.'

Ned swallowed.

'Is there perhaps anything I can do for you then?' he asked, clutching at straws, not wanting to leave Jenni here alone.

The different coloured magics seemed to be doing something behind Jenni, out of her eyeline. Purple seemed to merge with silver and blue. As they did so, Jenni shook her head a little, as if she were trying to clear her thoughts.

'I dunno wot's going on, Boss. Did I win? Last fing I remember, I was in the cave and then…'

'The Sea Witch's magic exploded when she hit the vortex. It blew you across the cave. I think you absorbed most of the blast. When you opened your eyes, they were black.'

'Black eyes? I ain't never 'ad that afore.' Jenni winced as her skin rippled with green-grey scales and she shook herself. 'Why is yor magic floating around, Boss?'

'You've been skimming, Jenni. Don't you remember?'

'Skimming?' Jenni's voice was faint and the magic seem to swirl faster around her. 'E just turned up out the blue. I never asked 'im to. I bin fine all this time wivout 'im. Why'd 'e 'ave to show up now? 'E came with trouble an'all. Momma K warned me, she said watch yor 'eart, but I didn't listen, I wanted a dad, didn't I? An 'e showed me some cool tricks.'

Ned felt guilty at neglecting Jenni since getting married and half moving into the palace. He'd had his own father-son relationship to figure out with Griff, and he had left Jenni to deal with her own magic issues. He knew she'd been struggling with the transition, but he'd figured she'd get there in the end. He hadn't really listened to her though, had he? He hadn't really had time to offer her an ear to bend. And he'd had no idea she'd been tempted into skimming by Norm, putting her very soul at risk.

Her accent was back, though, and Ned took that as a good thing.

'You know skimming is wrong, don't you, Jenni? All this time we've been investigating reports of stolen magic and all this time... it was you and Norm. Why would you do that?'

Jenni began levitating.

'Yeah, I know I ain't supposed to skim but... me magic ain't what it was and its bin 'ard to deal wiv that. I turned down the frone, and I lost a lot of power – I didn't like it. I wanted it back and then 'ere 'e was, me dad, showing me 'ow to skim. I knew it were wrong, I did, but I just figured if I took a little 'ere and there, no one would notice and Boss, it were like the finest scumble you ever drank.' The magics around Jenni started swirling faster and brighter. 'It made me 'ead tingle and me blood sing and the power danced for me.' She snapped her fingers and arched her back as all the power zoomed back inside her. 'It were wonderful.'

A sudden darkness fell over her and when she next

looked at Ned, the features of the Sea Witch shone out clearer than before.

'I've got real power now. I can do anything I want, be anything I want, take anything I want. I can take your magic. You're not using it, anyway.'

With the accent gone and the Sea Witch seemingly in control, Jenni's fingers made a grabbing motion and Ned felt his magic being ripped out of him. He thought he was going to throw up. He stumbled and sank to his knees, dry heaving, the most horrendous headache pounding in his skull and all his muscles feeling weak and trembly.

He made himself look at her.

'You can't just take people's magic, Jenni. You know that's wrong.'

'Pft. I don't need to listen to you. I can do whatever I like. I'm more powerful than the Source now.'

Ned supposed that was true, but what was also true was the fact that Jenni, part-controlled by the Sea Witch for sure, was still here talking to him and she hadn't left yet. He sat weakly on the floor and watched as the power flickered through Jenni's skin. The dark green rivulets that ran all over her were being constantly redirected and cut off by spurts of different coloured magic. Some were silver and blue, Jenni's own plus the Source's gold. The rest was the multi-coloured stolen power, led by a large streak of purple. Ned's magic. In places the green surged forwards and in others it seemed to recede, but Ned wasn't sure exactly who was winning. He needed to get Jenni remembering pure Jenni experiences.

'Do you remember when we first met?' he asked.

'Wot?' She looked at him and the Sea Witch features flickered on her face, giving her both black eyes then blue eyes, no nose then her nose, a healthy sprite complexion then a sallow Sea Witch one. It was most disconcerting.

'I was new, to the catchers, to Roshaven. Didn't have a clue what I was doing and Old Travvers had sent me to investigate a disturbance down at the market.'

'You didn't know the way,' whispered Jenni, coming back down to the ground.

'That's right. I didn't know the streets like I do now. I got lost. Instead of investigating the disturbance, I found you carrying a potato.' Ned smiled at the memory. 'It was just a normal potato, nothing special, quite large, if I remember correctly. There was Nick the grocer, screaming blue murder at theft and you standing there looking like a sprite caught in a flashlight.'

Ned coughed a little. He was feeling the aftereffects of having his magic ripped out of him. He was achy and cold, felt like he was coming down with the flu.

'I remember I asked you, *Excuse me Ma'am, is that your vegetable* and you looked at me like I had two heads or something.'

'It weren't my potato. I don't even like potatoes,' Jenni said with a small laugh. The redness was leeching out of her hair.

'But the grocer was yelling in my ear, demanding I arrest the thief and you were there with the offending item.'

'Which I returned.'

'Which you returned,' agreed Ned. 'And I took you in for questioning. Old Travvers nearly had a heart attack when he saw me come in with you.'

'It were well funny,' said Jenni in a small voice.

'I didn't know. Had no idea you were Momma K's daughter, a powerful fae and, coincidentally, the second newest member of the thief-catchers.'

'Yeah, that's right. We joined up at the same time, didn't we? I weren't sure at first if I was gonna like it, but then I seed you being all righteous over that potato and I figured you'd need all the 'elp you could get if you was gonna survive in Roshaven.' Jenni chuckled, and she lost all facial similarities with the Sea Witch.

'Best day of my life,' said Ned, holding out a shaky hand to Jenni. 'That first day we met, I thought you were a thief and had caught you red-handed. Look at you now, saviour of the realms, protector of the world. And if you decide to walk this dangerous path, Jenni, then you've got to know that I'll be walking it with you. It's my turn to help you if you're going to survive this massive power overload.'

She looked at him and tears welled up in her eyes.

'I dunno wot to do, Boss. I gots all this power in me and it's slithering around, looking for nooks and crannies, trying to get out and 'urt fings and I dunno wot to do wiv it. I'm scared.'

'Don't be scared. I'm here. We can face it together.'

Jenni took Ned's hand, and he squeezed it tight.

'Maybe we should call the Source,' he suggested.

'S'not that easy. We gotta go to the right place and say the right fings with one of the guardians and stuff.' Jenni blew her nose loudly on her sleeve and shuddered as a wave of dark green ripples ran across her skin.

'I don't think we need to do all that. I think if you just ask for help...'

Jenni stared at Ned, who gave her a nod of encouragement. He watched as she took a deep breath, steeled herself and then said,

'I needs 'elp.'

Chapter 42

The world ended. At least that's what it felt like to Ned. They stood on nothing. He couldn't see his body yet he knew it was there and everything was a pinky-purple colour except there wasn't a floor or a ceiling or sides. Ned's brain hurt from trying to quantify where he was.

'Hello, Jenni. Hello, Ned.'

'Are you the Source?' Ned was trying to concentrate on not panicking.

'I am.'

'She needs your help, please.' Ned tried to gesture with hands that weren't there to Jenni, who he felt sure was nearby.

The Source must have taken pity on Ned's brain because he and Jenni appeared. Granted, they were still existing in the middle of a pinky-purple nothing but at least he could see arms and legs now.

'I can't 'old on to it. It wants to escape.'

The dark green ribbons that Ned had seen rippling under Jenni's skin before now looked like a tangled web of seaweed that surrounded Jenni. It was pulsing and growing. Already it was hard to see Jenni's natural magical colours.

'Jenni, you need to surrender your magic.' The Source sounded calm, way too calm for Ned's liking. He was verging on the edge of blind panic.

'I can't. I gotta fight it.' There was a silver and blue surge and the seaweed webbing shrank back momentarily, only to fight back with several new tendrils finding their way into Jenni's body.

'Surrender to the flow.'

Again, the Source sounded exceptionally soothing. Ned wondered how it was doing it. His palms were sweating.

'Place your trust in nature,' continued the Source.

Ned had no idea what it was talking about. Somehow, they'd ended up in this magical realm. Then he realised. By asking for help in the first place, Jenni had surrendered somewhat. That's what had got them here, so if she continued to surrender, maybe the Source could purge the Sea Witch's magic out of Jenni.

'Yes, Jenni. Give in.' Ned winced at his word choice. 'I mean, surrender to the magic. I believe in you.'

Jenni focused on Ned. Her eyes flashing between her usual blue and the new, scary black. He watched her as she gradually unclenched her jaw, let her shoulders drop and take in a deep, yet shaky breath.

Almost at once, the green-grey scale dissolved from Jenni's skin while her nose and ears returned to normal.

'That's it, Jenni. You're doing it,' Ned said, urging her on.

Jenni closed her eyes in concentration. Ned watched as the dirty yellow colour flowed back into Jenni's hair, the last vestiges of Sea Witch red clinging on to the roots for a moment before being pushed out.

'One ultimate surrender, Jenni. Let it all go,' came the soothing voice of the Source.

Jenni's body hung completely limp now and as a deep exhale left her body, Ned watched the green tendrils seep out of her skin. The seaweed-like power still webbed around her body, but now the tendrils were outside of it, instead of being through the skin. The dark green mass had stopped pulsing and growing. Instead, it was contracting and writhing.

There was a definite tang of fish and salt in the air. Ned thought he heard a distant scream as the seaweed tendrils suddenly spasmed and finally disappeared with a weird squelching noise.

'Is that it? Is the Sea Witch gone for good?' he asked.

'Her power has been removed from Jenni,' replied the Source.

Not exactly what I asked, thought Ned, but he decided against pushing the issue. 'What about Jenni? Is she alright?'

'She needs to fully surrender all her magic. Only then will she survive this ordeal.'

'Survive? What do you mean survive?' Ned cast a desperate glance over at Jenni. 'Why isn't she going to survive?'

'Surrender.' The Source spoke again.

'I don't wanna,' she replied weakly. 'I gots rid of the bad stuffs, right? I'm good now, right?'

There was a desperation in Jenni's voice that Ned had never heard before. He realised she was begging the Source to keep the extra power she'd been given as well as that which she'd stolen. All the multicoloured magics that had previously ganged up on the darkness of the Sea Witch were now sparking at each other. Ned could see where this was going to go.

'Jenni, listen. If you keep all these different magics inside you, they're going to tear you apart. It's not all your magic. You've got to surrender it, please.' Ned's voice hitched. 'I don't want you to die.'

Jenni smiled weakly.

'I ain't gonna die, Boss. It's just a justment is all. Getting used to the juice and wotnot.' She coughed as her skin spasmed when two different colours of magic collided.

The silver and blue magical sparks and multi-coloured swirls which had previously coexisted in harmony were now fighting each other, causing Jenni to shudder and twitch as they bumped into each other.

'Please, Jenni,' begged Ned again.

'Surrender,' whispered the Source, its voice a lot quieter than before.

Ned got really worried when he realised he couldn't sense the Source as strongly and that the weird pinky-purple place they'd ended up in was fading. He could now see the ghostly outline of Justice Heights coming back into being.

'Wot if I ain't got no magics no more, Boss? Wot then? Who am I?' asked Jenni feebly.

'You're Jenni, my second-in-command and best friend. Superb thief-catcher and beloved citizen of Roshaven. You've got people who count on you and think of you as family besides me and Rose. I know for a fact that Griff and Fingers have a soft spot for you. Fred thinks you're his mentor and I don't know where Willow, Joe, and Sparks would be without you. You've got friends in the trollish and dwarven communities. The druids love it when you pop in. Hell, Aggie even created the cinnamon twist in your honour. Bet you didn't know that, did you? I also know that Ma Bowl has been experimenting with beetle cheesecake for your birthday. And that's not even counting the friends you've got among the fae. Roshaven wouldn't be Roshaven without Jenni, magic or no.'

Both Ned and Jenni had tears on their cheeks whilst the backs of Ned's ear were bright red.

'I ain't just magic to you,' Jenni spoke with wonder

in her voice.

'No, Jenni, of course not.' Ned held out his hand, hoping that she was going to do the right thing.

'I… surrender.'

Jenni's fingers gripped Ned's and the colourful magics that were shooting around her body abruptly left in a large, sparkly rainbow cloud that hung above them for a few moments before expanding and being absorbed in the surrounding space.

The ability to sense the Source's presence came rushing back to Ned and both he and Jenni were bathed in a warm, rosy glow with a myriad of golden sparkles dancing about them.

'Jenni, I am so proud of you,' said the Source.

'You are?' Jenni's voice sounded firm again and Ned was relieved to note that all her facial features were correct.

A small golden spark settled on Jenni's chest and was absorbed into her body. She glowed momentarily as her entire body lifted up before settling back down again to the non-existent floor she and Ned stood on.

'Wot were that?' she breathed.

'Your much deserved power. You gave up what you had stolen and put your trust in nature. Your fae magic has been returned. Use it wisely, Jenni.'

Ned was glad the Source had returned Jenni's magic, but he couldn't help feeling slightly disappointed at not seeing what she would have been like with no power at all.

'Um… what about my magic?' Ned asked nervously. It was unreliable at best but it was his, and now he knew it was a purple colour he felt more connected to it for some reason.

'Your power has been returned. As has all the stolen

magic.'

'Has all this all been some kind of test?' wondered Ned.

'Yeah, wot 'e said.'

Ned could feel the Source smiling at them both.

'Your fate is your own. It always has been. Depending on the choices you make, the paths you choose, the outcome changes. This was the journey hoped for, but nothing is set in stone.'

The Source's words explained to Ned why it had been proud of Jenni. She'd obviously taken the right paths and made the right choices.

'Still, seems like a precarious position to put yourself in,' he said. 'Anything could've happened. You might have lost.'

Ned felt like the Source was laughing at him now, not unkindly, but it was a surreal feeling.

'I had faith. So should you.'

Ned blinked, about to protest that he did have faith when he realised they had returned completely to Justice Heights, the Source nowhere to be seen or felt.

Chapter 43

It had grown dark, and the evening air had a nip about it. Ned flexed his toes in his boots while he shoved his hands into his coat, looking for his pipe and baccy.

'So…' Jenni broke the silence first.

'How you feeling?' Ned asked as he primed his pipe.

'Stretched, like a rubber band or summink that's snapped back but is all saggy now.'

Ned's eyebrows rose at Jenni's use of simile. She usually stayed clear of grammar.

'Maybe we ought to go sit down, have a drink,' he suggested, for lack of what else to say.

'Yeah, I reckon that'd be grand.'

And so the Chief Thief-Catcher and Consort to the Empress of Roshaven, together with his second-in-command and saviour of the world sprite, let their feet do the walking. The forest of kelp had disappeared, leaving behind a somewhat salty tang in the air, and Fred was nowhere to be seen. Ned suspected he'd gone to get help once the kelp disappeared.

Miraculously, they found an empty table in The Noose and were soon joined by Sparks, Joe, an extremely relieved Fred and Willow who had Slinky the dragon curled in and among some additional branches she'd sprouted. Ned had been right. The young palace guard had gone back to Thief-Catcher HQ for help. By the time Ned had caught them all up on everything that had happened, with lots of helpful additions from Jenni, at least a dozen empty glasses filled their table. Joe offered to clear the empties and get the next round in just as Fingers, Griff, and Rose arrived.

That Rose was heavily disguised was not lost on the patrons of The Noose, and an even wider circle than before was left around Ned's table.

'Are you allowed to be here? Is everything alright?' slurred Ned. He hadn't meant to, but the scumble was catching up to him.

'I'm disguised. It's fine. We just wanted to make sure you and Jenni were alright, after...' She paused, looking at Jenni uncomfortably.

'After I went all evil and stuff,' said Jenni helpfully.

'Yes, that. And to let you know that Norm escaped.'

'He did?' Ned made to get up but realised nobody else was moving. 'Is that a problem for tomorrow then?'

Rose nodded tightly and it dawned on Ned that his wife was potentially furious with him. He took a stab in the dark that it was probably because he hadn't kept her in the loop, although to be fair he hadn't had a chance to tell anyone, really. Well, except for his team. He gave her a sheepish smile.

'I was just coming to tell you what had happened,' he began, but she stopped him with a quick squeeze of his arm. Worry then, not fury. Ned felt fairly confident he could earn back some husband points if she'd only been worried about him.

'Why don't you fill us in now?' asked Fingers. 'I mean, we gave the bones back to the Spice Ghosts and all that, but what happened with the Sea Witch's power?'

Ned took a deep breath. He had a feeling he'd be telling this story for some time to come.

~THE END~

If you enjoyed reading *The Bone Thief* please leave me a review and let me know what you thought.

*****

**You can also listen to me sing the
Sea Witch Shanty:
https://youtu.be/e7mXFjw6zfE**

*****

**Catch Ned and Jenni in another Roshaven
adventure…**

***The Interspecies Poker Tournament,
Roshaven Case File no. 27***

NOW AVAILABLE ON AUDIO

https://books2read.com/u/m2Vk0R

Ned Spinks, Chief Thief-Catcher, has a new case. A murderous moustache-wearing cult is killing off members of Roshaven's fae community. At least that's what he's been led to believe by his not-so-trusty sidekick, Jenni the sprite. She has information she's not sharing but plans to get her boss into the Interspecies Poker Tournament so he can catch the bad guy and save the day. If only Ned knew how to play!

The Interspecies Poker Tournament, Case 27 of The Roshaven Files, is a humorous fantasy novella following the adventures of Ned Spinks and Jenni, a prequel to The Rose Thief.

Huge Thanks

My thanks go, as always, to my husband Kevin and my two monsters Leo and Belle as they put up with me going through the rollercoaster of writer emotions when penning something new.

Thank you to my brilliant crit group EM Swift-Hook, Darrell Nelson and Scott Tarbet for their valuable input into the first draft and to my wonderful team of beta readers – EM Swift-Hook, Jane Jago, Donna Tyrrell, Brent A. Harris, Ian Bristow and Martin Frowd. Your fantastic attention to detail is a life saver, as always.

Huge additional thanks to Ian Bristow, who created the fantastical cover for The Bone Thief. Did you spy the crab in the Sea Witch's hair? You can find out more about his artwork at www.iancbristow.com

About the Author

Sign up to Claire's newsletter for exclusive content and all the latest writing news: http://eepurl.com/csWd0f

Follow Claire on Twitter: @grasshopper2407
Like Claire on Facebook: facebook.com/busswriter
Visit her website: www.clairebuss.co.uk

Claire Buss is a multi-genre author and poet based in the UK. She wanted to be Lois Lane when she grew up but work experience at her local paper was eye-opening. Instead, Claire went on to work in a variety of admin roles for over a decade but never felt quite at home. An avid reader, baker and Pinterest addict Claire won second place in the Barking and Dagenham Pen to Print writing competition in 2015 with her debut novel, The Gaia Effect, setting her writing career in motion. She continues to write passionately and is hopelessly addicted to cake.